KU-558-585

# Antonin Varenne

# LOSER'S CORNER

*Translated from the French and with notes by*
*Frank Wynne*

MACLEHOSE PRESS
QUERCUS · LONDON

First published in the French language as *Le Mur, le Kabyle et le Marin*
by Éditions Viviane Hamy, Paris, in 2011
First published in Great Britain in 2014 by MacLehose Press
This paperback edition published in 2015 by

MacLehose Press
an imprint of Quercus Publishing Ltd
Carmelite House
50 Victoria Embankment
London EC4Y 0DZ

An Hachette UK Company

A CIP catalogue record for this book is available
from the British Library.

ISBN (MMP) 978 1 78087 782 2
ISBN (Ebook) 978 1 78087 7815

10 9 8 7 6 5 4 3 2 1

Designed and typeset in Minion by Jouve (UK), Milton Keynes
Printed and bound in Great Britain by Clays Ltd, St Ives plc

# Contents

# Introduction

In the aftermath of the Second World War, the European colonial empires begin to crumble.

The winds of independence sweep through Asia and then quickly over Africa. In July 1954, after eight years of war, France loses Indochina. Although the protectorates of Morocco and Tunisia did not have to fight to win their independence, the situation in Algeria is very different.

Algeria is the jewel in the French colonial crown. More than that, Algeria *is* France, its extension on the other side of the Mediterranean. Uniquely, the French *départements* in Algeria are settled. One million Europeans live there among the nine million Algerians.

In November 1954, the *Front de Libération Nationale*, which numbered no more than a handful of men at the time, mounted an armed resistance. This war, which had actually started in 1833, the beginning of the French occupation, would end in 1962. As a result of the exceptional situation of the colony, the conflicting ideologies at play, and the military and political choices of the Fourth and Fifth Republics, this war became one of the longest and most bitter traumas in the history of modern France.

The first French president with no ties to this colonial conflict was elected in 2007. The two generations of politicians that came before him had a past – either personal or political – that linked them to the war.

Now, as those who had fought in Algeria are beginning to die out, the work of historians is far from complete. Wrestling with emotions that are still raw, with the political ramifications of historical interpretation (in France as in Algeria), with nostalgia and family tragedies, with fading memories and guilty consciences, their research has nonetheless made steady progress. This novel, inspired by one story in this history, that of one French conscript, owes much to this research. And since this history is being written, literature should also contribute to this work.

Antonin Varenne
August 2014

# Translator's note

Algeria casts a long shadow in the French mind. Much like Britain's relationship with India, it is a source of mingled pride and shame. The brutal, bitter war that led to independence is often known as *La Guerre sans nom* – The War without a Name – since, for generations, none dared speak of it. The amnesty granted immediately after the war, both to French combatants and Algerian resistants, ensured this silence. And yet, few readers in France would fail to recognise many of the names and dates in this novel and most would know the scattered words of Arabic I have preserved in the translation since they have become a part of the French language.

This moving and powerful novel stands on its own, but for the benefit of those readers who wish to have some context, brief notes on historical events and political figures marked with an asterisk (*) can found at the back of the book where there is also a glossary of French and Arabic words.

*For the Algerian and the young Frenchman in the thick of the demonstration; and their somewhat insane idea that they might find a C.R.S. officer, precisely the one they went looking for, with a gun in their pocket. To this day, the C.R.S. officer in question knows nothing.*

I

# 1

April 2009

Days I've had this guy right in front of me.

It's changed, this boxing club; used to be different, but I know the place. Not the first time I've fought here.

Round four.

It's a hard ring. Old lags prefer a hard surface.

Kravine keeps his boys doped up. Two more punches and I'll take him down.

Bastard's got some arms. He's got the arms, but not the stomach. I'm going to beat the shit out of him. The dope will wear off, then all he'll have in his favour is the fact that he's twenty. What the fuck does anyone know when they're twenty?

Focus.

Handsome lad, this black kid. Legs like springs, a killer's shoulders, a good reach. This is a bullshit match.

Too much rebound. Ninety-one kilos. He's got the advantage in this bout. He's got twenty years on me. Forty-year-old Georges.

Don't make your move; wait till he tires himself out. I'm built to take punches. Georges, he can take punches like a brick wall. "The Wall". That's what they call me. Or Georges the Cop. Don't like it when they call me that.

3

Focus.

Easier to take the punches than roll with 'em.

But how long can you go on taking them? Things have to square up sometime.

Stop thinking! Just fight.

The kid shifts to his left foot, trying to get on my outside. I don't have an outside. Four walls. First-class hook. He comes from some island, this lad, I can't remember which one. A killing machine. He's looking me right in the eye.

Kravine chose the venue.

Paolo set up the bout. "This is your fight, Georges." Fucking bullshit match.

Another reputation. Kravine figures the new kid can cut his teeth on me. People say I'm washed up. But Kravine's cagey. The dope, this ring, this club full of guys who didn't come to cheer me on. Last bout on the bill. Oldest trick in the book. I don't have any fans.

Never did.

A fucking bullshit match too far, Georges.

Still gagging to get into the ring, now more than ever.

Shooting pains in my arm. Out of breath. The kid is panting like a steam train.

Me, pale as a ghost. Haven't seen a ray of sun in fuck knows how long . . . Him, young and black with teeth that could snap your bones . . . What the hell are you thinking, Georges? Pile into him, for Christ's sake, get stuck in, don't just stand there.

A wall, you're a WALL, Georges. What the f—? A quick right cross – I never saw it coming. Got right under my guard. Landed square to the temple. Still standing. A little stunner. Ears ringing, everything blurry. If he'd followed with a left hook, I'd have been fucked.

Focus. Something happened there, Georges, right there.

His right wrist is giving him gyp. He's raised his guard, no more mixing it up, no more quick jabs, he's running out of steam. He's worried about taking a hit. Gloves shielding his face, the peek-a-boo guard – this is what I've been waiting for.

His liver's mine.

Weak wrists. His weak spot, Georges, the chink in the armour that'll bring him down. Rossi, the piece of shit who claims to be his coach, is too fucking dumb to tell him to watch his guard, he's screaming for the kid to hit harder . . . But that's not the problem, the kid's already throwing punches that could stop a fucking train. Kravine has spotted it too. I hear his high-pitched voice from ringside screaming at his protégé not to change his guard. But his guard's not the problem either. It's your confidence, sonny, your confidence cracking like your knuckles.

Two more rounds playing punchbag.

My arm is fine. Ready to lash out when the time comes.

I let him throw a couple of jabs to my head. It's tough enough to take it. He thinks I can't move anymore. He jabs at my face, blood trickles into my mouth.

We're in a clinch now; bend, bend, push your head into his chest. That's it. He's ripping at my ears with his gloves; a couple of kidney punches while the sightline is blocked. I know all Kravine's tricks.

I shove the kid away, he's lighter than me. He's flailing. He's going again. The dope's wearing off . . . Thirty seconds to the end of round four. Kravine's obviously briefed him. Round six. Always round six, Georges.

I'm pissing blood, my eyebrows are mashed to a pulp. But I'll be here for the fifth round. Georges "The Wall" will be here.

The kid's riled now. He wants to take me out before the sixth. Move in. Push him, that's right, get your elbows in. That's it, keep pushing. Move your legs. Bring your head in. He's got no idea what I'm doing. Right there. He's confused. A quick right hook, gentle, a pitty-pat punch. Let him think I'm a worn-out punch-bag. He parries. Now! Left upper cut to his blind side, keep my feet nailed to the mat, back straight, follow through from the hip. Perfect.

Never saw it coming. Got him smack on the chin. One second to go before the bell.

He looks shocked. His brain is really rattling inside his skull.

Came within a second of hitting the canvas and he knows it.

And you know it too . . .

You fucked up, Georges.

Learn your lesson, not before time . . . The kid's twenty years old, Georges, you stunned him, but you wasted all that energy two seconds before he gets to take a rest.

Don't slump down on the stool, don't let him see. Paolo's hands on my face. My calves are starting to cramp.

The kid stares at me from his corner. He's jittery, his feet are twitching. He's capable of anything now, he wants to kill me. A minute from now, he'll have completely recovered; it'll take me ten times as long.

Paolo gives me the spiel, slathers my face in vaseline, dabs adrenaline juice all over my bleeding eyebrows which are worth shit now. Tells me to stop acting the maggot.

"Stop trying to play the heavyweight, Georges! Wait till he's worn out, otherwise he'll beat the shit out of you!"

I stare across the ring at the black kid. Two or three wins and he'll be a serious contender. He'll be a pro soon. An old hand and well on his way . . .

"You listening to me, Georges?"

The audience, people chattering, they don't give a shit what's happening in the ring. Paolo doesn't realise, I'm taking a beating the likes of which I've never had to take.

"What?"

"O.K., so he's dazed, but he's not completely out of it, don't try and box clever. Keep jabbing. Go for his belly. Two more rounds, don't go in for the kill before that!"

My smashed face, that's my coach's strategy.

Obviously, he reminds me of when I was twenty.

What has he got in his corner? Youth, a will to win for reasons he doesn't even understand yet, the need to get the fuck out of whatever shithole he grew up in. Carlier, a good cut-man, is spraying his face, smearing him with vaseline and camphor, massaging his wrists. I see you, Carlier, I see you fussing over your boy's cuts and bruises . . . Sitting ringside with some tart got up in pink and gold is the club owner, Kravine. How many careers has Kravine ruined? Do yourself a favour, kid, get out of his hairy clutches as fast as possible . . . But I can tell from that pretty face you know how to look after yourself.

Yeah, you've got people in your corner.

In my corner, Paolo, twenty years in the ring, thirty years sweating blood, liver shot to shit, one eye fucked up; Paolo the Portuguese, Paolo the Porkchop, a decent featherweight in his day, calls himself a trainer, but really he's a cut-man, a real surgeon, but completely incapable of tying a bandage. He took too many knocks to the head, did Paolo, but I'm happy to have him in my corner. What the fuck am I doing? I shouldn't be thinking about shit like this right now – the job, the apartment, the girls, the training . . . Shut the fuck up, Georges! No point thinking about a job that everyone in this room hates you for. The kid in the far corner, if he gave up boxing, he could be a model. My face is like a sack of potatoes, I'm a cop, a *brigadier* with fifteen years on the force who still pushes himself to jog five miles every morning, just for the sake of having . . .

"Hey, Georges! Jesus Christ, what the hell are you thinking?"

"Wha . . . ? What?"

"Shift your arse!"

The bell. Shit. Completely zoned out. Didn't hear a thing.

Still feel the urge to get back in the ring.

That bastard Paolo didn't rinse my mouth-guard. I can taste blood. He knows I hate that, but he's deliberately trying to get me riled.

Round five.

Back to the centre.

We stare each other down.

The kid is more canny. He's angry, but he's not dumb. He's not prancing around like some faggot anymore, he's more careful about where he places his punches. This isn't going to be a walk-over. I need to get a couple of punches in before the sixth. Paolo doesn't seem to realise if I don't slow the kid up now, he'll take me down. My legs are . . .

What the fuck? I'm down – one knee on the canvas. And one glove.

What's that voice . . . ?

The referee. The count. Already at three . . . Make the most of every second. Jesus, I need them.

Breathe, Georges.

Five . . . Six . . .

Head spinning.

Seven . . .

The kid is waiting for me.

Eight . . .

Back on my feet.

The ref looks me in the eye, his voice sounds weird, gives my Picasso features the once-over and doesn't much like what he sees. I tell him I'm fine, try to stare him down when actually I can see fuck all. He pulls a face.

Not a T.K.O.

Not now. Oh shit, not now.

I start to bob, everything's reeling.

The referee watches me bob and weave, but he's not fooled.

He says something I don't catch straight off.

"You're going to get your K.O., if that's what you want."

What did he say that for? Why did he glance at the front row?

White spots dancing before my eyes.

The ref lets me carry on, convinced I'm going to get myself K.O.'d. Kravine's got him in his pocket . . . What the fuck am I doing here?

I'm scared shitless.

First time ever. The kid's gloves are like iron, I'm going to die. I'm scared . . . The bell. It's going to start all over again. What th—

Put your guard up!

A sudden flurry; it's raining punches.

This whole thing's a set-up. They've planned my death, all of them. What am I supposed to do?

I'm still standing. You're still standing, Georges.

You're still here.

It's just boxing.

The kid's gloves aren't loaded. Your face is your own, it's taking the punches; your legs are your own, they're holding you up; your gloves are still there at the end of your arms, they're moving, they're yours.

I no longer feel the punches.

But I know they're still coming. The kid's not pulling his punches, he's putting his whole weight behind them, I'm taking a serious pounding. There's nothing rigged. This is boxing. This is my life.

Watch your chin, get behind him. No-one's taking me down in this ring.

I'm bricking it.

9

I'm going to fucking kill Kravine.

A black whirlwind. The kid's everywhere. Where's the ring?

Don't lose it, Georges! Your eyes, Jesus Christ, keep your eyes open. You've got the experience, he's flailing and furious. He's picking up momentum, like this was some sparring match. Jesus Christ, he's windmilling so hard he's out of breath.

Breathe.

Don't feel the fear anymore, feel the hatred, you've got experience on your side.

You haven't taken too much of a beating.

Let him push you back. That's it. Edge backwards. The ropes are right behind you. You're getting your second wind, your guard's holding up. Lean on him. Throw your arms round him. Get him in a clinch. That's it. You disgust him, you stink of sweat and old age, Georges. You're glued to his skin. He screams and swears, tries to bite your ear off.

The ref isn't even looking anymore.

Go back and bawl on his shoulder. Lean your whole weight on him.

Let him push you.

You've still got your arms. He's worn himself out, you've held up, Georges, you're still standing.

Kravine is shouting at his boy to get the fuck out of the clinch, he's screaming harder than Rossi, who's finally woken up.

Nostrils flaring like a galloping horse, puffed up as hard as possible.

Kravine knows me, and he knows boxing, even if he is prepared to shit all over it. They roar at their protégé to get clear, but the kid can't hear anything now. He's back in the schoolyard, throwing wild, uncoordinated punches. Behind me, Paolo must be pissing himself laughing, baring his toothless gums.

Fall into the black kid's arms, you're nothing but an old wreck. Let him think that, let him roar.

He viciously shoves me away.

Now, bounce off the ropes, it's your only chance.

A little aikido, kid; feel your own twenty-year-old power coming back to smack you in the face.

Arms above his head, he's forgotten everything he knows about boxing, he's flailing wildly.

Eight kilos in a single glove. A jab to his solar plexus, winding him. I could have killed him. Didn't have the strength.

His face is grey, his toes turned out, his eyes wide.

I manage to bend my knees. Little steps. Push him, Georges, push him all the way back across the ring.

Move, for Christ's sake, don't let up now or you're truly fucked.

God, these gloves feel heavy. Hang in there. Jab, cross, jab, they're weak pitty-pat punches but they're enough. I'm going to take him. Look, Paolo, look, I'm going to take him down! Careful, he knows how to box on the back foot, close that gap, don't give him a chance to recover. He lashes out with all the strength he's got left. He's got the power, but he's forgotten how to use it. Don't give him any reach or you're dead meat. Right, you've got him now. Christ, I've got no strength left. Dodge, he's about to crumple. Too many questions on his face; he can't think anymore. I've got no strength left.

Jab, right hook, left hook. These aren't punches now, this is pure showmanship.

Liver, ribs, heart.

Accuracy, it's your only hope.

No strength left, only weight.

Cramps in my shoulders, hands burning, blood pouring into my eyes. This is the end, for him or for me. There'll be no purgatory.

The kid takes the beating, the post is holding him up. He's not going down, he's not crumpling, Jesus Christ! Sheer willpower, a pair of twenty-year-old legs. I've nothing left.

I don't want to lose. I can't go on. What's he waiting for, why doesn't he just kill me? Don't fuck with me, just finish me off, I've got no strength left. What are you waiting for?

He . . . It's over. He's giving up. His arms fall to his sides. I can see his head right there in front of me, I can't see his gloves anymore. What do I do?

Box, Georges, box, for fuck's sake, if it's the last thing you do before you croak.

Hook to the temple, once, twice.

The chin, rattle his brain inside his skull. Upper cut, my arm is shaking, my last ounce of strength, pitiful, just enough, *in extremis . . .*

I can't believe it.

Twenty years of raw power crumpled at my feet.

I almost feel like picking him up.

I can barely stand. I'll sleep for ten years after this.

He's slumped to a sitting position. The count starts.

Six. Seven. He's not dead, his eyes are still throwing punches at me. I'm scared shitless. Stay on your arse, kid. Don't get up, please . . . don't get up. Let me have this match. Eight. The kid grabs the ropes. There'll be other bouts, kid, let me have this one. He slips. Nine. The ref is counting off seconds half an hour long. The kid shakes his head. I stare at him as though my eyes could add weight on his shoulders. He manages to get a knee up, he is magnificent, he struggles to his feet. He slips, falls back. The ref can't string it out any longer. Just say it, for fuck's sake!

Ten.

It's over . . .

One second.

One more second and he would have been back on his feet.

I'm still staring at him. He's gasping, half choking.

The crowd roars, I can't even see the auditorium.

I'm standing there over the kid.

Carlier takes out his mouth-guard, tells him to breathe through his nose. The kid looks me up and down. That's it, he closes his eyes, lets the cut-man spray water on his face.

An old horse foaming at the mouth, beating him scares me.

I feel like thanking him.

You won. Try to smile, Georges, you're happy. You won.

He opens his eyes. It's over. He gathers his wits, he thinks. He smiles at me.

I haven't got the energy to do a victory tour of the ring.

Always in the sixth round, Georges. Except when someone gives me a chance in the fifth . . .

Don't kid yourself.

It's the kid who really won, sitting on his stool already recovering his strength.

Paolo throws my gown around my shoulders. I feel cold. I'm sweating like a pig and I feel cold.

A good bout, all things considered.

Even Kravine can't tarnish everything.

Paolo is smiling, the old bastard is happy. He's the one who raises my arms. I'm about to collapse.

The tall black kid is on his feet, he skips into the middle of the ring, I place one glove on his killer's shoulder and say:

"You might have lost, kid, but it's gonna take me a hell of a lot longer to recover."

He presses his mouth to my mangled ear.

"Thanks for the lesson, Gramps. See you next time."

He smiles.

A decent boxer.

*

The crowd trudged out of Juvisy Sports Centre in sluggish columns. Men of all ages, a few women, drunks, ex-bruisers, kids from the local boxing clubs. Now the heavyweight bout was over, the hall was emptying out. Meagre betting, the half-hearted enthusiasm of a weekday night. All that remained was the stench of sweat mingled with the acrid tang of bleach a council worker was using to swab down the ring, wringing out his floor cloth into a bucket.

Out on the street, the stragglers chewed over the last bout.

Georges "The Wall" – 38 wins (23 knockouts, 15 decisions), 5 losses (5 decisions) – had beaten André Gabin – 11 wins (7 knockouts, 4 decisions), 2 losses (1 K.O.) – in the fifth round by a knockout. In a half-empty hall, Georges "The Wall" Crozat had been the first boxer to knock Gabin out; a desperate effort that went almost unnoticed.

In the empty hall the circuit-breakers crackled. Only the solitary changing room at the rear of the building was still lit.

Crozat was sitting on the massage table, wrapped in a navy blue robe. His bare feet dangled in the empty air. His swollen right hand was plunged into a bucket of ice while Paolo was cutting away the last of the tapes from his left. In the tiled gloom of the changing room, the old sparring partners looked like melting lumps of wax. After the referee finished the count, every movement was marked by the slowness of routine, by a brittle homesickness.

"You're fucking crap at handwraps. I tell you, next time, I'll get the commission to fire your sorry arse."

Paolo snorted, ready to play the game.

14

"*Caralho!* I didn't notice my handwraps giving you no problem in the ring. From the state of Gabin's face, I figure they held up pretty good, huh? Tight enough to fuck his face up good and proper."

Georges flexed his right hand, numbed by the ice.

"Yeah, that'll do for now."

Paolo slapped The Wall on the thigh and gave him a wink, an old habit he'd kept up even after his left eye gave out. He ripped off the final piece of tape.

"Go take your shower, I'll pick up your cheque."

Georges looked down at the bucket.

"How much?"

"Four hundred, same as always. We can't hit 'em up for any more, you know that."

"So what's your cut, you old fucker?"

"Same as always, the whole wedge."

Still Georges didn't crack a smile.

"Paolo . . ."

Embarrassed, Paolo buried his face in his first-aid kit.

"The fucking kid's twenty years old, Georges, and you beat the shit out of him. You won twice as much as he lost. Go take your shower and I'll stand you a meal from my cut. We should celebrate."

Georges slid off the table, but his legs gave out under him. He leaned on the trainer's shoulder.

He allowed the hot water to course down his neck, then slowly turned on the cold tap. Not recommended after a bout; the shock of switching from hot to cold can bring on a heart attack. But Georges needed it to dispel the thoughts whirling in his head.

He'd come to win; he had won, and it felt worse than losing.

He hung up his gloves.

No more boxing? Nothing but the day job. And the money?

15

No more fights meant no more girls. He spat out a thick gob of spit and blood and watched it eddy around the drain.

He could find a couple of amateurs and train them. Work with Paolo. A little boxing club out in the *banlieue*, coach a few kids. Or maybe The Ring out in the 14th *arrondissement*, where the other cops trained; Marco could get him a gig there . . . Spend all day grafting with his colleagues, and all night too . . .

No thanks.

Keep fighting? Third-rate bouts . . . Plug away until you lost an eye or some young rookie permanently fucked your brain.

Georges stepped out of the shower, towelling his cropped hair, careful with the slippery tiles. The door of the changing room slammed.

"Paolo, I'm not sure I want to eat – I'm shattered, I don't suppose you could . . ."

He balled his fists, his knuckles cracking like breaking glass.

"Evening, officer. Good bout."

Kravine, a cigarette dangling from the corner of his mouth.

Georges looked down, tied the towel round his waist.

"What do you want?"

"Just came to say congratulations. Straight up, you deserve it."

"With you, nothing is straight up, or for free. What do you want?"

Georges pulled on a pair of boxers and a T-shirt while Kravine, his hands behind his back, prowled around the massage table.

Kravine had boxed as a kid, though not for long. A thug, a middleweight who never managed to find a style, brute force but no technique; he'd given up the ring to become a trainer and, later, a promoter.

The boxing world was full of guys like him. It clearly needed them, one way or another. Kravine peddled success, money, winning, he never talked about losing; he fixed a few fights, made sure his kids got enough of a taste of winning to sucker them in. Only to be crushed later because they hadn't had enough training. Rigged bouts, steroids, dodgy rankings, risk-free investments, careers on the slide. This wasn't about sport. It was about money. These days Kravine had to travel further and further afield to find his marks. Farm boys from the sticks weren't enough for sharks like him. These days he had to go all the way to Africa to find fighters prepared to sign away their talent for a wad of cash and a handshake.

Georges might be from the skanky suburbs of Montrouge, but he knew a thing or two.

Kravine was the kind of guy who came round feeling sorry for you after he'd dumped you in the shit.

The Wall slumped down onto a bench. A rictus grin tugged at the scars on his face; he imagined Robert Kravine in an African slum, standing in a pile of goat shit, dusting down his three-piece suit.

"You've got an eye, always have had, that something that can't be taught. It was a great bout, Georges, straight up. You could have had a great career, everyone knows that; you were made for championships . . ."

"Don't fuck me around, you know as well as anyone what went down."

Kravine took a few steps, turned his back on Georges.

"Like I was saying, a good bout. But you know you haven't got much left in those gloves of yours."

Georges dressed slowly so as not to show how much pain he was in as he bent double to pull on his socks. Just get the hell out without having to listen, knock back three Nurofen and get some sleep.

"Spit it out."

17

"I've got a proposal for you. I'm not gonna bullshit you, you've heard it all before. I'll hire you to work on my team. Spar with my lads, give 'em some advice, work with Rossi and you could be slipping two hundred into your pocket every week."

"And . . . ?"

"Good old Georges! Like I said, you've got the eye. I'll find you a couple of bouts from time to time. These days, all you get offered are bullshit fights for fuck-all money. I'll find you some class action. You can hold out another year, maybe two, the shape you're in. I can guarantee you a couple of prize bouts to keep you afloat, we split the cash fifty-fifty. You get to pocket the take as well, and you fight whoever I tell you to, whenever I tell you to. If you don't retire from the circuit right now, you'll still have money to buy yourself some ladies . . . See how well I know you? Two years from now, I'll hire you as a coach, training people with real talent. Whaddya say?"

Georges was afraid to get up off the bench. His swollen eyelids barely opened halfway, he couldn't look Kravine in the face.

"You've got some nerve, you two-faced cunt."

Paolo came back into the changing room, cheque in hand.

"Done and dusted! I've got the money, champ . . . What the fuck is he doing here?"

Kravine glanced at his watch.

"Hey, Porkchop."

"Hel— What the fuck's he doing here?"

"I just came to say congratulations. Got to go see André now, build him back up after the pasting Georges here gave him. Think it over, cop, you've got my number."

Paolo crumpled the cheque in his arthritic fist and stepped aside to let Kravine leave.

"Go fuck yourself, you and your fucking scams."

Kravine turned back.

"Be seeing you."

Head in his hands, Georges still did not get off the bench.

"Go bring the car round, Paolo, I'll meet you at the entrance."

"You gonna tell me what he wanted?"

"Just get the fucking car, now."

"You need a hand to . . . ?"

"Paolo!"

"Alright, alright, I'm going. Chill."

Georges could think of only one thing: having a whore rubbing up against him, telling her about the fight, winning for just one more night. He'd made 300 euros tonight. Tomorrow . . . tomorrow what?

You haggled over your own remains. While they were still worth shit.

It was a bullshit offer, but probably the best one he would get. A boxer paid by a crooked fight promoter to help his rookie fighters rack up a few wins. Keep raking in the money by taking a dive when he was told.

Should have smashed the slimy fucker's face.

Take a deal at the end of his career from the very guy who had fucked him over at the start . . . because at the bottom of the hole he was in now, no-one else was going to come knocking.

Kravine knew exactly what he was doing.

Take the cash? Or play it safe, get out with his hands clean? Because there were worse things than ending your boxing career as a cripple: the shame of ending it with a battered reputation. The shit that went down inside the ring had a habit of spreading outside. The fighters who took steroids were the cops who never got promoted. Georges knew this from personal experience. Two years it had taken to persuade the Boxing Commission he was clean, his best years as a fighter wasted, suspicions that never really went away, his career as a pro down the can. Fucked.

Permanently.

Then Paolo had shown up and pulled him through.

He'd say yes. Maybe not straight away, but he'd take the deal.

So he could go on boxing.

Georges wasn't dumb enough to delude himself that anyone was forcing his hand.

The door swung open. He shouted:

"What's the deal? You forget your keys?"

"What you talking about, Mister Wall?"

Tonight was teeming with shits, it was like they'd all decided to drop by his dressing room.

A shock of wiry hair, a skin-tight T-shirt bulging with biceps pumped with helium, a bronzed complexion – the Pakistani. He boxed to impress the girls and worked as a bouncer at some club in Passy. He was so ham-fisted, no-one wanted him as a sparring partner, though they all felt the overwhelming desire to punch him in the mouth.

"What do you want?"

Georges knew he also hung out down the cop shop and it was no accident that he went training at the gym in the 14th, where lots of cops worked out.

The Pakistani bobbed and weaved around the dressing room, dodging and feinting, a series of punches that he wasn't capable of pulling off even without an opponent.

"O.K., I didn't come down here to chat technique, Georges. It's like, I've got something to ask you, innit."

The guy was hopped up on coke and meth.

"It's a favour, right, but not for me, yeah? It's for a mate, well,

20

a punter down the club, this guy I know. It's right up your street! I mean, I'd do it myself, but, well, it's a bit sketchy, so I can't."

"Stop fucking dancing around, you're giving me a headache. So what is it, this favour?"

"Well, it's like, I mean, you're a cop, Georges, but you know . . ." He thought for a moment, stopped weaving; the word escaped him. "But you ain't like other feds. You proper worked him over, that little *bamboula*! Smashed his face up! Yeah, safe, man! But, like, this favour I'm gonna ask, don't take it the wrong way, yeah?"

"Spit it out, I need to get home, get some sleep."

The Pakistani calmed down a little, started jogging on the spot.

"So, anyway, I got this customer who's got this situation. You wanna make five hundred, easy?"

Georges raised one bald eyebrow, half-covered with a plaster.

"I can't make speeding tickets go away."

"This ain't about no speeding ticket, man, this guy's don't got no ticket."

Georges slung his bag over his shoulder.

"Then I can't do anything for him."

"You're wrong, Georges. Guy like you can do a lot. Actually, it's a sex thing, you feel me?"

The more the Pakistani tried to be cunning, the more Crozat became convinced he was being taken for an arsehole. His head was still fuddled from the exhaustion, his hearing screwed up by the tinnitus.

"Get to the point, Paki, I've other things to do."

"See, this guy, he's got a problem with this other dude."

Georges smiled foolishly.

"So he's gay?"

The Pakistani froze, completely taken aback. He spoke as if to a child:

"Nah, man. He got a wife, that's the problem."

How could you complain about having a woman, wondered Georges, without realising that he did not have one.

"So who has he got this problem with? Look, I'm sick of this, I don't know what the fuck you're on about. I'm outta here."

"Chill, blud! His wife, she's sleeping with this other guy. Five hundred if you do him over, the guy, the guy she's sleeping with. That clear enough?"

Georges lifted his tattered balloon of a head. His cauliflower ears flushed red, his crudely patched-up eyebrow had started to bleed again.

"What?"

"You said you wouldn't take it the wrong way!"

"I didn't say anything. What do you think I am, some kind of thug?"

"Forget it, I was just messing with you!"

Before Georges could grab his T-shirt, the Pakistani bolted.

Paolo was waiting behind the wheel of his clapped-out Citroën.

"You took your time."

The AX's shock absorbers screeched.

"Run every red light, for the love of God; I need to sleep."

# 2

The whole of France is working eight-hour shifts to keep alive the illusion of full employment. A dream is being forged, a struggle leading to just reward for national effort. The fruits of Reconstruction. The right to work, to recognition, the right to live in a decent home or not to starve to death. In 1957, everyone is working towards their dream.

Hard graft, pride, the future, everything has been nationalised. Algerian oil, the French Sahara, nuclear testing. France desperately needs its last remaining colonies, they need the land and what lies beneath, they need the men if they are to build, to progress. The paradox of a colonial empire in this modern era of modernity has not yet struck people. For the past three years, Algeria has been laid waste by war. In February 1957, military service is increased to 30 months and those who did national service in '55 are called up again.

By April, there are 200,000 conscripts fighting under the flag, and 200,000 enlisted soldiers, most of whom have just limped back home from Indochina with their tails between their legs. De Gaulle's name is omnipresent, in every conversation, every newspaper. Censorship and propaganda are no longer enough. There are the dead, the bombs, the ambushes and reprisals in Palestro*, the Battle of Algiers, the first damning news reports. Prisoners tortured. Summary executions. The nameless war is already a dirty one.

The great dream of the nation is dead, eaten away from inside by political cancer. The Fourth Republic is on its last legs, there are calls for a new constitution. The political leaders of the F.L.N. are in Egypt, in Tunisia, in Germany, in France, a "revolutionary tax" is levied on immigrant Muslims and the "tax collectors" use the money to arm *fellagas* in working class *banlieues*, the M.N.A., supporters of Messali Hadj* clash with supporters of the F.L.N. on the streets of Paris; bombs are set off in Arab cafés, men are gunned down in the streets, policemen too. Algerians disappear, the police overrun the streets, the factories, the ghettos.

In the shanty towns, old beliefs are blown away. Communities close ranks, people spy on each other. Everyone is told to stand their ground, not to make waves. On the far shores of the Mediterranean, "terrorists" are making their voices heard. Factory fumes mingle with the smoke of dream towns ablaze. A different struggle in pursuit of a different reward: independence.

The Battle of Algiers is still raging and the psychological warfare of General Jacques Massu's* paras is being exported back to the metropolis. Arrests are mounting and with them the pleas daubed in the streets, on the factory walls: "Independence. F.L.N. Peace in Algeria."

*

Baptiste Provost looks out the window at the vast Aluvac factory yard below. The doors of the foundry and the workshops are wide open. The temperature soars with the sun. Thousands of workers pouring with sweat are waiting for the day to drag to a close.

He opens the window. A warm breeze rustles papers on the drawing boards. The bustle from the factory drifts up, the rumble of engines, the belch of the furnaces.

On the far side of the rue Pereire, two patrol cars and three police vans are waiting outside the huge wrought-iron gates. The officers patiently wait inside their sweltering vehicles. Provost shudders. The police presence reminds him of the Nazi Occupation, of the forced labour, of another factory being kept under surveillance. He gazes up at the two tall chimneystacks, follows the plume of black smoke that spreads across Nanterre towards Puteaux, the shanty towns of La Folie and beyond, towards the horizon and the rusting girders of the C.N.I.T.

Baptiste flinches as he hears the nightly wail that terrorised Paris, the silence shattered by the electric siren, the *muezzin* of the eight-hour shift.

Men in blackened overalls spill into the sun-bleached courtyard. On one side, the French gather with a handful of Italians and Spaniards; on the other, the Algerians with a few Tunisians and Moroccans. The usually raucous end-of-shift is eerily silent.

He recognises some of the workers. He studies his hands. Ten years he has worked at Aluvac. He remembers coming back from Germany, glad to find work, free, like everyone else, to pursue his dreams. These days, dissension has hardened men's faces.

Some twenty men shuttle between the two groups. The police clamber out of cars and vans and spread out in parallel lines blocking the street. The gates remain closed.

Should he join the trade unionists trying to reconcile the French and the Algerians? The Algerians who refuse to capitulate, who for the past three weeks have endured this daily confrontation.

When exactly did the police first show up? Have they always been there, lying in wait?

The *préfecture de police* has drawn up lists: those under surveillance, those to be arrested. In the desk drawers of the factory bosses there are similar lists: union members, sympathisers . . .

With world-weariness as his only guide to history, Provost struggles to understand all sides, and he gets confused. The only things that matter are tolerance and peace. Two things that are no longer to be found in Aluvac, in the *banlieues*, or in France itself, as people watch young men set off again for war, not knowing whether to cheer or to protest. How many have left the foundries here with nothing but the pathetic promise that they can have their jobs back when they return? The insidious notion that war won't change a thing, that everything will go back to how it was, as though nothing had happened.

War does not shape young men; it breaks them.

Baptiste bows his head, then turns to Verini, slumped in his chair, hands in pockets. Verini is twenty years old.

Square head sunk into his shoulders, he has been brooding since morning, his silent resentment adding to Provost's despondency.

In the factory yard, the personnel director goes to meet with the trade unionists. The endless disputes begin again.

A month ago, a strike at the foundry gave the police the excuse for this indefinite vigil outside the factory gates. The industrial action has lasted for some time; the police are not only there simply because of the Arabs. Every evening, at clocking-off time, a dozen Arabs are carted off to "have their papers checked", a process followed by all-night interrogations. The police are trying to get a sense of the chain of command of F.L.N. members in France. Aluvac is no exception to the rule. Only a few firebrands from the union have attempted to interfere in the name of working-class solidarity.

26

Cigarette dangling from his lips, Verini gets up and joins Baptiste at the window.

The gates have been opened, and the union men have lined up to face the police. Provost turns to his colleague.

"What did he say?"

The young man stares at one of the twenty-odd militants, clenches his teeth, his dark eyebrows lowering over his green eyes.

"Wanker!"

They can hear slogans: "Solidarity with our Algerian comrades! Free this factory!"

"He said: 'No enlisted men in this family.'"

Verini exhales a plume of cigarette smoke.

"Two-faced bastard!"

Provost looks down at the swarthy man raising a clenched fist.

"Don't talk about him like that."

Verini shrugs.

"The guy's an arsehole."

The Frenchmen march towards the gate. The members of the C.G.T. shout at them. They move between the serried ranks of police, who let them pass. The management applies what pressure it can: any Frenchman who has not openly expressed solidarity is to be allowed to pass unmolested, the factory has to remain open. Stick to the Algerians.

"He has his reasons."

"Party orders? Fucking pacifist!"

Verini slips on his linen jacket and heads out.

Plain-clothes officers point to faces in the crowd. The police hurl themselves at the silent Algerians, pushing aside the trade unionists who try to intervene. They drag the Arabs into Citroën vans with bars in the windows, a dozen of them. The vans drive away.

"What are you going to do?"

Verini goes out, slamming the door of the technical department behind him.

Provost, slumped in his chair, thinks back to the strapping teenager with grubby fingernails who showed up in his office three years earlier. A boy with little more than a primary school education, a *certificat d'études* and three years' experience in the workshops. He had been transferred to the technical department when one of the foremen spotted him coming out of the library. Provost had trained him to work at the drawing board, but he recognised that, though the boy made progress, he did not belong here. Too closed-minded, resistant to authority, too curious. Pascal Verini brought books into the office.

"Do you read much?"

"Not really ... now and again."

"What are you reading at the moment?"

"Alain Gerbault."

Provost had glanced at the title: *The Fight of the Firecrest: The Record of a Lonehand Cruise from East to West across the Atlantic.*

"Where did you find that?"

"Here, in the library. Old Mother Licoux gave it to me."

Licoux was the widow of a member of the *Francs-tireurs et partisans* shot by the Milice. She ran a skeletal library – an attempt by management to seem progressive – by commandeering second-hand books wherever she could, keeping back any money she got from Aluvac to spend on more expensive works. She encouraged curious workers. When she managed to corner people who showed they were interested in books, she was tenacious. In his three years with the department, Verini had borrowed three books a month. Old Mother Licoux had worked out what he liked. Tales of adventure, of travel: Jack London, Herman Melville, Alain Gerbault. He had read them all.

Three years during which Provost, twenty-six years his senior, had taken a shine to the lad.

1954: Verini is seventeen. He is studying draughtsmanship, he is a hard worker, happy to be out of the workshops, happy not to be slaving away on the production line with his father. Baptiste encourages him: "Don't stay here, Pascal, get out. You're young, you can do whatever you like, you don't have to be trapped here doing this." In the Aluvac factory, Algeria is little more than a rumour. 1955: at eighteen, Verini is bored, he doodles during working hours. "Go travelling! Leave your books, leave this factory. Get the hell out, Pascal, you have your whole life ahead of you." Already, the volunteer reservists and the first wave of conscripts are leaving for Algiers.

January 1956. Nineteen. Fort de Vincennes. The three-day military service assessment. Verini is found fit for duty and, in June 1957, he is called up. Things are starting to go wrong in Algeria, Provost's encouragements have become desperate pleas.

May 1957. Provost is slumped in his chair, the police have left and with them the last of the workers, the factory is deserted, silent. The sun's glare is still dazzling, the day seems determined not to end. Provost wants to leave. At forty-six, he has raised his children, fought a war and, since 1947, he has worked as a engineer at Aluvac. A month from now Verini will leave for Algeria. They had fought the war to end all wars; it was never meant to begin again. Verini could have escaped. A working-class lad with a fondness for books and dreams of travelling. Only one in a thousand, one in a million, managed to escape. Provost well knows the determination it takes to uproot yourself from the streets of Nanterre; it is a strength he never had. To be disloyal to a class, a world that is sensitive to the slightest betrayal.

Verini will finally get to travel. A troop ship to Algeria. Provost can feel his fury mounting, with no other vent than the hope that one day a boy like Verini will rebel.

*

Raoul Battaza was an old schoolmate from Mont Valérien primary school. Like him, a second-generation wop. Ten days earlier, Pascal had run into him in a local bar, celebrating his departure. He was buying rounds, laughing loudly, proudly wearing his army uniform. Pascal had a drink and asked him why he was so happy about being sent off to have a bullet put through him: "I tell you, my friend, no-one's going to put a bullet hole in this uniform, because this here's a Navy uniform and there are no boats up in the *djebels*! The most I'll see of Algeria is the coastline, if we even get that close." Raoul had enlisted without waiting to be called up, had signed up for a two-year tour. In return, he had been allowed to choose a branch of the military. To Pascal, this news was as much cause for celebration as Raoul's departure. It meant that he could still escape. He might get to sail, even if it was on an old army tub, it would have nothing to do with the war. He had a month to enlist before his call-up.

But Battaza has turned twenty-one while Verini will not come of age until November – five months after his call-up. To volunteer, he needs his father's consent. Last night, his father threw the papers back in his face. "I'll have no enlisted men in this family." This is the policy of the *Parti Communiste*, a pacifist policy of *cocos* who offered no other means to support Algerian nationalism.

Arsehole.

Pascal rides through Nanterre on his Vespa. He is not heading back to the rue de Garches, he is going to see Christine.

A committed pacifist has condemned his own son to war. Pascal spits and curses. Graffiti streams past. He will be the one doing the peacekeeping. Does he have to die to prove his father wrong? Fuck the factory, fuck the *banlieue*, fuck Algeria.

What if he goes A.W.O.L.? In *l'Humanité*, he has read articles about *les insoumis* – the draft-dodgers. How would he go about it? Where would he hide? For a son of Nanterre, Switzerland is a long way. Not that he gives a damn about running away, about leaving this place, but is he really prepared to risk going to jail, or being shipped off to Marseille in handcuffs? His twenty years are slipping away.

He tells Christine his father has refused to let him enlist. She cries. Despite his misgivings, he agrees to talk to Mercier. Anything rather than Marseille.

Madeleine, Christine's mother, phones Mercier. The conversation is strained.

Eventually, Mercier agrees. They arrange to meet the following day.

Christine and Pascal have been stepping out for a year. Christine is deeply in love, while Pascal worries whether he loves her as he is supposed to do: from the first, for the rest of his life.

Christine's mother is divorced; she and her daughter moved to Puteaux to avoid the moral opprobrium of their old neighbourhood. Madeleine considers Pascal intelligent. Her political principles do not prevent her from worrying about him.

She is seeing Bernard Mercier, a widower and captain in the infantry reserve forces. A veteran of the Indochinese war who came home in 1954, Mercier has always been suspicious of Verini, the son of a diehard, insubordinate Communist.

It is only for Madeleine's sake that he agrees to pull some strings for Pascal; he cannot have him declared unfit for service, but he can ensure he completes his military service in France. Pascal knows what this means. It is that chance of a lifetime, but the offer is thrown in his face like an insult. Right now, the insult does not matter; all that matters is the result.

Thirty months in a garrison on the outskirts of Paris: Algeria will be nothing more than a grubby, distant skirmish. He drives through town on his moped, the wind streaking tears across his face. He will find another job, live in Paris, buy a car. In thirty months, he will be able to do as he pleases. I'm free, he thinks to himself, and for free men things are different.

*

Camp de Frileuse, Yvelines
August 1957

Civilian life is a distant memory, the army is his family now. There is talk only of war, it is petrifying. In a few short months, these timorous raw conscripts must be turned into well-oiled machines. Everyone knows that on the ground, high up in the *djebels*, there will be no place for hotheads. Verini is champing at the bit: the slightest eccentricity is a risk the army cannot accept. A lone voice expresses the thoughts of a dozen conscripts. It is a life of constant drudgery, brutalisation, infantilisation and verbal abuse. The drill sergeants work in relays. Efficiency, speed, every single second is accounted for. In a few weeks, the rookies need to learn they are no longer in charge of their destinies. Verini laughs to himself, he plays along, knowing none of this is for him. He will not be heading for Algeria, he is staying here. He suffers the warrant officers' roars without flinching. He does exactly as he is ordered because he only has to put up with training for a month. Mercier promised. In the first month after he was called up, he went through Army Safe Driver Training to get a licence for ordinary and heavy goods vehicles, and felt he was learning something useful. The food here is repulsive; he eats it. The atmosphere reeks of testosterone and tension – a cross between summer camp and boarding school – the new conscripts all determined to come across as hard nuts. At night, around the card tables, playing *belotte*, he hears things that he finds shocking. "We're going to fuck them over, those *bougnoles*. We're not gonna just hand over Algeria to a bunch of sand monkeys." He realises not everyone reads *l'Humanité*. He learns to hold his tongue, to mistrust his brothers-in-arms, he declines to play cards, keeps himself to himself. Twenty years old. People repeat what they hear, they don't think for themselves. Orders, he is surprised to discover, easily get through these thick young skulls he had assumed would be as tough as his own. He only has to hold out until the end of basic training, endure the barking of the drill sergeant, Adjudant Fauchon, fresh home from Indochina with a scar across his cheek and a reputation as a nasty drunk. Just one more month. He avoids coming to blows with cretins looking for trouble, lets comments slide which in Nanterre would immediately start a fight. Wop. Commie. Bolshie. Traitor. Yellow-belly.

He keeps a low profile, holds out for a letter from Christine and, very soon, a cushy job.

Three days they've been on manoeuvres. Thirty degrees in the shade. The tension mounts, more and more conscripts set off from camp, their kits on their backs and a knot in their bellies. Verini carries on joking, but emotions are running high and the fear is contagious. The weak are singled out, ridiculed, humiliated; the strong hold sway, led by *les sous-officiers*. Ravening hunger, three days on manoeuvres, has turned the group into a baying pack. Verini is exhausted, Fauchon's ranting bores into his eardrums. Out of bed, standing to attention, a morning briefing after yet another sleepless night. This is a test: what will trickle out of a young man when you put really put him under pressure: deference, acceptance, defiance, insubordination? Exhaustion makes him want to laugh.

Radio contact: an attack on the yellows' artillery positions. They are the blues. Verini giggles, says loudly: "When we've finished beating the shit out of the yellows, you can make us eat our greens." Fauchon barks for him to belt up and move it, get going, finishes his order with: "Shut your hole, you little wop shit, and get marching." Verini's laughter turns to spluttering fury.

"Go fuck yourself. I'm not marching anywhere."

The other conscripts are speechless. Unless he starts marching straight away, he risks being banged up for thirty days. But it's too late.

"Bang me up for thirty months for all I care."

The warrant officer roars. Verini tosses his rifle at Fauchon's feet and takes off.

He crosses the practice ground and returns to barracks, blood pounding in his temples. He is fucking everything up, all he had to do was bite his tongue for one more month. Well, fuck the lot of them. He thinks about the letter from Christine he received the day before they went on manoeuvres.

Mercier had had his reasons for helping Verini. The "favour" had been an affront, a form of blackmail. To a boy born in Nanterre to a family of Commie wops, nothing comes for free. Mercier was prepared to save Verini from Algeria on condition that his stepdaughter did not see him ever again. In despair, Christine begged him in her letter not to write, not to try to see or contact her until after his military service. Then we can talk about the future. The future? A future he has just watched a match being put to. Verini may be unsure that he loves Christine

34

as he should, but there is one thing he knows for sure: he despises Mercier.

He sprawls on the bed, snickering as he remembers the look on Fauchon's face.

Insubordination, refusal to obey a direct order, assaulting an officer, laying down arms. Court-martialled. Adjudged a deserter, a traitor to his country. No strings left to pull. A prison sentence is commuted in favour of disciplinary action. Wartime exigencies. He is to leave for Marseille on August 25. Board a ship for Algiers. Pascal grits his teeth as he listens to the verdict of the officers lined up before him in a makeshift courtroom.

War. Death. Fear. Algeria.

Verini does not write to Christine.

The train leaves Paris.

France is not at war. All the newspapers say so. Only the army is at war. France is hard at work. Our sons will keep the peace in Algeria. A bunch of *bougnoles* planting bombs. Two hundred thousand conscripts. There is no war in 1957, France is a modern country. Where has Verini gone?

# 3

May 2009

The two days' leave he had were just about enough to put him back on his feet. Crozat lay in bed in the mornings, sinking into the too-soft mattress, face pressed into the pillow. Feverish, his sleep fitful, he emerged still groggy. When he woke, he swallowed a litre of water and 400 mg of Nurofen. He watched as the room slowly grew brighter; at 7.00 a.m., he got up. A few cautious stretches. In the fogged mirror he studied his face, mottled with bruises, swollen downturned lips, lifeless eyes.

A cafetière full of arabica, a hole in his stomach but no appetite. Sitting at the kitchen table, he wolfed down a couple of eggs. A thin thread of egg white trickled from his numbed lips onto the old boxing robe that doubled as a dressing gown. His whole body ached, but pain – an old friend – never bothered him.

For hours he sat, sipping cold coffee, replaying the count that had ended the bout. *Six.* Thanks for the lesson, gramps. *Seven.* You could have had a great career, everyone knows that. *Eight.* You get to pocket the take. *Nine.* Five hundred if you do him over. *Ten.* Do you take me for an idiot? . . . *Six. Seven. Eight.* Thanks, gramps. *Nine. Ten.* Fuckwit.

He hadn't gone out whoring.

He stretched his fingers, his body seemed to move independently, like a machine.

He needed to shake it off. Physio, training and hard work, sort his head out, blot out the faces of Kravine and the Pakistani, postpone the inevitable.

Georges pulled on a tracksuit, put on a baseball cap, went out. Heading for Ring 14. The gym was usually pretty empty around 4.00 p.m. The twenty-minute walk eased the stiffness in his legs, but the pounding of his heels on the pavement echoed inside his head. He attempted a few sprints before getting to the ring, but had to give them up. A ten-metre dash left him panting, he slowed his pace so as not to show up breathless at the gym.

Marco was in the office, his broken nose buried between a stack of papers and an overflowing ashtray. The office was decorated in the typical dusty, maudlin style, all smoke, autographed posters, trophies, medals, framed black-and-white photos. A little world of heroic tales that crackled like an old record, a constant reminder that boxing is only for the young.

"Hey, Marco."

The boss of Ring 14 looked up and a pair of cheap regulation-issue glasses slipped from his nose where nothing now could perch.

"How you doing, you old bastard? I see the kid got a few punches in. Handy with his fists, young Gabin. They say you rattled his teeth?"

Georges pulled the visor of his baseball cap lower.

"I got him, but it was a close call."

Marco stared up at him from beneath the droopy eyelids of an old man, or a dumb basset hound. His lips curled up on one side, down on the other.

Georges clenched his teeth. He knew that rictus grin, the one that plastered you onto the wall of a gym to join the rest of the photographs.

"Yeah, Paolo said it was a top-notch fight."

Georges turned towards the room.

"I'll head . . ."

"Hey, make yourself at home, Georges. Hang loose."

*Hang loose?*

Marco cleared his throat.

"Kravine swung by last night. He was looking for you."

Georges paused in the doorframe.

"Yeah?"

"Said he'd be back. Any message you want me to give him?"

"No." Georges sighed and walked away.

The punchbags were too hard, the weights too heavy, his sweat was acid, his breath short. From the office Marco kept glancing at him, watching him wear out his aching body.

Stubbornly, The Wall kept going, one eye on the door to the gym, increasingly regretting his decision to come here. He thought about the *commissariat*, about everything he hadn't had the guts to take on; he thought about Georges Crozat, that pathetic sack of shrivelled muscle who would soon get precisely what he deserved: fuck all. Kravine's deal. He tried to keep under the radar, in the vast, deserted boxing gym echoing with the squeak of his trainers. He felt like laughing, to take the piss out of his life before he chucked it on the scrapheap. But Kravine's face came back to him, that pasty smile; suddenly his fury found its sparring partner. He threw punches harder, faster, his face contorted with pain and he collapsed again, evicted from his own body: an ageing brawler shadow-boxing with the guy he used to be. Shit, Georges, what the fuck's wrong with you? Don't give in, Georges, hang in there. Keep moving those feet, Georges, keep shuffling.

Towards 5.00 p.m., when he saw a group of boxers come

through the doors, he went and shut himself in a shower stall, turned the water on full, and only emerged after the others had changed and left. As he left the changing rooms, head down, he bumped into someone going in. Georges apologised, his face flushing.

Then he pulled himself together. Stand up straight, at least in front of this worm.

The Pakistani, like a cat on hot bricks.

"Damn, just the dude I was looking for! How's it going, copper? Fucking hell, you've got some face on you. Hard to believe you won!"

"Fuck off."

Georges pushed past, but the Pakistani put a hand on his shoulder.

"Hey, champ! Not so fast."

Georges turned; the bouncer smoothed his hair which was tied back into a ponytail.

"You think about my little deal? Don't get bent out of shape, O.K.? Just saying, if you're interested it's still on the table, yeah?"

The Wall looked down, clenched his fists and spoke without thinking:

"Have to see."

The Pakistani lowered his voice, leaned in and whispered.

"Sweet. Five hundred notes, that's the deal. I'll talk to my guy, yeah? We cool?"

"Mmm."

"Like I said, blud, it's right up your street. I said to my bro, I said, 'I got just the guy you need!'"

Georges raised his hand, grabbed the pumped-up parasite by the scruff of the neck and stared him in the eye for a second.

"Now listen up: I don't want you talking about me anymore,

39

are we clear? I don't want you giving out my details to the fuck-wits who hang out at that club of yours."

The tip of his baseball cap brushed the forehead of the bouncer who was standing on tiptoe.

"Chill, bruv, it's all cool, don't sweat it. It's just this one guy who's got a problem with his wife. It's nothing sketchy, swear down, it's just this one thing."

"Who are you whoring your services to down at the station?"

The Pakistani swallowed hard, held his palms up in surrender.

"Hey, Georges, you know I can't talk about that shit, even to you!"

"I'm warning you, if any of this gets back to the *commissariat*, if I have any problems because of this, I'll fucking kill you. I'll rip your face off. Are we clear? . . . How do we do this? How do these things work?"

Georges unclenched his fist, the Pakistani tugged his T-shirt smooth.

"Chill, Mister Policeman, you trust me, yeah? So this guy, he lives in Paris, he needs this thing done in the next few days. Listen, I know you're the pro and all, but I'm gonna say this anyway: we don't need you giving this guy a heart attack, just a bit of a scare, yeah? I'll get the info to you tomorrow. Meet here, same time?"

"No way. Put it through my letterbox – 3 rue Copreaux – I need the address and the money upfront. After that . . . after that I don't want to hear from you again."

"Works for m—"

"What's up, girls? Having a catfight?"

Georges jumped but the Pakistani managed a lopsided grin.

Roman. As tall as Georges but stockier, and half a head taller than the bouncer.

40

"Any chance of getting past?"

A thug who's not worth shit who used Ring 14 to maintain the calluses on his knuckles that he got from hitting anything that moved in the street. Georges knew him by sight and by reputation. Roman was in Organised Crime, a *lieutenant*. Roman knew Georges, not as a colleague, but as a boxer.

"What the hell hit you, Crozat, a freight train?"

"No way, bro, Georges K.O.'d this Algerian kid Saturday night, it was a wild bout!"

The Pakistani started bobbing on the spot again.

"Was I talking to you?"

Roman was a piece of work, happy to sell his services to anyone who was paying. Bent cop or Super Cop, depending on your view of the force. A hoary police cliché, work with the underground during the war, get your stripes after Liberation, wind up in some minister's contact books. Roman feared nothing and he treated the whole world as his enemy.

He and Georges never hit it off, they had the sort of grudging respect of boxers who share a weight class and constantly wonder which of them could take the other if it came to it.

"That true, Crozat? You won?"

"Yeah," Georges muttered and left the changing room, touching the brim of his baseball cap by way of goodbye, or as a greeting to Roman.

He needed to get out, to get home and stick his head in a tub of ice until his brain froze. Anything so he would not have to think about the fact that he and Roman were in the same line of work now, that the Pakistani was turning up at his place and that it would take him no more than a second to rat him out.

Pouring sweat, he slunk out of the gym, which was now teeming with people. Besides the four guys already sparring, a dozen men were hanging around in police uniforms or business suits, sports bags at their feet, chatting with Marco. Georges edged towards the door. Merleau, a fellow officer, a *brigadier* down at the 14th, shouted after him.

"Hey, Georges! Where d'you think you're going . . . ? Come back here, fuck sake, we want to hear about the fight!"

*Six, seven, eight,* keep on your feet. *Nine, ten,* smile for the cameras.

*

Standing in front of the mirror in the lobby, Georges adjusted his collar. Putting on his uniform, he hated the feeling that it was like climbing into the ring with tampered gloves. To say nothing of his gun. This morning was worse than most. It was as though, for the last time, he was hiding his boxer's body under his police uniform.

Bergolio showed up briefly just before noon and, without bothering to knock, popped his head round the door of the office where Crozat had spent the past four hours shuffling through the same twenty police records. The *commissaire* usually gave him paperwork to do after a fight, not out of the goodness of his heart – Bergolio was not a fan – but so that he wouldn't frighten old ladies in the street.

"Hey, Crozat. Not finding your comeback too tough?"

Bergolio laughed to himself. Georges didn't register the joke, disconcerted as he was by the fact that the *commissaire* had dropped by to say hello.

"Not too bad. I managed to rest up."

"Two days isn't much. How long's it been since you last took a proper break?"

"A holiday?"

"A week, two weeks, the beach, the mountains, a trip to the countryside. A proper break, not just a two-day rest."

What the hell did Bergolio want? What was with these questions?

"I don't know, a while I suppose . . . I mean since I took a holiday."

"I want you back on patrol tomorrow. You're not cut out for paper shuffling, you need more physical challenges. Am I right?"

Hands in his pockets, Bergolio stared at Georges for a moment, a smile tugging at the corners of his lips, then he left as abruptly as he had arrived.

Georges broke into a cold sweat. As far as he could remember, this was the longest conversation he had ever had with his boss. A shot across the bows. The Pakistani, Roman, Bergolio. What was with all this talk about holidays? A desk job? He was none the wiser by the time he got to the canteen.

Sitting among his fellow officers, who seemed to find his bruised and swollen face hilarious, he mulled it over.

What did they all want from him?

He tried to calm down, chewing his steak slowly. If the Pakistani had grassed him up, why would Roman have told Bergolio? And why would his boss seem not to give a damn?

Jibes and catcalls echoed around the canteen and along the corridors, but Georges didn't hear them. He just smiled idiotically, so as not to have to answer. Georges the Wall, a ninety-one-kilo simpleton, built to take a beating. He didn't give a toss, he'd found a way to tell Kravine where to shove it, for now at least; later, he would have to see. In spite of his misgivings, he was getting worked up – though he had no idea how he might drum up a Don Juan to work over every month and a husband prepared to shell out five hundred notes; the Pakistani would probably run out of marks pretty quickly.

But he had other prospects.

Roman.

He liked the idea of sitting at his desk, blowing hot air, trying not to think about the ring, about his need to slip on a pair of boxing gloves and stare another guy right in the eyes for a few minutes.

He spent the afternoon dealing out reports, he tried to joke with his colleagues, but his voice sounded strange in his ears and no-one laughed. Maybe he should suggest they go for a drink one of these days after work, now he didn't have to worry about training anymore. He could talk about the bouts he'd fought, these guys loved boxing. He'd have stories to tell them. Talk about the girls, without mentioning that they were hookers. What difference did it make? If they asked how he managed to pull so many women, how he paid for the restaurants and nights out, he would just wink and say: "I do alright, don't you worry."

When he found the envelope in his postbox, on rue Copreaux, he came back to earth with a jolt.

Up in his apartment, he ripped open the unmarked envelope. A handwritten card read: "Alain Dulac, 2 place du Maroc, 75019"; attached to the message were a photograph and five hundred-euro notes.

Georges pinched the notes between his fingers, rubbed them against each other, inspected the watermark. The bills were real, alright. A fine chain of connections, he thought, stunned that the money had reached him so quickly.

The guy whose wife was playing away had to be an ugly son of a bitch, because Dulac was no oil painting. He looked like the sort of guy who pays for it.

Five hundred euros. More than he could expect for an amateur bout. And no fist in the face.

The envelope contained no message for Alain Dulac, nothing but his address. And a beating. The guy would work out why he was getting a beating. It was the sort of wordless logic that appealed to Georges.

And yet, the face of this Lothario upset him. He looked like a geek, an intellectual type. There was no danger of him fighting back. He probably weighed in at 30 kilos less than Georges. The moral qualm was less troubling when expressed as a weight category.

Even so, Georges found it hard to sleep, he felt an inexplicable resentment. Something was bothering him. Sprawled in the bed, he dozed, his half-closed eyes staring at the .38 Taurus hanging in its holster on the back of a chair at the end of the bed. An image flickered in his head, one he couldn't dispel. André Gabin, muscular, determined, dancing round the ring. He remembered his name now, certain he would not forget it again.

The image of the boxer dissolved at last into an inchoate thought, which exploded into scraps of dream.

*

The first few hours he spent watching Dulac's building, Georges felt like a detective. The tracksuit and baseball cap made it feel as though he were working undercover, though he remembered this area of Stalingrad as being more working class. It had been years since he last came here; back then there were no cinemas, no trendy bars along the banks of the artificial lake at la Villette.

The pavements were teeming. Gangs of youths and occasional couples were sitting on the flagstones, feet dangling above the water. Some areas of the city became younger, hipper, while others – like his own – seemed to age and wither without his noticing. The longer he waited, the more preposterous his track-suit seemed to him. In this new life, he would have to think about dressing differently.

After three hours loitering around the place du Maroc – a roundabout with no trees, no benches – he began to think that a car would have made the stake-out easier. Georges had never owned a car, he drove only patrol vehicles. He added this to the mental list of things he needed to buy, and started to look out for models he liked. With the extra work the Pakistani could put his way, and a small loan, he would be able to afford one second-hand.

When he recognised Dulac, the man was walking towards him with another man – also fortysomething, weedy and with a grey-ing three-day beard. Corduroy jackets, leather shoes, they were almost identical. The briefcase Dulac was carrying was black, the other man's was fawn. Deep in conversation, walking quickly, they entered number 2 place du Maroc at 8.00 p.m. Dulac's friend emerged at 9.00 p.m., Georges spotted him as he was returning to his observation post with a kebab.

He ate the kebab. Half an hour later, he saw Dulac pull the curtains of his living room, a third-floor window that overlooked the square. Seeing his shadowy figure, once again Georges had the uneasy feeling that reality would not bend readily to his plans. He waited until 11.00 p.m. Dulac did not re-emerge.

He went home.

He had a few days to do the job, according to the Pakistani. Then again, Georges had no desire to spend his evenings hang-ing about outside. He had better things to do.

It was a busy neighbourhood, there was no way he could whack Dulac on the street. He would come back after his next shift, wait for Dulac to get home and then ring the man's doorbell. There was no need for cunning, two punches would be enough to knock him out, it would all be over in twenty seconds. Georges assumed he would do it in the doorway to Dulac's apartment, gripping the man by the collar so as not to make too much noise.

*

His face had recovered its ruddy complexion, the bruises from the bout had faded, and he was out on patrol with Merleau. His partner kept himself to himself. Merleau was only interested in women, played bad cop with shopkeepers and pedestrians which kept any conversations to a minimum.

The beat was an endless round of stop and search, gossiping grannies, motorcyclists without helmets, truck drivers double-parked; hours with nothing to do but pound the pavement, truncheons slapping against their legs, service pistols, handcuffs and tear gas canisters beginning to wear them down. Back to the police canteen at noon, Merleau running his mouth off to other officers about the women he had chatted up that morning. The afternoon spent tramping the streets of the 14th *arrondissement* again. There were the people who became nervous at the mere sight of a policeman and crumpled under Merleau's glowering stare and those who looked them in the eye – *I've got nothing to feel guilty about, so fuck you*. There were the people who said hello, those who studiously ignored them, and those who eyed them with contempt.

Merleau was a cop through and through and towards the end of a shift day, when he got tired, he became more aggressive. Which was bad news for anyone who crossed his path. Despite appearances, Merleau was no dumber than the other officers he regaled with his stories: shopkeepers sucked up to cops in the hope of protection, whores flashed a smile in the hope of avoiding a fine. Georges hadn't uttered a word all day. In his mind he was already on the place du Maroc, ringing Dulac's doorbell.

He was less excited, he hadn't slept well. Outside of a boxing ring, beating someone's brains out was no simple matter. Especially if you want to make an impression but don't want to be seen. And remember, dickwad: screw this up, and you can kiss your career in the force goodbye . . .

"What d'you say?"

"Huh? . . . Nothing . . . it's time to head back."

"You think I'm dumb or what? You're not looking yourself today, Georges. Everything O.K.?"

\*

Georges stepped out of Dulac's building, looking around for an escape route through the yellow night. Shit, which way had he come? He whirled around, looking for an alley to duck into. He turned left, walked as fast as he dared, he passed a few people, tempted to turn round every time a car behind him raked him with its headlights. He rubbed both hands on his sweatshirt, cursing himself for wearing light clothing which was now smeared with patches of blood. In the end he pulled off the sweatshirt and tied it round his waist. He took the dark, narrow streets, lengthened his stride, then broke into a run. His lungs began to peel away from his aching ribs. He slowed down, realising he was heading the wrong way, into the 19th *arrondissment*, towards Maréchaux. He turned right on a hunch, he was calmer now, he came to the canal de l'Ourcq and crossed over, turned right towards the Buttes-Chaumont. He hated feeling that he was retracing his steps, circling Dulac's flat, unable to get away.

He suppressed the urge to go back.

Had Dulac called the police, an ambulance, a doctor? Were

there crowds milling on the place du Maroc? Sirens, people peering out their windows, neighbours on the landings? Or had Dulac simply dragged himself into the bathroom and cleaned himself up?

Dulac clearly wasn't used to taking a punch. Had he alerted the whole neighbourhood or taken his beating like a man? That's what Georges would have done, but Dulac was probably scared he might die. It was a close thing. The hail of punches, many more than he had imagined. It was the silence that most surprised him, nothing but the sound of bare fists on flesh.

Actually, there had been something else. Dulac had managed a few gasping words, his nose and mouth filled with blood. Words Georges did not give him time to scream.

*Who are you?*

Stop.

Stop.

Then came the stammering, the questions Georges could not and did not have the time to hear because he was already hurtling back down the stairs.

Sirens wailed across the city, one of them might well be headed for the place du Maroc.

The flurry of punches came naturally, automatically. A dozen, maybe fifteen blows. Georges had pulled his punches, but it was enough to rattle Dulac. Maybe he had been too brutal? Maybe he should have thrown a few more punches, knocked the guy down? Though of course Georges had held him upright, dragged him to his feet when he collapsed, and hit him some more. Because just looking at the weedy little runt, he felt a dull rage. Maybe it was triggered by the way Dulac looked at him when he opened the door. Arrogant? Yeah, that was how he remembered it: an arrogant look. Later it had been the man's tears that goaded him, his terror, his passivity. He hadn't even tried to defend himself, he simply grovelled and asked why. Transformed from hero to zero with the first punch. If he'd shut his hole and taken the beating, maybe it would have been over sooner.

Georges had let anger get the better of him. He chalked it up to inexperience.

He walked quickly, it would take him an hour to get home, he focused on the money – the takings – the better to forget Dulac's pitiful face as soon as possible. How the fuck could a man get to the age of forty without realising that one day the world will cave in on you? In the final analysis, it was Dulac's innocence that had made Georges angry. That air of entitlement that comes from being born with a bullet-proof vest.

He climbed the three flights of stairs to his own apartment without slowing down, the smell of Dulac's stairwell still filled his nostrils. He closed the door behind him and sat motionless at the table for an hour, trying to clear his mind. A month's reprieve, he had enough to ward off Kravine for three or four weeks now, enough for a pretty whore, he needed a woman, someone to listen to him tell the tale of his latest victory before he forgot it.

\*

Georges listened to the radio as he drank his coffee. His sleep had been fitful, there was no escaping the haze of conscience that whirled around him like a hangover. Nothing on the news, on any of the stations he listened to as he twisted the dial and scanned the airwaves. No beatings reported in the 19th, no sign of Dulac's name in the newspapers. There was nothing the next day, or the next. One more anonymous assault, there had probably been dozens since then. There might have been a report, a complaint lodged against some unidentified suspect at the local station, but Georges made no attempt to find out. Dulac had kept his trap shut.

For a week, he couldn't bring himself to touch the money. He didn't go to the porte de Champerret to visit the whores. He felt pretty low and Gabin was still haunting his dreams.

Ten days after the job on the place du Maroc, he came home from his shift to find a white envelope in his letterbox. On the card: "Good Work". Below this, an address, a name, another photograph and six hundred-euro notes.

He had not seen the Pakistani again. Another envelope had arrived. Georges smiled.

# 4

As the train surged onward, the South melted into the sunset, the rocky landscape of Provence veered to yellow, red, then black. Men began to peel their faces from the windows and stared blankly at the darkness. In the compartments, drowsy, fretful men took comfort in looking around to see other soldiers bound for the same destination. Knowing they were all in the same boat meant they did not have to question their fate.

There were no bawling officers, and the fact that there were civilians on the train eased the tension. They felt a surge of freedom as they watched the countryside flash past. It was absurd. In Frileuse or in any other barracks, the war seemed further away than it does now, in the blaze of the setting sun as the train heads towards Marseille.

Verini listens to the clank of helmets against the kitbags tied to the luggage racks above their heads.

Night is drawing in, and with it a warm, scented breeze that streams through the open windows. Verini had smoked a few cigarettes in the corridor, suppressing the urge to join in with the other rookies catcalling to women on the platform whenever the train stopped at a station. He didn't wave, didn't acknowledge the people who saluted them, cheering on "our brave boys".

Those smiling people. There were not many of them, but even so, they had come to show their support. Verini felt like screaming abuse at them, he felt like grabbing someone and pushing him onto the train so that he could take the man's place, could laugh from the station platform as the train pulled away. Meanwhile, his fellow soldiers waved back, they smiled, they saluted. Stupid arseholes.

Verini, *soldat de deuxième classe*, is far ahead of them: for him, Algeria is a punishment detail. What other horrors lie in wait for him? There can be nothing good there. At best, a peaceful garrison in a town, far from the mountains and the *fellagas*. Algiers, maybe: girls in skirts, sunshine, cafés, beaches, mopeds – just like Nanterre. The war is being waged out in the countryside, where the F.L.N. are hiding, out in the *bled* where he will never set foot. He feels relieved: two years of dumb fatigues in Algeria. A waste of time. Nothing to do out there but safeguard the sunlit streets. Maybe a job as a driver, now that he's got his licence. He clings to his uncertainties, shuffles through them as he listens to the thin metallic clinking from the overhead racks.

It is pitch dark now, the train slows as it passes though villages, the constellations of lights become more dense. A suburb. Men look up, excitement surging through them, those from Paris mimic the thick Marseille accent, stable-boys open their eyes wide like marbles. Faces are pressed against the windows smeared with greasy shapes and fingerprints.

Then fear explodes. He is breathless, he can feel the fitful pounding of his heart deep in his belly. He is leaving. There is nothing more he can do.

On the platform at Saint-Charles, other soldiers direct them to waiting trucks, engines idling. It looks like a police round-up. The trucks move through the muggy darkness. From beneath

the tarpaulin, a fleeting glimpse of busy streets, of bars and restaurants, of people sitting on the terraces turning to watch the
convoy. Then the harbour buildings, the damp air coming from
the sea, the screech of gulls, the smell of fuel oil, the heat of the
engines. Faces pale now, men toss kitbags down onto the ground,
jump down from the trucks, pick up their bags again and follow
the bellowing voices urging them onward amid the clatter of the
flat-bed trucks, the squelching of boots through slick puddles;
the sickening smell of a commercial port, the shriek of cables
loading military equipment. Searchlights pick out a ship, its hull
painted white: the *Charlton Star*. A cruise ship commandeered to
transport troops. The men join hundreds of other conscripts.
How many of them are there? A snivelling mob, tense and half
asleep, stumbling forward in their beige uniforms, pushing and
shoving so as not to be trampled. A gangway. Officers check each
man's military papers and distribute boarding passes.

The windowless hold is dimly lit. On the steel deck, they find
hundreds of deckchairs lined up on which they pile their belongings. Verini stands next to a white deckchair in the ship's prow,
hard against the hull. He had looked around for some way out,
but he is surrounded, trapped, bewildered.

Finally they are given a bone to gnaw on: word goes round
that soup will be served on deck after everyone has boarded. Verini is surprised to realise that he is hungry, that he had barely
eaten anything since Paris, that he has needs, that he will not be
able to simply put his life on hold for two years.

Waves of men stream into the fetid, overheated hold. The
smell of marine paint, of oxidising chemicals, or rust and salt
water catches in the throat. He thinks about the call he made
from the Gare de Lyon. About his sister's voice. "Tell the folks I'm
being shipped off to Algeria. Tell them I'll be in touch." Stricken
with remorse, he had made the call just before boarding the

train. In the crowded hold, he realises that he is terrified that he will be forgotten, that there will be no-one waiting for news, no-one to care about him. Over and over he mutters his parents' address, like a secret message that he would rather swallow than allow to be ripped from his mind.

Doors slam, levers clang, the foghorn of the *Charlton Star* wails as they cast off. The conscripts cheer. Somewhere, a group of two or three lads starts singing the Internationale, soon switching to a whistle. The muffled thrum of the engines grows louder and the hull begins to shudder. For a second the noise stops as hundreds of faces stare up at the quivering light bulbs. The cruise liner judders and almost imperceptibly pulls away from the quay.

They are allowed to venture out, a nameless horde of men already seasick, faces green, hands clasped over their mouths. They are counted as they come up on deck, boxes are ticked on registration forms.

How long since they arrived at Marseille station? Two hours, three? Verini has not even had time to think about Fauchon, about running his mouth off, about the court martial, about Christine, about Mercier. He leans against the ship's rail. Aluvac is another world, a present relegated to the past. The quay disappears in the distance.

They are leaving for two years in Algeria.

Thousands of eyes straining to see the unfamiliar scrap of France that is the harbour. They stare so hard that it is the coastline that seems to move, wheeling around the fixed axis of the *Charlton Star*, around this need for one last glimpse of dry land.

There is no-one on the quays. All too quickly the city is no more than a shadow against the orange sky pricked with yellow lights. Soon it is a halo of tiny stars, then a barely visible point, and still they continue to stare.

They are served a thin broth swimming with a few chunks of

meat and some small white dots. Stringy mutton with couscous. Their first taste of Algerian food, wolfed down half-heartedly only to be quickly thrown up again.

Not two hours out of Marseille, the *Charlton Star* is heaving and yawing. In the hold is a maelstrom, deckchairs sliding around and crashing into each other. The rumour spreads. A storm is brewing. Verini never thought there could be a storm on the Mediterranean, in mid-August. The ship pitches and rolls. Conversations trail off into silence.

The toilets set up for them become blocked. Puddles of urine and vomit stream across the floor. Tossed against the sides, some conscripts have lumps on their heads, some are bleeding. Others have put on their helmets. Cold and damp seep through their uniforms. They swaddle themselves in their bedding. It is impossible to sleep. Verini manages not to be sick; perhaps the grim fury with which he clenches his teeth has kept his stomach calm. The choppy Mediterranean waves pound the steel frame like hammer blows. The hull judders, crumples several inches under the blows. Is this a hurricane, or merely a storm that they can weather with ease? The cruise ship that had looked indestructible, a building moored to the quay, is now pitched about like a fishing schooner. Hours pass, the engines never slow, still the *Charlton Star* slices through the waves.

The conscripts are distraught, exhausted. Officers, pale and nervous, come down into the hold to reassure them the storm will not last long. Some of the rookies scream to be let out; others try to calm them, fearing that panic will spread.

Little by little the rolling of the ship becomes less violent, the sea becomes calmer. The deckchairs are put back in place, the soldiers slump in the uncomfortable seats in the vain hope they might catch some sleep, or at least some rest. It is 5.00 a.m.; the sun will soon be up.

How far are we from Africa?

At 6.00 a.m., the hold is opened and the soldiers abandon any hope of sleep. They scrabble onto the deck. Will the count be the same when they reach Algiers as it was in Marseille? Have any of the men thrown themselves into the sea during the crossing?

The men are dumbfounded. They have not arrived. They are in the middle of nowhere.

The high seas. The sun to the east is low on the horizon still. The men climb back down into the hold to fetch jackets and blankets against the wind and the salt spray. Those who are sickest sit, arms folded over their stomachs, and refuse the breakfast served in mess tins that still smell of mutton broth. Conversations start up, names exchanged, awkward introductions. In the dawn light, friendships are quickly cemented; no-one wants to be alone staring at the horizon.

They are not the men they were the night before, the storm has emptied their stomachs and minds. The dazed conscripts in this contingent brood on what lies ahead, any illusions that this might be a routine military service shattered.

Verini drinks a cup of coffee leaning against the gunwale, facing south. But he does not want to look that way, he turns back towards the stern, towards a France that has vanished during the night. He does not want to see over there, either. In his mind, he sketches out a rough map of the Mediterranean, strides across the deck and stares out to the west, to a horizon that presents no terrors, offers no hope. Somewhere out there, unseen, lie the Straits of Gibraltar, and beyond them, the Atlantic. He smokes a cigarette, offers one to the lad standing next to him and introduces himself.

"Pascal."

He realises that he has not uttered a word since Marseille.

"Christian."

He doesn't know what to say.

"Where you from?"

"Compiègne. You?"

"Nanterre."

"I have a cousin in Nanterre, he works at the Simca factory."

They stare out at the sea, the conversation trails away. The seascape creates a feeling of malaise; their platitudes seem suddenly absurd. Verini is sorry that he spoiled his first encounter with the sea by offering a cigarette to some prole from Compiègne. Christian puffs nervously on his cigarette.

"Do you know where you're going, where you've been posted?"

Verini tosses his cigarette stub overboard.

"No."

"Me neither."

Verini walks off along the gangways. A sailor tells him he cannot go any further. They are about the same age. They exchange a look. Verini does not insist, he considers engaging the sailor in conversation but decides against it. It would be worse, somehow, to talk to someone who is not planning to disembark.

By noon, things on deck are better.

Lunch is served.

Shouts come from the bow of the *Charlton Star*.

The men race over to see, not the coastline, but another liner on its way to France. A mile apart, the two ships pass each other. Foghorns wail a greeting. A troop carrier? Soldiers heading home, shouting for joy? Do soldiers leave Algeria with the urge to shout for joy? Probably. On the voyage home, Verini thinks, he will shout himself hoarse.

Now and then officers appear on the upper decks. Surely they know little more than their men about what awaits them. But all that matters, their military bearing announces, is that the ship is surging on, moving in the right direction: all eyes turn to look, with the proud humility of those who know that glory means sacrifice.

Relics of bygone days, legends of heroes, their swords drawn, writing earnest letters from the edge of Empire to far-off wives, clutching pictures of well-bred children to their anguished hearts. Their aristocracy makes him want to throw up. Verini knows. He will be sent to keep the peace in a vast, sunlit farm, where a century of moustachioed officers and shopkeepers chose to settle. Realising that his idiot father was right, he spits into the sea.

The sun is waning now, the afternoon has passed.

There are shouts from the bow of the *Charlton Star*. Verini does not budge.

The coastline is a dark smear on the horizon, growing brighter as they approach. The crew goes into action, the ship is gripped by a sort of frenzy. The conscripts climb back down into the hold, fold their blankets, tie up their bags. The spurious intimacy created by a few short hours at sea dissolves. Each in his boots, nervously tapping his heels, at the sound of the foghorn, their hearts, and their stomachs, leap into their throats. The engines suddenly slow in a shuddering of metal. The hold of the *Charlton Star* becomes a stinking nave where 2,000 men commune, praying to the stars whose luck ran out during this ill-starred crossing. Verini thinks back to Frileuse, surprised at how much he can remember of what he heard, what he saw. The pacifist is scared stiff of disembarking without a weapon. What will happen when the gangplanks are lowered? When they step ashore, will they find themselves in a sunny, lively, charmingly exotic town, or on a battlefield raked by gunfire and shells?

He listens carefully, his helmet on his head, his thumbs hooked into the straps of his rucksack.

The glare, the heat: his uniform is stained with sweat, he lifts his arm to shield his hollow eyes from the sun. His helmet itches; he

59

glances around, anxious to know what will happen next. The harbour depots, the hills and buildings of the city. No plumes of black smoke, no ruined houses, no gunfire, no explosions. Suddenly he feels the concrete quay beneath his feet, he scans the harbour machinery, the vehicles, the faces, looking to see how they are different, what they have in common with France. A group of Arabs begins to unload the *Charlton Star*. They unload the crates and pile them onto lorries, trailers, wagons. They are wearing sandals and baggy trousers, their heads are protected from the sun by turbans or caps. They far outnumber the Frenchmen on the quays. They work silently, ignoring the hundreds of young soldiers who stream from the hold of the ship. Verini had expected the relationship between French and Arabs to be hostile since, in Nanterre and at his parents' house, Algeria had always been described as a savage colony, a country reduced to slavery by colonists who ruthlessly exploited it. He never imagined he would see Arabs and Frenchmen working side by side. He formulates his first Algerian thought. The immediately apparent hierarchy between Muslim labourers and French foremen, and the silence of the men, seems not very different from what he experienced in the Aluvac factory.

In Algiers harbour, there is no war.

Disembarking in the blazing sunshine is slow and painful, but a sea breeze tempers the 30-degree heat, dries out the dampness he felt in the hold, dispels the stench. In single file, clutching their papers, the conscripts march into a building . Once again, he has lost sight of the few familiar faces from the ship, replaced now by others which are tense, their eyes narrowed, focused. The slightest contact causes the men to flinch and offer nervous apologies.

At a desk, Verini hands over his papers. An officer scans the interminable list of names. Pascal panics when his name is found and the officer gestures to a subaltern and pronounces the abbreviation: C.C.I.* The non-commissioned officer leads him to the far side of the building. He clambers into a covered G.M.C. truck in which six other conscripts are waiting on wooden benches. No-one speaks. Five other soldiers join them. Dusk is drawing in, the truck door slams, an engine starts up and the tarpaulin closes. They see nothing of Algiers. They pass through a checkpoint, see a red-and-white barrier being lowered behind them; the truck stops. An officer orders them to get out and follow him across a courtyard: a guardroom; camouflaged jeeps are parked in front of a four-storey concrete building that seems to be an office. Above the doorway, a French flag flutters. A countertop, a mute officer. Their papers are handed back and they are led to a dormitory with some fifty beds, just for them.

Sitting on their beds, they wait until they are called. Verini cannot work out the officers' ranks, their uniforms are unfamiliar. They are taken to an empty mess hall. Self-service, no-one is behind the food counter. They help themselves to couscous and vegetable stew. The heady scent of spices amid the glacial glint of stainless steel is unsettling, at once tempting and toxic.

Hesitant yet sheep-like, they sit at the same table beneath the white fluorescent striplights. They glance at each other, and the introductions begin. A few lads from the country, the others are from Grenoble, Bordeaux, Nantes and the suburbs, and there is a *ch'ti* – a northerner – from Lille.

After the meal, they head back up to the dormitory; they stand at the windows, staring down, past the red-and-white barrier to the short illuminated stretch of street beyond. Though it is dark now, the heat is still oppressive. Verini talks to François – the *ch'ti*. With a group of other conscripts, he was taking part in a protest in Lille when he should have been taking the train. The skirmish was broken up by police and earned him a beating, a couple of days in jail and an official charge.

"Punishment," Pascal adds.

"Too fucking right. As if this weren't punishment enough, this Algerian bullshit, you with me, pal?"

François is a trade unionist, a member of the C.G.T.

Of the dozen conscripts sleeping in the dorm, half are there as the result of disciplinary action. The other half is a cross-section of rural France, provincial, biddable and utterly bewildered.

At six o'clock in the morning, orders are bellowed for them to get up.

Breakfast in the mess hall.

An officer, black beret tucked beneath an epaulette, comes to find them and leads them to a dark room, the blinds drawn.

Hanging from a blackboard is a screen. In the cone of yellow light cast by an anglepoise lamp, a guy in civilian clothes is tinkering with a projector.

"Sit down," the officer says and leaves the room, followed by the projectionist.

The reels turn, the film countdown, white letters on a black background: *The Truth about the Algerian Rebellion.* Then another caption: *The Palestro Gorges, May 1956.*

The contorted face of a man, his head grotesquely thrown back, the jaw much too high, jutting. His throat has been slit, the gaping wound exposing taut shreds of flesh, this is what has made his face loll at an impossible angle. The camera pans round the corpse stretched on the coroner's slab. There is no voiceover. The dozen conscripts are mute.

Every day for two weeks they are forced to watch the same silent screenings, until the nightmares start, until fear takes hold and with it loathing, hatred. Corpses that have been tortured,

62

mutilated, burned, flayed, amputated, stoned, gaping bellies filled with stones, genitals cut off and stuffed into mouths; the remains of French soldiers, of Arab men, children, of Arab women with their breasts hacked off. Whole families with their throats cut, an impossible jumble of naked bodies whose lives have been snuffed out, sprawled in the dust.

Two soldiers stand sentry at the door; there are two hour-long sessions every day. Verini and François can no longer bear to look, they stand by the windows, draw back the curtains and look down at the jeeps entering and leaving the parade ground. Others are numb; they sit open-mouthed as the images flicker, they blink, they whisper "My God", "Jesus Christ", "Fucking *bougnoles*". Sick to their stomachs, they come every day and sit in the same place, on the same chair, and they stare. Photographs of bombings, ruined shops and cafés, bloody faces – the same brutal atrocities, over and over.

After one screening, an officer from the C.C.I. – the *Centre de coordination interarmées* – came to explain what they have been watching, to explain the F.L.N. He spent two hours describing the nationalist struggle: an uprising of bloody terrorists who attack not only the French soldiers and civilians but even their own brothers. This handful of men are forcibly trying to turn the Muslim population against France. But the Muslims of Algeria want to remain French, they are being manipulated by the F.L.N., a monster that we will soon have destroyed. Soldiers, you are dealing with cut-throats, with baby-killers who – with the help and the propaganda of the Algerian Communist Party – are trying to portray these acts of terrorism as a political struggle, a battle for freedom, for independence. Without France, Algeria would be nothing; France has brought it everything that is good, everything this is modern. The F.L.N. represents everything that is brutal, backward and ignorant in Algeria. Remember that when you fight against the *fellagas*, remember that when you have them in your sights: if you give them half a chance, they'll kill you without a second thought.

Verini is sickened. After the initial shock, he tried to make sense of it all. Were all new conscripts forced to watch these films before taking up their posting? Was this their punishment? Is it preferential treatment, a right to know, or simply propaganda? What were the arseholes trying to do? Drive them insane?

A dozen twenty-year-old men rendered speechless and traumatised. All they are offered is horror, fear and hatred. Try as he might to distance himself, those images have already burned themselves onto Verini's brain. He speaks to no-one. How could anyone cut . . . how can anyone do that, why would they do that to me? . . .

They are not permitted to leave the barracks. They see nothing of Algiers, they are left to stew, going from the dorm to the mess hall, from the mess hall to the screening room. Algeria is right outside, but before they are allowed to set foot there, they are made to believe that they are stepping into a world of blind terror and brutality. There is nothing to challenge this vision, and most of the men cling to it as gospel truth.

Two weeks have passed. Verini, François and three others are given orders to pack their kit and be ready within the hour.

Queasy, exhausted, emaciated, conditioned by the images they have seen, the orders they are given, they leave the C.C.I.

At Algiers train station, they are once again split up. On the platform, Verini says goodbye to François, and the *ch'ti* spews a volley of abuse as he boards a train headed for Constantine.

According to his travel warrant, Verini is to wait for a train to Orléansville, on the Algiers–Oran line. In the crowded station, amid the throng of Algerians and French, Verini experiences the same curious feeling he had when he first disembarked. Here are two parallel worlds, gliding along side by side, never meeting. The Arabs and the French do not touch, do not speak to each other, they keep their distance. Algerian boys look down when a French girl passes. Whites and Arabs do not travel in the same carriages. The notable exceptions – a few well-dressed Algerians, richer perhaps, or better educated – only further add to the confusion.

A sweltering furnace. Everywhere there are soldiers carrying sub-machine guns, police in blue uniforms and peaked caps. Verini still cannot work out where the war is. A world of hats, of light clothes, of old men sitting on the ground, of orange sellers and children, of elegant women, straight skirts, flimsy jackets, bare arms and yet, as in the Aluvac factory, behind it all is silence. *Les événéments* – the innocuous euphemism for the war in Algeria – have been raging for three years, emergency powers have been passed, the army has taken responsibility for national security, there have been dozens of bombings in the capital, the Kasbah has been cordoned off, the terrorists hunted down, the paratroopers rule the city.

Verini boards his train with his travel warrant. Destination: the 9th Infantry Division, Orléansville.

As it pulls out of Algiers, a freight car carrying soldiers and a machine gun is coupled in front of the engine, and in front of them, two more cars filled with sandbags.

Verini sleeps for a spell. The flickering images. He wakes with a start. He cannot bring himself to admit that he is relieved to find himself surrounded only by white men and soldiers.

Orléansville. The railway station is teeming with soldiers; the windows of the station building are boarded up.

His papers and his travel warrant are checked. He is directed into a truck. The quiet streets are lined with shops, cafés, a cinema, there are strolling Arabs, Frenchmen, soldiers.

On the outskirts of the city, the logistics are impressive. Buildings, tents, vehicles, helicopters. The numerous soldiers here seem more relaxed, they wear their shirts unbuttoned over T-shirts, machine guns slung over their shoulders. Verini is shown to his dormitory. He tosses his kit onto the bed and once again wonders: is this where I'm supposed to stay? Is this where I'll be living for the next two years?

The mess hall, the routine, the cliques. This is a community. Pascal Verini feels a nagging fear. In Frileuse and on the ship, it had not occurred to him. Here, it is the first thing he notices: he's going to live in a community. The atmosphere is friendly; other conscripts introduce themselves, ask where he's from. Always the same faces, the same stories, the same mess-hall jokes, the same platitudes, the same gripes. He can see the weariness in their faces, the hunger for something new. A new arrival is something of an event.

No, he doesn't know where he is being posted; no, he doesn't know anything. He has just arrived from Algiers. He doesn't mention the screenings. Have these men seen the same films? He is careful about what he says. He refers to the C.C.I. I spent two weeks at the C.C.I. in Algiers. That's all he knows. A few heads stare down at their plates, there is an awkward silence. Yeah, no-one tells us anything. You don't say! Not a thing. Don't sweat it, it's the same for everyone, you'll get used to it. How long have you been here? Six months. A year. I'm being demobbed in four weeks, pal! We've got a cushy number here, you'll see. If you're clever you won't have to do much. Not too many ops. Yeah, we don't leave the base much.

Verini struggles to breathe, to relax, take things in.

As he lies on his iron bed, a captain in full uniform who looks about thirty comes over to him. Verini isn't sure how to react, military discipline seems lax on the base; even so he gets to his

66

feet and comes to attention. The captain does not return his salute.

"Private Verini? You'll be going on the supply run at noon tomorrow, D.O.P.* Rabelais sector, Harka Commando*."

D.O.P.? Rabelais sector? Harka Commando . . . ? He doesn't understand a word, but he knows that this will be no cushy number. Harka Commando? Tramping through the mountains, skirmishes. Two years. Somewhere in this string of words and acronyms lies the deep shit that has been waiting for him. Three weeks after his journey began, he has finally been given his posting.

At noon, in front of the Supplies office, a Frenchman helped by an Arab is loading jerrycans of food into a dusty G.M.C. truck.

The Frenchman has a southern accent Verini does not recognise.

"You Vareni?"

He is taller than Pascal, slovenly dressed, insolent and friendly.

"I'm Verini."

"Well, I'm your taxi driver. Sylvain Casta."

To clarify, he adds:

"I'm from Bastia, in Corsica."

He proffers his hand.

"Pascal."

"This here's Ahmed, he can understand most things, but his French is not too good."

Ahmed is wearing an ancient battered helmet that looks like the something worn by Rommel's troops. Pascal reckons him to be about fifty. The Algerian busies himself with the jerrycans, rolling them up a wooden plank into the truck. He touches his cap by way of greeting but his expression does not change.

Pascal puts his kit into the truck and asks if they need a hand. Casta turns to the Arab:

"Ahmed! What do we need?"

"Stiks and beer!"

There is paperwork to sign. The Corsican seems to know the quartermaster, they are laughing and joking; Casta manages furtively to negotiate a bottle of whisky, a few banknotes change hands. Pascal carries two cases of beer to the truck, comes back to Casta.

"What are 'stiks'?"

"Steaks."

They head out of Orléansville, crossing a large bridge that spans a river which looks more like a creek – though it is a hundred metres wide, in August the riverbed has dried to a trickle. A tarmac road follows the stream for several kilometres, then they turn right onto a potholed dirt track. Casta steps on the gas, swerving to avoid ruts, potholes, he swerves even when there is nothing to avoid. He looks grave. Resting against his leg, his machine gun clatters with every jolt. Ignoring the road directly ahead, Ahmed is studying the upcoming bends, the overhanging rocks, the ditches and the hillocks along the track. Verini grips the door handle and winds down his window to be able to warn of any hole or rock. Ahmed turns to Casta without a word.

"Close the window, for fuck's sake!"

Verini winds up the window again; he no longer wonders why the windscreen is so dirty it's almost impossible to see through, except directly in front of the driver, where a porthole has been wiped clean. Snipers? He doesn't dare ask: from now on, any answers will just plunge him deeper into the shit.

The road climbs and twists, leaving the river behind, then it narrows; on one side is the sheer rock face with, on the other, a narrow ravine that plummets down to the valley floor. Hundreds of metres below, Verini sees two mangled wrecks, a jeep and a truck identical to theirs.

The tension mounts. This stretch of the journey clearly has the other two scared stiff. He clenches his buttocks and glances around, not knowing exactly what he has to fear. Casta is still weaving and swerving, he all but tips them over the edge.

Two kilometres further on, the track widens again. The Corsican sits back in his seat and seems to relax a little. Ahmed smiles at Pascal:

"Casta, he a god driva', the bes' Fangio in de commado!'

After the narrow gorge, they turn right onto a less rutted track that winds upwards towards the brow of a low hill where Verini can clearly see a few whitewashed buildings: a farm.

"You can wind down your window now."

Pascal does as he is told; he sticks his head out. He can see the valley now, its lush green slopes cutting through the arid rocky terrain. For the first time he considers this landscape of ochre, yellow and beige; he is struck by the vast emptiness, the expansive view, there is a special quality to the pure, clear air. Far to the south, the jagged mountains cannot quite encircle the boundless blue-white sky of the horizon. To the north, beyond the farm, closer, steeper mountains completely fill his field of vision. The farm buildings, built right into a rocky plateau, overlook the valley and are surrounded by orchards planted in neat rows.

He recognises the orange trees by their fruit, he knows some are olive trees; the others, he has no idea.

At the brow of the hill, leaning against an orange tree, a soldier stands guard, his machine gun at his waist. He waves them on. Casta gives a curt nod in response.

The Rabelais sector D.O.P. is an isolated farm: two rows of facing buildings separated by a dirt yard three or four metres wide. Off to one side is a large two-storey house, rectangular and neat, styled as a cross between a Mediterranean villa and French winery, there are a few outbuildings and garages, the whole compound is surrounded by an adobe wall two metres high. A soldier guards the entrance to the yard, a wrought-iron gate reinforced with bars and thick wire netting. In front of the house, another wall surrounds two barns of different sizes. This is where Casta drives the truck.

"What's a D.O.P.?" Verini says.

"It's a new thing. Three months ago, they didn't even have a name for it. Now, they call it a *Détachement opérationel de protection*."

For the first time in almost three weeks, Pascal smiles. His punishment has been to be sent to the most godforsaken hole in Algeria.

"Protection? What's to protect all the way out here? Oranges?"

Ahmed and Casta do not crack a smile. They stare straight ahead at the courtyard and the barns. Two soldiers in dishevelled clothes, a number of Algerians wearing scraps of uniform. Verini swallows hard, his smile fading, fear boring into his belly. What exactly is this place?

At the door to the main barn, they unload the jerrycans, which are rolled inside by two uncommunicative Arabs. There are two dozen beds lined against the walls, in the centre is a wood stove with a stainless steel flue that runs horizontally along the wall for ten metres before coming to a right angle and rising to the roof. There are pieces of makeshift furniture next to the beds; calendars are stuck to the wall.

The two soldiers Verini saw earlier are now busy overseeing four Algerians digging trenches at the foot of the walls surrounding the courtyard. Leaning against the smaller of the barns are metal posts, some three metres high, and rolls of barbed wire.

The two overseers standing in the shade, smoking. The Arabs shovel and pickaxe at a leisurely pace and no-one seems keen to force them to work faster. They appear to be building a gate.

Casta ushers Verini into the barn and tells him to choose a bed. Verini walks round in circles. This is where he will be staying. His journey is at an end; the twenty-four months of his tour of duty begin here. He sets his kit down at the foot of a bed next to a rolled-up mattress.

"Tell Ahmed if you're hungry, he's making some grub."

"How many people live here?"

"There are fourteen of us in the commando unit. Right now there are a dozen Arab *aides-de-camp* who sleep in the other barn. Then there's the *caporal-chef*, Colona, he's a Corsican like me."

Casta winks.

"He's not bad, he's a veteran of Indochina. He bunks in here with us." Sylvain points to the rear of the barn where a small area has been curtained off using ropes hung with brown blankets.

"Lieutenant Perret, he's in charge of the detachment, lives up in the house. We report to Orléansville, more or less, to the 9th Infantry Division Headquarters. Actually we report to the C.C.I., but we don't give a shit about any of that, they're the generals and we're just cannon fodder – *basta*. So, anyway, this is Rabelais Sector. So you've got some idea what I'm talking about, this is Z.O.A., the *zone ouest algérois* – the western Algerian zone. Here, the 9th Infantry run everything. There are six sectors controlled from Orléansville, extending as far as the sea to the north, and to the south just past the Tazamout Pass in the *djebel* to Ténès and El Marsa which is run by the 22nd Infantry. We've got a radio operator here, he's called Martin. We've also got a police officer from Orléansville and two local *gendarmes*, though not always the same ones. And then there's Rubio, the interpreter."

"Police? What the hell do you need them here for?"

"The others will be back soon, they're out on manoeuvres with Colona. Now go get some kip, get some grub. You'll start sentry duty tomorrow. There's no hazing here. Colona will put you in the picture and he'll sort out your gear."

Pascal sets up his bunk, unpacks his belongings. Will he be able to find books here?

Ahmed brings a tray with a plate of food and a bottle of beer. He sets it down on the next bed, gives a perfunctory bow and walks away. Pascal thanks him. Is he supposed to consider Ahmed and the other Algerians as soldiers, as servants, as prisoners? Should he be afraid to be alone with him?

Verini eats. The nicest meal he's had since Paris: he is hungry.

He slinks around the courtyard, feeling idiotically wary. Unlike the others he is not wearing a bush hat, and his forage cap affords little protection from the sun. In his brand new uniform, he looks like a boy from a genteel family.

He wanders over to the soldiers overseeing the Arab labourers, two strapping blond-haired lads, their downy cheeks red from the sun. Henri and Paul; they roll their rs. They're not brothers, they don't even hail from the same part of France, but each holds out a hand calloused from years of farm labour. Henri is from the Vendée; Paul from Touraine.

Sitting in the shade of a tarpaulin, Casta is cutting an iron bar with a hacksaw; there is a workbench, a few tools, a soldering iron. He is making frames for the gates that will protect the yard. Back in Bastia, he explains, he works at a garage. Does odd jobs. Verini takes off his jacket, he is wearing only a sleeveless vest, he gives Casta a hand.

"You're not bad with your hands."

"Comes from working in a factory."

The heat dies down as the afternoon draws to a close. Casta calls Ahmed over and tells him to bring a couple of beers.

"We allowed to drink whenever we like?"

"When Colona's here, you'd do well to ask his permission. But yeah, long as you're not on duty, nobody much minds."

"How many are on manoeuvres?"

"Six of them went off with Colona."

"So who exactly is fighting the w—"

War.

In his belly, ringing in his ears, he feels his legs give way. Pascal slowly turns towards the white house. Behind the gate, the guard does not move, the two blond farmhands do not move, the Arabs go on digging. Casta bows his head, stops for a second to chalk cut-marks on his iron bars.

War. There it is again.

The second howl is louder than the first. It is a man, not an animal. A howl of pain and helplessness. A howl that makes his stomach lurch, that shrieks from the courtyard of the white-washed villa all the way to the orange groves.

Verini has found it. This war that everyone is pretending to ignore.

He wants no truck with this war. Who should he tell?

He blinks, he looks down at Casta welding and, seeing him bow his head and tremble, wonders how long the Corsican has been here.

# 5

One of the springs creaked loudly, accompanying Georges' last breathless grunt as he clung to the whore's fat hips. For thirty seconds he held his breath, trying to prolong the moment, his eyes squeezed shut, then opened them to see the woman straddling him.

Perspiration beaded in the whore's armpits, trickled down the sides of her heavy black breasts and dripped coldly onto the boxer's pale chest. She wiped herself with the back of her hand, ran her fingers through her hair and stretched.

An uncomfortable orgasm in the stink of sweat.

Planting one hand on Georges' stomach, she lifted one leg. Georges watched their genitals disengage and his penis flop back against his thigh. With her fingernails, she removed the condom. The latex snapped.

"You like that, *chéri*?"

What would he do with all these hours?

The hotel room did not have a kitchen or even a minibar. Nothing but a bed with a lumpy mattress. Georges felt like a coffee.

They had been naked for ten minutes. Perfunctory foreplay, she kneading handfuls of flesh as she undressed him, murmuring sweet nothings as mechanically as a photocopier. Three

74

gentle strokes from her polished fingernails as she slipped on the rubber, the sex itself was unremarkable, a few moans of encouragement and a badly faked orgasm. Ten minutes. Not even as long as the haggling before they had come upstairs.

Georges was lost from the start, on the stairs as he followed her plump arse. He could take punches for fifteen rounds, but he could not resist a caress. He should have taken his time. Ten minutes, his eyes fixed on the cracks in the ceiling wondering how come he hadn't been able to make the pleasure last.

How old was she?

Forty? Maybe older?

She went into the bathroom, Georges pulled the sheet over his legs and his traitorous prick.

Maybe he could renegotiate? Claw back half of the four hundred euros, leave her the price of the fuck and go home? That sounded like a good idea. But what would he do for the rest of the night? Besides, he'd already paid for the hotel room, another hundred notes down the drain.

Shit. Georges swore to himself as the woman stepped into the shower. What with the urgency and his passion spent, the illusion had been shattered. Ninety-one kilos lying rigid on the bed like a marble sarcophagus surrounded by flowery wallpaper worn out with twenty years of sighs and moans. Wandering through this moribund dream, he pulled several hundred-euro notes from his wallet, his nostrils filled with the mildewed smell of the room.

The girl re-emerged from the bathroom, strutted around the bed with the bearing of an indolent queen. She had slipped on a faded nightie and a fresh pair of knickers, cleaner and plainer than the lace panties that Georges' stubby fingers had not had time to caress. She had removed her make-up, and her hair, untied, hung dishevelled around her face. Hand on her hip, her back arched, her huge breasts thrust forward, she said:

"You gonna order some food, *chéri*?"

Her eyelids drooped over her big round eyes. Exhausted.

Georges had insisted; he had offered a good price for her to spend the whole night despite the fact that she had already worked all day.

She looked like an old biddy ready for bed.

And yet her plain cotton knickers turned him on. Georges stared, they were sexier than all the stockings and suspenders in the world, they rekindled a distant memory of the sixteen-year-old cousin he had glimpsed, half naked, during a summer holiday when he had been helpless and desperate, a twenty-year-old virgin. The size 18 cotton pants had the magical quality of something picked at random from a drawer stuffed with frayed underwear with loose elastic, the pants she wore when she was not turning tricks. Despite the lie, the stale taste in his mouth, the defective plumbing, Georges now had no desire to leave this hotel room.

"Food?"

The €400-a-night queen of the savannah pointed a long red fingernail towards the telephone.

On the nightstand, Georges found a pizza delivery menu for a restaurant a few doors from the hotel. He picked up the receiver, dialled, and ask if he could order. With the speed of a flame-thrower, the girl on the other end of the line rattled off the list of pizzas. Sitting on the chair at the end of the bed, filing her nails, the whore did not even look up.

"Order me a Four Seasons, *chéri*, extra cheese, and a bottle of Vittel."

"One Four Seasons pizza, extra cheese, and . . ."

The girl on the other end of the line said "a bottle of Vittel" just as Georges did, then asked what he would like.

". . . You got any salad? Can I have a green salad? No, no dressing, just the salad."

He looked over at this hooker who drank mineral water. He wanted to talk, but he didn't know what to say. She got to her feet, pushed a pillow back against the wall and sat cross-legged next to him.

"You wanna' talk, *doudou*?"

Georges' gaze drifted towards her crotch and caught a glimpse of the blue cotton panties against her black skin.

"Go on, *chéri*, you can tell me anything, mebbe after, I'll show you a good time."

Georges turned away. This woman had probably heard it all before, but half the whores he knew were snouts and even here, on the far side of Paris, it was best to keep his mouth shut. Or at least mention no names. The words came in clumps, tangled and confused. Georges bit his lip, stared at the blue panties, he blushed and blurted out:

"I'm a cop."

She looked up and the nail file paused in its sadistic sawing motion, her large brown eyes opened wide.

"You ain't vice?" she whimpered, her voice rising to a shrill whine.

He sat up, stared at the wallpaper, filled with shame.

"God, no! Just a *policier municipal*, not even a real cop, I mean I'm not . . . Look, what I meant to say is . . . actually . . . actually, I'm a boxer."

"*Chéri!*" she growled. "You ain't gonna go crazy on me now, are you?"

"What? No! I'm not going to . . . I'm not going to do anything for fuck sake."

He wanted to grab her arms. She leapt from the bed before he could touch her.

"Listen, *chéri*, don't worry 'bout it, on the house – next time I give you fiddy per cent, but don't go arrestin' me, *chéri*."

"Jesus Christ! I don't want to arrest you, all I want is to spend the fucking night with you! I'm not looking for a discount, I want to spend the night in this fucking bed with you, I want to talk to you, I want you to take care of me, that's all. I'm not a cop, I'm just some sad bastard who doesn't know how to do anything other than hit people with his fists, a sad bastard who wants you to take care of him."

He bellowed this, kneeling on the bed, his shrivelled prick hanging out, his every muscle contracted, every tendon tensed and leading to his throat. The hooker with the taste for Vittel batted her eyelashes, weighed up her chances. As she slinked towards the door, she said in an hesitant voice:

"Talk to me, *chéri*, tell me eveythin', I'm listenin', you some big shot boxer, some big shot fighter, yeah, c'mon, *chéri*, tell me 'bout it."

Three knocks rang out. The woman glanced towards the door and blinked. Georges stared at her. From outside in the corridor came a voice: "Pizza!"

Georges hung his head.

"I just want to be with you, just for tonight."

"This ain't no joke, *chéri*, you scared the shit outta me."

"If you want me to, I'll leave."

The delivery boy knocked again. The woman walked warily past the bed and opened the door.

In the hall a lanky, acne-pitted boy wearing a red-and-blue uniform held out a pizza box ringed with grease marks and a plastic bag containing a bottle. He glanced into the room, spotted the muscular man kneeling up on the bed with his balls hanging out and raised his eyebrows.

"Everything O.K., Mireille? You want me to call Romolo?"

She shot Georges a petrified glance, then looked back at the delivery boy.

"It's all good, Doudou Beau Gosse, ain't no problem. Don't you go botherin' Romolo. Can you put this on my tab, Doudou, honey?"

"You sure?"

"Sure, you tell Romolo."

Doudou Beau Gosse handed over the food, turned towards the bed again and then left.

"O.K., *chéri*, I wan' you to promise you won't do nothin' stupid, I wan' you to promise you won't take me down the station, O.K.?"

Georges sat back on the bed and nodded.

"I'm trustin' you here, a'right? Cos otherwise, Romolo, he's just down the hall and big an' all as you are, he's a sight bigger. You feel me? Cos Romolo, he don't give a shit about cops, yeah?"

Georges nodded again, though if necessary he would have been happy to put the fear of God into her pimp.

"A'right, then, you get comfortable in that big ol' bed and we gonna make sure you get your money's worth, you gonna tell me your troubles, you gonna tell me everything."

She piled up the pillows, gently laid her hands on Georges' shoulders and settled him as though he were an invalid. She sat beside him, next to the door, then she heaved a sigh.

"Go on, then, what you got on your mind?"

"So your name is Mireille?"

"Sure is, *chéri*, you can tell Mireille eveythin'."

She watched the john out of the corner of her eye; he seemed more dumb than dangerous.

"Two weeks ago I had a bout, a boxing match. A shitty little bout with some young boxer who comes from some island somewhere – I don't remember where, but I remember his name: André Gabin. He was a first-rate boxer. A fine athlete, a good reach and the shoulders of a killer . . ."

With the rhythm of a long-distance runner, Georges gradually filled the room with the ghosts that had been fighting it out inside his head for the past month. Boxer, ex-boxer, cop, bent cop. Kravine, Gabin, Paolo, the Pakistani and the worrying shadow of a shark just below the surface, the fascinating, fearsome Roman.

He shifted the numb fingers laid against the silken thigh. He was just going to tell her about the second envelope, about the second man whose face he had smashed in last night, but a gentle snoring interrupted him.

Lying on her back, Mireille was sleeping like a log, her wide mouth gaping, one hand in the pizza box reaching for a last cold slice.

He cleared the remains of the food off the bed, pulled the sheet up over the woman and pressed himself against her. He slid his hand along her body millimetre by millimetre, forgetting he had paid four hundred notes to tell some whore his life story and that, at that price, she would let him do whatever he wanted.

He fell asleep, his boxer's hand buried to the wrist in her cotton panties, cupping the warm roundness of her sex.

*

The Wall unbuckled his belt, set it on the kitchen table and brought the mobile phone to his ear.

"It's Paolo, where the fuck you been? I've been trying to get hold of you for days!"

Georges dithered a little before finally confessing to the Portuguese that he was having trouble recovering from his fight with Gabin. Paolo didn't hear or he didn't care because he went right on roaring.

"Yeah, yeah, you could at least answer your fucking phone. I mean, you don't expect me to go down the cop shop to find out how you're doing, huh?"

"What do you want?"

"Whaddya mean, what do I want! I'm your fucking coach, yeah? And your cut-man and your manager if it comes to that, it's not like you've got options. Well, guess what, I'm calling to talk to you about boxing! Georges? You listening to me?"

"It's pretty hard not to hear."

"I've got a bout lined up. You at your place?"

"Not right now, Paolo, I just got in from my shift, I'm shattered."

"Don't move, I'll be right over."

Paolo had been to Ring 14, he'd seen Marco and they had had a little chat: Georges was down in the mouth, he'd stopped coming to training, he was obviously depressed. And the two ex-brawlers had come up with a brilliant idea, and Georges was pretty sure it was the same idea boxers always hit on when things are bad. "Let's set up a match. It's the only way to get him back on his feet." Now, Paolo was on his way over, and having the bit between his teeth it would be difficult to dissuade him.

"A month and a half! Don't talk shit, Georges, that's more than enough time for you to get in shape. Forget about Gabin, it's over! You won the bout, for fuck's sake. Don't go turning it into some neurotic bullshit. You won, you're tired, O.K., I get it. But a month and a half – in six weeks we can turn you into a combine harvester."

"We? I knew that Marco was in on this thing. You know how Marco treated me when I went back to the gym? Huh? Do I need to draw you a picture? Jesus Christ, Paolo, you've been through it yourself, you should understand. You know I have to hang up my gloves, just like Marco did, just like you did . . ."

"I never hung up my gloves, those fucking quack doctors put me out of business."

Here we go again.

Dumb fuck. Georges screwed up his eyes, resigned to having to listen to the story once more.

"Don't give me that fucking look like you're bored of listening to me! You know that it was bad luck that I got saddled with some shit-for-brains surgeon who shouldn't have been allowed to use a butter knife, so don't go giving me that look. Everyone knows I was unlucky. I never hung up my gloves, my fists and my legs were good for another ten years. *Caralho*, I was headed for the big time, everyone knows I was a dead cert for the feather-weight title. The world fucking title, my friend, the sort of fights they show on the T.V. news. Everyone knows it, you know it, so don't come over all superior on me, don't go biting the hand that feeds you. I was a good boxer, you know I was, so don't treat me like some piece of shit when I say I was unlucky. After thirty years in this business I know more about fucking boxing than anyone, I know that luck is never on your side, but I never hung up my gloves, my career was taken from me. And not because I was caught doping, not because I let myself be conned by that arse-hole Kravine. I lost it in the ring! I wasn't allowed to fight on account of my eye, I wasn't brought up in front of the Boxing Commission! Dickhead! . . ."

Georges held his hands up in surrender.

"Paolo, please."

The Portuguese fished a bowl from a pile of dishes and poured himself a coffee. A derisive whistle escaped his dead lips. Sure, he was making a big deal of it, but he was right: he had no right being snide about the past of a guy like him. Especially when Pablo was busting his balls to set up a bout for him. Respect was due to ageing boxers.

He rubbed a hand across his face, narrowing his reddened eyes. His palm rustled over his three-day beard.

"You already know what I think about the whole story, so stop giving me a hard time. It was a slip of the tongue, I'm on auto-pilot here, Pablo, I'm knackered. So give me a break, yeah? All I'm saying is that I'm not up to this match. Not yet."

Paolo stopped shovelling sugar into his coffee, looked up through his yellow eye, his teaspoon squeaking against the china bowl.

"It's a good match. Take it, you need it."

"It's too soon."

"That's not true, Georges, the truth is if you don't take it, it'll be too late."

Georges got up from the chair, took off his police shirt and tossed it onto the table next to his gun. At the sink, he splashed water on his face and dried it with a dishcloth.

"It's already too late, Paolo, you know that as well as I do, I'm not going to kid myself."

He kicked off his shoes, took off his uniform trousers, wandered over to the fridge in his vest and boxers, took out two bottles of beer and opened them. Paolo drained the last of his cold coffee and poured the Löwenbräu into the same bowl. Having no feeling in his lips, he sloshed beer all over himself. His dead eye, half closed, was still fixed on Georges, who buried his face in his own bowl.

Jesus Christ, they made an ugly pair.

The Portuguese set down his bowl of beer, cradling it between his hands as though to warm them.

"Listen, Georges, I'll forget everything you said if you tell me."

"Tell you what?"

"Don't play dumb, Georges, I might only have one good eye, but I can still see. What the fuck is going on?"

"I don't know what you're talking about."

"You think I don't know you? I've seen too many guys who had problems recovering from a bout to know that that's not the problem here. What's going on with you?"

Georges gave him a sidelong glance, looking for all the world like a sulky child refusing to talk.

"Something tells me you need this bout a lot more than you think. If you don't want to talk, that's your look-out. If you've done something stupid, it's not like this is a confessional, I'm not going to lecture you, you'll just have to deal with whatever it is. But I need you to tell me one thing, and I'm not leaving here until you spit out your mouth-guard: has it anything to do with the son of a bitch Kravine? Because if it is, then you can forget about me watching your back."

He spat on the floor.

"That's a promise, Georges, you know I mean it."

Georges chugged half a bottle of industrial-strength beer.

"It's not Kravine."

"Perfect," Paolo roared. "In that case you might as well tell me what the hell's going on, dipshit. Don't just stand there in your boxers like a sack of wet cement, tell me what you've been doing the past three weeks that's kept you from running your laps and working the punchbags."

By the time the doctors stopped Paolo fighting, his body was already fit for the scrapheap. But he could still K.O. a man through sheer determination.

"Give me some time to think. I'm not saying no, I'm just saying I'm not ready."

"Think? When did you take up thinking?"

"Oh, Paolo."

"Don't be so fucking prissy, Georges, we're both as dumb as each other."

Paolo finished his beer and got up.

"I'll swing by to see you in a couple of days. And do me a favour, champ, open the windows once in a while, you need fresh air for those lungs of yours."

Georges looked at the window and at Paris beyond.

"Fresh air? I'd need to go a long way to find some."

Paolo gave a grunt, a sort of high-pitched choking sound, he smiled fit to split his face in two and slammed the door behind him.

At 5.00 a.m., shrugging off his tiredness, Georges had dragged himself out of bed and was out running, pounding the pavements. Rue d'Alésia, right onto the rue Coty, past the parc Montsouris, along the broad, deserted boulevards Jourdan and Brune where the grass between the tramlines in the central reservation was still damp with dew. The street lighting flickered off as he jogged along the boulevard des Maréchaux. Behind him, the dawn was breaking, he quickened his pace as he passed the porte Brancion. Porte de Versailles, a line of trucks streaming into the parc des Expositions, a few cars heading towards the city centre, outriders for the tailback that would shortly invade the city. He followed the cars, turning right onto the rue de Vaugirard. He was dripping with perspiration, his head ached. His sweat smelled of days of too much food and beer.

The second man had lived way out in Sartrouville, a nightmare to get to by public transport. Martin Brieux. Two kids, a wife and a fucking dog, white leather sofas in the living room, standard lamps and shelves full of books. He was a guy with a routine, he took the same train every night, was always home by the same time. After dark, in the yellow light of the rooms, Georges watched scenes of family life that seemed banal, even happy, but they were misleading since Georges knew that Brieux was banging someone other than this wife, who was still pretty for her age. They were both in their fifties, their kids looked like A-grade students. Georges let a weekend slip past and returned to the scene on Monday. Baseball cap, tracksuit, the same ones he was wearing that morning. He had jogged up to Brieux and slammed him against the garden fence in a quiet residential street a hundred metres from home. Hidden between the branches of the leylandii that overhung the footpath, Georges had rearranged the guy's face. Like Dulac, Brieux hadn't said a word, hadn't even asked why. In less than a minute, using only his left fist, Georges had beaten him and left him crumpled on the footpath as he jogged away again.

Like the first, this assault also went unreported.

Georges jogged on, but his lurching stomach refused to settle to the rhythm of his running.

At Convention *métro* station, he picked up his pace as he always did, but his legs and even his breathing refused to keep up. Still he did not slow. Reach the point of exhaustion, drain himself of his last ounce of strength, collapse if that was what it took.

After Brieux, Georges had understood, or perhaps when he received the second envelope, or perhaps he had known from the very beginning in Juvisy. He had lied to himself for as long as possible, but on the train back from Sartrouville, he stopped. Stop deluding yourself, this is not a kids' game.

He came to the rue Copreaux, still sprinting but dead on his feet, staggering, sucking in air without oxygen.

Not a kids' game.

Knees trembling, he walked up and down for a few minutes outside his building until he had caught his breath. He hawked up the last of his spittle to be rid of the taste in his mouth.

Paolo could go fuck himself. He was done with jogging, with

pumping weights, with coaching sessions and a training programme that consisted of taking the punches. As long as no-one found out what he got up to in the evenings, he didn't have to worry about screwing up his reputation. He wasn't ashamed of himself. This wasn't some kids' game, it was a money game. I don't give a fuck, he thought as he climbed the steps. So, he did know who he was really working for? What difference did it make? In the ring, everything is clear. But outside the ring, there's no point even trying to understand – you just get fucked over, it's all below the belt. There you are with your fists clenched, lined up with your neighbours like an idiot, standing naked in a courtyard, and someone tells you that you have to punch them if you want your life to be the way you'd hoped. Yeah.

I, Georges Crozat, have climbed out of the ring, but I'm still punching people for a living, because I need to pay for my little luxury, for my little vice; it's my reward for being a punchbag to everyone in this fucking city for the past forty years.

Mireille. Yeah.

If he was going to sleep badly for the rest of his days because he'd fucked his bones up in the ring, he didn't give a shit. Being with her now and again, he could sleep like an angel, his nose buried in her armpit. When that's all you ask of life, the whole world could go fuck itself.

He washed away these negative thoughts along with his stale sweat under the cold shower, pulled on his uniform and headed off to work without wondering why. He had no answers. He had nothing but a single room with flowery wallpaper on the outskirts of Paris, until he moved into a retirement home which would have the same wallpaper, the only difference being that right now he could still get it up.

At the 14th *arrondissement* police station, his fellow officers were surprised by the fact that Brigadier Crozat was not smiling, his manner seemed suddenly stiff, they didn't make their usual jibes. Cops know when one of their own is at the end of his rope.

\*

No new envelope. Strapped for cash. Three weeks since Brieux. Georges had carried on jogging, he'd swung by Ring 14 a couple of times for some work on a punchbag. Paolo hassled him to get serious about his training, Georges avoided him and dragged his feet. He'd seen Mireille twice, she'd given him a discount and taken all his cash. The envelopes were empty; his salary wouldn't hit his account for another week.

The bout Paolo and Marco had arranged wasn't rigged. Toni Esperanza, a dago who, despite his tacky stage name, was a decent boxer. He'd been a pro for a while, but his career as a southpaw didn't quite work out. Southpaws didn't bother Georges, his style was sufficiently even-handed that he could adapt. Toni was about thirty, a big bruiser who had returned to doing amateur bouts because he loved boxing, he took it seriously, he never compromised. He was no killer, but he had a winner's instinct and he knew how to handle himself. This would be a real bout, not some walkover. But there was no cash involved. And most of all he was shit scared. Time passed, and still he didn't admit this to Paolo. The less time he spent training, the more scared he was. He was allowing the situation to fester, he wanted to find a white envelope in his letterbox, to stop pretending to be a boxer.

How could he fight, knowing that this was the end? Paolo and Marco had found him an opponent against whom, if it came down to it, he could lose with dignity. It was a nice gesture, but the prospect gave him knots in his stomach. The thought of collapsing at the finish line. A bad start and a terrible finish.

Yesterday, at the gym, he'd pushed the door open and immediately did a U-turn. Kravine had been there, prowling around the kids who were training. Georges had run away.

As he left the police station, he let out his belt. He was a little heavier, he weighed in at ninety-five kilos. He no longer bothered talking to Merleau, who had applied to be partnered to Bergolio who had ignored the request.

At the intersection of rue d'Alésia and rue des Plantes, they heard a squeal of tyres and a car screeched to a stop in the bus lane, two wheels in the cycle lane. Merleau ran ahead, hand on his truncheon. The passenger window rolled down and Roman popped his head out. Merleau snapped to attention and made to salute, Roman ignored him and leaned out to talk to Georges.

"I thought it was you, Georges. You got a minute?"

Georges reluctantly walked over to the car. Roman tossed a cigarette butt, burnt down to the filter, into the gutter.

"Look at you! I see you've got your playboy swagger back since that last bout of yours!"

Roman gave a brief laugh. The Wall bent slightly towards the car and noticed the driver, a guy of about thirty, jaws clenched. Georges did not recognise him.

"You got a fight coming up soon? I heard you know how to handle yourself."

Georges was about to say yes, then realised that Roman was not talking about boxing.

"We should grab a beer one of these days. Talk about boxing. I've always been fascinated by guys who know how to use their fists."

Roman shot a glance at Brigadier Merleau who had taken a step back, but had his ears cocked, trying to listen in on the conversation.

89

"Guy like you, it's a waste to see you pounding the beat. Don't you think maybe it's time you looked for a promotion?"

The driver gave a thin smile. Without taking his eyes off the far end of the street, Roman signalled to him with his left hand.

"Be seeing you, Crozat."

The car started up again and pulled away.

Merleau bounded up to Georges excitedly.

"That was Roman, wasn't it? From Organised Crime? You know the guy? What did he want?"

"Not much. To talk about boxing."

Merleau cackled.

"With you?"

Two photographs, two names, two addresses. Twelve hundred euros in cash, all new bills. Georges no longer needed to worry about finding out who the Pakistani was running errands for. He'd been working for Roman from the start, and he wondered whether Roman had dropped off the envelope before or after accosting him in the street. He felt sweat trickle down his back and from his armpits.

Roman didn't get involved in kids' games, that much was certain.

Georges made no attempt to puzzle out the whole situation. In all likelihood, Roman was just another lackey – though in a very different category. And behind Roman . . . Shit, Georges, you don't want to know who's pulling Roman's strings. The fanned-out banknotes trembled in his hand. He unfolded his map of Paris, found the addresses, then studied the pictures.

There was something similar about the faces. Though the two guys looked innocuous, their eyes both had that same glint of fear. Or maybe he was just anticipating.

He had been hired. The job this time was more complicated.

On a small card, there was a message: "Same day."

The Wall thought about Mireille and smiled.

90

# 6

They spent three weeks building cells. A dozen brick enclosures two metres by two opposite a barn where discarded farm machinery was stored. Roofs made of corrugated iron, straw mattresses. In the barnyard next to the one used by the commandos, they built another, slightly larger, unit for Caporal-chef Colona.

Verini learned bricklaying to the sound of prisoners howling in the cellar. Within a few days, the straw mattresses were covered in brownish stains that attracted flies.

Casta had quickly become an invaluable friend. In the face of the absurdity and the violence of this place, their meeting was the first solid support Verini had found. Then there is Philippe Chapel, the son of a Parisian restaurateur, who throws up while the others laugh. The three men understand each other, they stick together.

They have lots of volunteers at the D.O.P., not everyone is obliged to get involved. When Colona first asked Verini to take a prisoner down into the cellar, he had refused. As much from fear as on principle, though it was assumed to be the latter. But saying "no" entails consequences, and it costs dearly: deductions from pay, days spent on fatigue duty at the 9th Infantry in

Orléansville – though there, at least, they managed to sleep at night – and worst of all, days confined to barracks which, though they are no different from any other day, would be added to their time in Algeria.

At night, Pascal buries his head under the pillow so he can sleep.

Of the thirty men in the detachment, he, Casta and Chapel are the "Nos". The *cocos*, the chickens. But this little group keeps up its morale. The others are called Paul, Henri, Roger, Christophe. They have no trouble sleeping, they volunteer for everything, they cross the track that separates the house from the barns and offer their services.

Verini is beginning to think that the real enemies are the men eating at his table, the ones who talk about what they're doing down in the cellar in front of the Algerians who serve the meals. Old men who were tortured and turned. All those who work for the French because death is waiting for them outside. Everyone is terrified of setting foot outside the D.O.P. even though everyone longs to leave.

Verini gets used to the sentry duty, to the fear and the darkness, to being responsible for the security of this place, these men he despises. And he learns to sleep knowing that the guard making sure he is safe is a man who hates him.

He has been on his first sorties, his first operations. Walking in silent columns through the *djebel* at night. Using a pair of binoculars to keep an eye on the donkey tracks, watching for passing traffic, for women and children. Sleeping under the stars, a rifle gripped in both hands. Searching caves and houses, ransacking miserable rooms where what little they find has already been trampled. Getting to know the D.O.P. sector: the maps, the names of the gorges and the passes, the *mechtas* and the local wells.

He has become one of the appointed drivers, chiefly responsible for bringing supplies to the Farm. Casta showed him how to drive on the dirt track, taught him a few basic reflexes. Pascal often brings Ahmed along and teaches him a few words of French. They talk.

"Ahmed, why do you work for the French?"

"Why you think I no working for F.L.N. no more?"

No more questions for Ahmed. Take him on the trips to Orléansville – maybe the *fellagas* won't toss a grenade and blow up the truck if Ahmed is with him.

The "Fangio Results Table" pinned to a wall in the barn records the speed records between the D.O.P. and Orléansville. Games as an antidote to fear. According to Casta and Chapel, attacks are rare, but speed can kill too. Verini has taken over the job of a driver who died two weeks before his arrival, sending his truck plummeting to the bottom of the ravine. Three months before that, a jeep was blown up by a landmine, tossing all the passengers clear: one soldier lost a leg, Lieutenant Perret walked away without a scratch. Two corpses lie rotting in the ravine.

The most important thing Verini has learned in the six weeks he has been here is the language. He now knows the lies hidden behind the metaphors that seemed mysterious when he arrived. When someone talks about "firewood duty", it has nothing to do with heating, any more than "gathering mushrooms" has to do with food; both mean a prisoner is to be executed. In the words of Martin, the communications officer, the phrase "special canisters" means a plane is about to drop napalm on some village or *maquis*. "Intensive interrogation" means electric shock.

One man in particular takes responsibility for these duties. Rubio, the *pied-noir* interpreter from Orléansville. Spanish by birth, he used to be a regional amateur boxing champion. He speaks Arabic and works for the French army. After dark, he leads the prisoners he has already dealt with in the cellar out to one of the pits and cuts their throats. He is accompanied by a *gendarme*, or by Paul and Henri, the farm boys, who know a thing or two about slaughtering pigs. Sometimes prisoners are shot in the back – a prisoner from the Rabelais Sector D.O.P. attempting to escape. Another one.

Pascal refuses to think about the fact that he is here for two years. His fear and his hatred will have destroyed him long before then.

*

It is shortly after dawn, the nights are cold. In those areas still in shadow and those whipped by the wind, the dew has turned to hoarfrost. At the main gate, Verini is standing guard while also keeping watch over the cells. Half of them are occupied. Five men.

Ahmed, the designated chef, comes along the path carrying a billycan of steaming soup. Verini opens the gate and lets him inside. The Arab does a tour of the cells, filling the plates held out through slots crudely cut into the doors. Parched, trembling hands of all ages. The youngest is not even sixteen, the oldest probably seventy. Companies in Rabelais Sector who capture prisoners send them to one of the Orléansville assessment centres where an Intelligence officer makes an initial selection. Those suspected of knowing more are sent to the nearest D.O.P. The more an Algerian knows, the less chance he has of leaving the D.O.P. other than with Rubio, in the back of the black six-cylinder truck requisitioned with the farm buildings: it is a fast vehicle much favoured during the previous war by the Gestapo, the Milice and by criminals. Less important prisoners are sent back to the assessment centres, ideally after they have been turned. The few officers of the A.L.N.* who are captured are sometimes sent to Algiers where they are interrogated about subjects unrelated to the sector. Algiers means death, and they know this.

Verini listens to the sucking sounds, mouths pressed to mess tins slurping down the soup. He hears an old man talk to the chef. Ahmed leans down, glances towards him; Pascal turns away. Ahmed serves more soup to the old man who has probably called him "my son", called upon Allah the most merciful for a little more broth. Verini does not want to see. The old man might well have his throat cut tonight. Men as dangerous as these cannot be allowed to return to the battle. The lives of French citizens are at stake, our hectares of vineyards, our tarmacked roads.

"Pascal, you wan' some *frichti* for the dogs?"

Ahmed smiles, his French is improving. The Algerians have a sense of humour.

"The old man, he have seven children, have four son. What you think they do, this sons, when the old man dead?"

Ahmed goes out through the gate and heads back to the barn to make breakfast for the French soldiers. Pascal turns his back on the cells and waits to be relieved. Rubio is not here, today is Sunday, he is visiting his fiancée. Does she know what her boxing champ does here at the D.O.P.? Rubio sometimes comes to the commandos' mess hall to drink a beer with his admirers. Verini, Casta and Chapel shun him. Caporal-chef Colona ignores him. When not in the mess hall or in the house getting his orders from the *lieutenant* or out on operations, the *caporal-chef* does not emerge from his hut. He drinks. Colona saves their lives when they're on marches, telling them:

"Listen up, lads, the army is just a job to me, I'm not about to snuff it out here, so let's be careful, let's not go looking for shit to step in. We follow the *lieutenant*'s orders, but if we don't need to play the hero then as far as I'm concerned we don't. I didn't come here to kick the bucket and I don't want to see one of you lot take a bullet."

Colona is on his last legs, booze has destroyed his body, but he's a capable officer. The bottles of whisky they bring back from Orléansville are for him; from time to time he buys a round, usually when they return from manoeuvres.

They don't go out much, and most of the missions are close to the Farm. The intelligence collected by the various D.O.P.s in the country are sent to Algiers by a radio network independent of the normal frequencies used by the army. Intelligence is the sinew of this war; the more the army knows, the worse it gets.

Their mission, first and foremost, is to keep tabs on the D.O.P.s, their prisoners and their secrets. After he had spent his first night here listening to inhuman howls, Verini was granted an audience with Lieutenant Perret, who works for the Intelligence Service – *le deuxième bureau*. He is forbidden to talk to anyone about what he does and hears in the detachment. Military secret. Since then, he has seen Perret only from a distance. The *lieutenant* never comes over to the barns, which are Colona's sole domain. Officer Pradel of the Judiciare d'Orléansville comes out into the courtyard to get some fresh air, to smoke a cigarette, but he never speaks to anyone. He is pale and looks sickly, nauseated. He turns up stoically every Monday. There is some strange judicial reason for his presence here: in the interrogation room, he represents the French legal system. An absurdity he does not appreciate. Working for the army, the cop is given the rank of *sergent-chef*, a better salary and danger money. A doctor from Orléansville comes by from time to time to treat a badly beaten prisoner who still has secrets to give up. He is a military doctor. One night, Colona, soused on whisky, announced that the doctor had kicked up a stink about the state in which he found one of the *fellagas*. He never came back; he was replaced by another doctor.

All the men at the D.O.P. have permanent passes so they can move about freely by day or night. They have the right to dress in civilian clothes and to carry weapons while in civvies. They have standard-issue uniforms, the only addition being a black beret which some of them wear proudly in town: this is the beret of the Intelligence Service. Verini, Casta and Chapel stuff them in their pockets. Everyone at the Orléansville camp knows what happens in these detachments. No-one talks about it.

Verini's sentry shift ends. Another soldier comes to relieve him. Christophe has been here for two months, and has literally fallen apart. His face is grey, his eyes hollow. He is terrified, he gives everyone a curious stare. It is disturbing to see him with a machine gun, he seems hardly aware he is holding it and often, when in conversation, will aim it at the person he is talking to. Every week, he asks Colona for a transfer and Colona promises to speak to Perret. But Christophe never gets an answer. Sometimes his nightmares are so bad that he wakes up screaming. Out of fear or a lack of resilience, he joined the pack.

Verini sits on his bed and rereads a letter from his uncle telling him his parents are thinking about him. The parents who never write to him. He sent two letters, one from Nanterre, one from Puteaux. Orders are strict: no details, no acronyms, no place names. The letters are strangely vacuous though they have so much to say. Censorship, a lack of words. Every letter is opened and read: the slightest infringement results in the soldier being called before the *lieutenant*. Letters from the conscripts begin with an innocuous "Everything here is fine", and end with "Thinking of you". Those reading them in France must surely believe that nothing terrible is happening in Algeria.

Nothing seems to be happening in France either, the letters that arrive from home begin and end in the same way; they too are opened and read.

He is hoping for a letter from Christine, but at the same time thinking about the Algerian girl he met in the whorehouse in Orléansville. It was the first time he had ever been to a brothel. The fact that most of the soldiers treated going there as completely normal meant he did not question himself. With the money in his pay packet, there was little else to do.

Tomorrow morning, he and Casta will head off on the supply run; they are free all afternoon. They come back just before dark. And he thinks about Adila. He has no illusions, but perhaps she will remember him.

The patrol comes back from manoeuvres. Six men and one more, a prisoner. About thirty, quite tall, light-skinned, probably a Kabyle. He seems quite calm. His clothes are caked in dust, but there are no signs of a beating. Colona makes sure that the operation goes off as smoothly as possible. The prisoner is locked in one of the cells, then the patrol leader goes and reports to Perret.

Verini is happy to see Chapel and Casta again. He offers them a cigarette.

Anxious faces begin to relax. It takes hours to acclimatise to the safer universe that is the Farm. Tonight, over a beer, Verini will hear how things went, where they were, what they saw, who the prisoner is.

Everything reminiscent of a normal life is treasured. Fear slows time to a crawl, life is a ritual timed by a stopwatch and regular habits the best possible exorcism. They lose themselves in routine. The price for this small comfort is crippling boredom, and even this is cherished because it makes them feel safe. Verini has been at the D.O.P. for two months now and he feels as though he has sat around this brazier a thousand times, turning the lamb chops on the grill. They have set the brazier up outside in the barnyard, they open cans of beer. Casta and Chapel tell their story.

They went up to their "second home" – the adobe house up in Rannsou *djebel* which is used as a hideout – to leave rations and tins of food; they sometimes have to spend the night here. It is easy to guard and more comfortable than sleeping on the rocky ground in the open air. Especially now the nights are getting colder (Ahmed claims that it snows here and that in winter, everything is covered with ice; Verini does not believe him). There was a surprise waiting for them. The tins of corned beef had disappeared. The house is not in a deserted no-go area, but there have been so many incursions by the rebels and the French that everyone has fled. They did not sleep easy. Who but the *fellagas* could have been in the house?

Colona had known exactly where to catch the prisoner. Someone down in the cellar had obviously given reliable information. Two hours before dawn, on the road to the mountain pass, they found him disguised as a woman, leading a donkey laden with firewood. Chapel bites into a lamb chop.

"That bastard Paul shot the fucking donkey."

Casta nods.

"Yeah, the idiot put a bullet through his forehead and stood there giggling. Colona really tore him off a strip! Obviously, seeing he's from Corsica, he gets sentimental about donkeys. Usually, when you let off a round, the *fellagas* get panicky, but this guy, nothing, didn't move a muscle."

"The other conscripts were making fun of the woman's dress he was wearing, but, without waiting to be asked, he calmly took it off and draped it over the dead donkey. He hasn't uttered a single word since we caught him."

Chapel tosses the bone to the half-blind old dog that lives on the farm and is constantly getting under their feet. The poor animal is losing its hair. Most of the soldiers just call it "the dog", except for a few wiseacres who call it Raghead. Its masters abandoned it with the farm machinery when they went back to France. It sometimes barks for no apparent reason in the middle of the day or the middle of the night. When they're woken up, the conscripts joke about killing it. But maybe it did hear someone coming; so they listen in the darkness until they fall asleep again. Verini tosses the dog a bone.

"Aw, shit."

Rubio pushes open the gate – "Evening, lads!" – and comes into the barnyard. Heavy-set, he is one metre seventy and weighs about eighty kilos. He is not yet thirty and a spike of black hair falls over his forehead; when he emerges from the cellar in the morning, his cheeks and chin are blue with stubble. His physical appearance and his accent make it easy to forget that the man is not stupid.

The three "Nos" look down. Conversations start up between Rubio and his fan club. In town, he plays the big man, using his reputation as an ex-boxer and his more recent fame working at the D.O.P. He's a loudmouth but one too useful for them to do without.

Rubio bursts out laughing.

He goes on his way, yelling back that he's got work to do. It is dark now. He salutes the "leftists". It is a strange nickname. Chapel has never been political, his ideas are resolutely his own. Casta, despite his gangster airs, trails a dose of Catholic guilt around after him; it is hereditary in Corsica. Verini is a non-practising anarchist who reads *petit-bourgeois* books. What they do have in common are their brushes with the authorities.

Leftists as a synonym for draft dodgers.

Until 1956, Rubio had worked here as a foreman on a large farm. He knows the Arab soul and he more than anyone can say that he is doing everything he can for French Algeria. When Rubio talks about the Spain of his father, he is talking about Franco's Spain; he knows nothing of France besides what is African, nothing of Algeria besides what is French.

Verini thinks about the new prisoner and is sorry to have seen him. Never look at the prisoners.

Ahmed offers them some wine. He is the only member of the back-up crew allowed to remain out of doors after the curfew that has been set for Algerians: after performing *salat al-isha* and a hurried meal, they are locked up by 8.00 p.m. They sleep in the little barn whose windows have been bricked up. The door has been reinforced so no-one has to stand guard. Ahmed has to be locked in at 10.00 p.m. by whoever takes the second guard duty. Tonight, that is Verini. His two friends, exhausted having been on ops, head off to bed. He is waiting for his shift, from 10.00 p.m. to midnight and again from 2.00 a.m. to 4.00 a.m.

Ahmed stays with him. He seems a little nervous.

"What's the matter?"

Ahmed politely asks whether he will be going to Orléansville with them tomorrow.

"Yeah, sure, same as always. Why?"

Verini is alert to Ahmed's moods, especially since he started making jokes about the F.L.N.

"Pascal, my brother, you take me to brothel, yes?"

"What?" Pascal laughs. "You don't need me to take you, you can go by yourself."

Ashamed and embarrassed, Ahmed splutters that yes, he can go there himself, but only to the Muslim brothel, but he wants to fuck a white woman.

Pascal laughs and says he will see what he can arrange.

The dog barks. Colona comes back from making the rounds of the sentry posts.

"Verini, time to get to work, lad!"

Tonight, he has been posted to stand watch by the house, by a long wall with only a single bricked-up basement window. He gets to his feet and gestures for Ahmed to follow him; he is thinking about Adila, about seeing her tomorrow. Maybe she knows a white whore who would be prepared to go with Ahmed.

Verini ushers the chef into the small barn reserved for the Algerians, closes the door behind him and secures it with a chain and padlock. He finds doing this repugnant.

No-one knows what goes on at night in this building, what these men talk about.

What do the others think of Ahmed, the only one who is paid, the only one allowed to leave the camp, to fraternise with the French soldiers? Having become an auxiliary after his time in the cellar, he cannot but be suspect. To both sides. One of Ahmed's sons is fighting with the *fellagas*, yet here he is, living with those who torture and kill the rebels, terrified after every mission that he might find himself serving food to his son's killer; or that his son will be taken prisoner and land up in the cellar with Rubio.

Verini turns the corner, giving a low whistle so as not to startle Roger and die in a hail of machine-gun fire. He hands the sentry a cigarette to smoke on his way back to the barn. Roger tags along after Rubio, Paul and Henri. Not the worst maybe, but a dumb farm boy and as racist as he was taught to be. No words are exchanged; they will see each other again at midnight. They see each other every day, but they have nothing to say to each other.

Verini waits for a few minutes in the darkness, then walks towards the abandoned shack near the orange trees some ten metres from the wall. He slings his machine gun over his shoulder, grabs a low branch and hoists himself into the tree and from there onto the roof of the toolshed. Verini prefers to perch up here rather than staying by the wall as the other sentries have done for months.

The shed is far away from the basement window, but the bricks used to seal it are not enough. He has not been perched there ten minutes when he hears the first cry. The surprise of a weak electric shock. When Rubio is at the top of his game, you can hear his panting breath as he ratchets up the shocks. Verini feels ashamed that he would rather they were using the bathtub. Those drowned with a garden hose make less noise.

But Rubio and Perret have a penchant for electroshock, since it is less tiring and more straightforward to ask questions at the same time. For them, the bathtub does not make enough noise. Alert ears are constantly prowling around the Farm. This is psychological warfare.

Verini stares into the night, strains to listen to the sound from the direction of the trees.

The Kabyle's screams grow louder.

*

The dirt track. Exhausted from spending the night on sentry duty, Verini grips the steering wheel. Sylvain and Ahmed clutch the door handles. The G.M.C.'s engine whines as the truck winds upward towards the pass. Their instructions, if there is a gunshot or an explosion, are to floor the accelerator, drive towards the rock face, pull the handbrake, leap from the truck and hide in the ravine.

As they leave the narrow pass behind, they can breathe more easily. For some time now the *fellagas* have been less active in this sector. The Battle of Algiers, waged by the paras in the Algiers autonomous zone, and the arrests of the F.L.N. resistance leaders in the capital have a knock-on effect in *wilayah* IV of which

Orléansville is part. The respite is only temporary and might just as easily end today. Like all other conscripts, Verini knows nothing about such strategies: beneath the skin, all dangers, real or imagined, are the same. He drives as fast as possible along the open road; they can see the bridge that spans the Chélif river near the Farm.

The truck is left outside the camp storehouse and the three men scrabble into a jeep which a liaison officer drives as far as the city centre. He drops them off outside the Café la Rotonde. On the terrace, there are other soldiers and a few civilians; there are no women. French Algerians are friendly, quick to strike up a conversation, but they hide their daughters. Soon, when the outcome of the war looks uncertain, the penniless *pieds-noirs* will do everything they can to push them into the arms of the nearest soldier in the hope of marrying them off to a Frenchman.

Casta buys the first round. Ahmed asks for a beer. He rarely drinks, but today he is nervous. Verini is going to try and get him into the brothel.

It takes several drinks before they shake off the terror of the drive, this is the price they pay for time away from the D.O.P. and the others. They drink a toast to Chapel who is still stuck up there in the mountains.

The streets are quiet, there are no bombings in Orléansville. People work, open their shops, they have lunch, they chat. The Muslims here know their place; life glides along in a state of permanent distrust. Out of the corner of their eye, soldiers watch every movement. Terrorism is a war without a battlefield, it can strike anyone anywhere. M.A.T.-49 submachine guns are slung over the backs of chairs.

Verini suggests they have one for the road. Ahmed sniggers like a little boy until people start to turn and look. They leave La

Rotonde and club together to pay for a taxi as far as the whorehouse on the outskirts of the town

It's not an army brothel, though a lot of the regular clients are soldiers. The prostitutes are French and a little over the hill. Like any other French *département*, Algeria offers commercial opportunities for the criminal underworld. The younger, prettier girls are Algerian, daughters of poor families who are well aware how they make their living. Some of them are married and their husbands split the take with the brothel.

The French management and Algerian staff maintain a respectful distance from white clients and those in the military, most of whom are armed. Verini and Sylvain are wearing their pistols on their belts and their machine guns over their shoulders. A piece of advice from Colona, who refers to both the beds and the brothels as "a bug's nest", since most of them have been infiltrated. In Algiers, several have been subjected to grenade attacks by terrorists.

Outside, at the back of the building, is the area reserved for Muslims; here there are only Algerian girls who work in rotation behind blankets strung up to create "tents". The doorman scowls but allows Ahmed in since he is accompanied by two soldiers. The spacious bar on the ground floor is busy, given that it is still afternoon. Some Paul Anka hit is blaring from the jukebox, girls dolled up in the oriental style, or the French, crowd around officers who are already drunk. Then there are the bashful guys, farm boys from the *bled*, who blush and stammer as the girls playfully steer them towards the stairs. Behind the cash register, the boss, a Frenchwoman of about sixty, welcomes them and gives Ahmed a wry look.

Casta has a girlfriend back in Bastia. He has a couple of drinks before going upstairs with a French girl. Verini requests

Adila and the manageress tells him he'll have to wait. He leans over the bar.

"Listen, I've got a favour to ask."

Ahmed is embarrassed. Negotiations with the madam are concluded.

"But not in one of the rooms, out there in the tents. I'll send him one of the girls who does *bougnoules*. There's no way I'm letting him do it on the premises."

Ahmed will get to fuck a white woman, he doesn't care about the madam's contempt, and Verini laughs to himself, imagining what she must look like, this white girl "who does *bougnoules*". Ahmed heads for the back of the brothel. Verini has stopped drinking; not that he doesn't feel like it, but eventually they have to drive back down the dirt track, along the ravine.

A soldier comes down the stairs, the madam glances over at Verini.

"You can go up now, handsome."

He goes up.

Adila remembers him; after the sex, they talk a little. They are almost the same age, she is twenty-three, she speaks good French, her family live in Oran. Her husband, a taxi driver in Orléansville, was much older than she was. A few months ago, he had his throat cut for no reason anyone can determine – whether because he was a pimp, whether he was working for the French or for the F.L.N., whether he had anything to do with the war. When she asks him about his life, he tells her about Christine. He is alone. The young woman tells him that she likes him and what can he do but believe her?

"You know, in Paris, I wanted to be a taxi driver. Just like your husband."

Adila smiles.

He will come back. His time is up. He has to leave, to head back to the camp.

By the time they leave, Casta is blind drunk. Ahmed is waiting for them outside. They take another taxi. The blazing sun, the booze and the frustration have their heads reeling.

Sylvain sleeps in the truck while Verini goes to buy two bottles of whisky for Colona, and he and Ahmed load the billycans. Then they set off. They are running late, the dirt track is beginning to get dark and the wind whistles through the ramshackle cab of the truck. To buoy their spirits, they try to joke. Ahmed has fucked France, Verini has fucked Algeria. It was a sweet betrayal, even if Ahmed grumbles a little about his paramour's age.

Casta opens his eyes as the first potholes slam his head against the window. He emerges from his befuddled nap, sees the yellow road and roughly clutches his M.A.T.-49 to his chest. After a few seconds, the alcoholic haze dissipates. The ravine. Ahmed keeps a careful eye on the rocks, on the road. Verini puts his foot on the accelerator, he has a bad feeling about this; he glances over at his companions. Casta grips the butt of his machine gun, flicks off the safety. All three men come back to reality with a jolt of fear. Guilty of bunking off for a couple of hours. The god of war punishes the infidel, the reckless and the coward.

Verini pulls his pistol from its holster, releases the safety catch and offers it to Ahmed. The Algerian, forbidden from carrying a weapon, looks at Casta. The Corsican glances at Verini, who nods silently. Ahmed takes the gun and lets it dangle between his legs, both hands gripping the butt. Verini breaks all previous speed records; three times he rights the truck as it swerves towards the ravine. Still the three men feel they are not going fast enough. The billycans rattle on the flatbed of the truck. The low sun draws the shadows into yawning chasms amid the rocks, on the road.

"Left!" roars Casta suddenly.

The truck swerves, scraping along the rock face. Verini rights it without slowing down. They have successfully avoided something – a shadow, a pothole, a landmine, a rock – they don't know what.

They emerge from the gully, driving faster and faster and, without braking, head up the steep track to the Farm; only when the buildings are finally in sight do they slow down. Ahmed hands back the M.A.S.-50 and, head down, gives thanks. If there had been an attack, would he have picked sides? Everyone seems to think so, but the old Arab shivers.

Paul is on sentry duty in the orange grove. He waves as the truck passes, Verini scarcely nods in response.

They are back at the detachment.

# 7

1 July, 2009

Georges checked the time, glanced around at the landing, listened carefully. He knocked three times and took a step back.

"Who is it?"

He shouldered the door, smashing it open. Vasquez took it full in the face.

More walls lined with bookshelves. Vasquez, clutching his hand to his nose, staggered, fell on his arse, scrabbled to his feet, made a run for it. His blind dash ended by his desk, which he upended as he fell, taking with him the computer and the lever arch files. He grabbed one at random and hurled it behind him. It sailed over Crozat's head, knocking a painting off the wall and sending a few ornaments flying. Vasquez was crawling towards the window, probably to try to open it and shout for help. Too late.

Crozat grabbed his ankle and dragged him into the middle of the room, his fingernails scraping on the wooden floor. Georges grunted, grabbed the leg with both hands and slammed the guy into a bookcase. Before he had time to come round, a knee jabbed into his solar plexus and the blows began to rain down. In a few seconds, his cheekbones were raw and bleeding, and Vasquez passed out. Georges stopped punching, took off his black sweatshirt and used it to wipe his hands before tying it round his waist. They had made a lot of noise. The Wall cocked his ear and listened before leaving the apartment.

Now, in a red T-shirt, tracksuit bottoms and baseball cap, he turned right on the rue de Clignancourt and broke into a jog. 7.10 p.m. As long as Scheffer stuck to his routine, he was in good time.

Two weeks of mapping out the hit, two weeks of preparation.

Twenty minutes to reach the rue Lacroix behind Montmartre cemetery. A leisurely stroll.

He bobbed along the pavement, keeping a steady rhythm, never sprinting, never slowing, all the way to the 17th *arrondissement*.

At 7.27 p.m. he entered the building. A door code was only required after eight o'clock. His face hidden by the peak of his cap, he turned right in the inner courtyard, pushed inside the area where the communal bins were stored and left the door ajar. He stood at an angle so that he could see the main entrance, the courtyard and the bicycle shed opposite. There was no way of knowing whether Scheffer had got home early; he would have to wait. Gradually he caught his breath. Scheffer's timekeeping was erratic, but for the past ten days he had been thoughtfully punctual.

At 7.31 p.m., the main door opened. A woman wheeled a bicycle into the courtyard. Georges stepped back towards the bins and a cloud of flies took off and landed on his sweat-drenched face. He heard gearwheels turning and echoing in the courtyard. The creak of the door to the bicycle shed, the clank of a chain lock and a muttered curse as the padlock refused to cooperate.

"Do you need some help?"

Georges flinched. Scheffer must have followed the woman

110

into the building; Georges had not heard him come in. His bicycle was leaning against the wall, the front wheel visible through the half-open door. Scheffer struggled for a minute with his neighbour's padlock, grumbling somewhat more politely, before admitting defeat.

"It's seized up."

"Doesn't matter, I'll get Denis to sort it out tomorrow, it's not like anyone is going to steal it from here."

"Do you want me to lock it to mine? I'm out early in the morning, so it would be unlocked."

"Oh? Sure, why not."

"O.K., I'll do that."

"Thanks. Thanks a lot. Have a good evening."

"You too."

The sound of footsteps retreating. Hunkered down, Scheffer was busying himself threading the lock chain through both the bicycles and closing the padlock. Broad-shouldered, balding on top, twenty kilos heavier than Vasquez. This would take brute force, surprise would not be enough. Georges stepped back, took a run at him. He could tell from Scheffer's legs that the man was sporty, that he had good reflexes. The man spun round and his jumper slipped from Crozat's grasp. Scheffer put his guard up.

"What do you want?"

Georges blinked, looked at the raised fists and dropped into a sideways stance.

"Who are you? What do you . . ."

Quick sidestep, curve the torso. Hypnotised, Scheffer could not take his eyes off Georges' head and took a right jab straight to the nose. His head snapped back in a crack of cartilage, his eyes rolled back in his head. Before he could cry out, a second vicious jab slammed into his mouth, splitting his upper lip all the way to the base of the nose. Georges grabbed the man by the scruff of the neck and shoved him into the shed with the rubbish bins. Scheffer rolled on the ground and Crozat jumped on him, held him there, and beat him senseless.

"What were you expecting, arsehole? Huh? What were you expecting? Huh?"

Scheffer's head bounced between his fists and the concrete.

"You think you can get a punch in? Huh, fuckwit? You think you can land a punch on me?"

He felt warm splashes on his forearms. Finally he stopped, his hands sticky with blood up to the wrists. Out of breath, his joints aching, Georges fell backwards and leaned against the wall. Lying on his back and wheezing, Scheffer's larynx spasmed as his thoracic muscles expelled a mouthful of blood. Unless he was put into the recovery position, he would choke. Georges got to his feet, grabbed the man's shoulder and heaved. The body was heavy. A voice made him freeze.

"Monsieur Scheffer?"

The neighbour with the bike was back.

"Monsieur Scheffer? I heard a noise, are you hurt?"

Flies were already beginning to land on the ruined face, sucking blood from the wounds. Georges let go of Scheffer. His head lolled obscenely, his nose and his teeth pressed against the concrete.

The woman hesitated between the two doors, peered into the bicycle shed, called again, then walked towards the rubbish bins and pushed the door open with her fingertips. A triangle of light spread across the floor, from the feet to the head of the splayed body.

She stifled a scream, suppressed the urge to vomit. Georges panicked as he saw the bloody, butchered face in the light of day. He shrank back against the wall. She sensed his presence and froze as her eyes met those of the crouching beast.

She took a step back and then broke into a run, shouting at the top of her lungs. Georges stepped over Scheffer's body and made a run for it while she was screaming for help.

He sprinted as far as the place Clichy, spreading panic on the pavements. He turned off into a narrow street, turned left a dozen times, right a dozen times, and when finally he no longer knew where he was, he collapsed, panting, in a doorway.

Twelve hundred euros.

Four nights with Mireille.

He wiped his face and his hands on his sweater and then jogged on.

*

He would not have cared if Scheffer were dead as long as no-one found out. He would not have cared if he himself were dead as long as no-one found out. Keep things strictly between him and Roman and the others, and not have people who didn't understand sticking their noses in.

The front page of the newspaper, a photo of a hospital bed, Scheffer's bandaged head, tubes snaking from his mouth, his nose.

Coma.

FREELANCE JOURNALISTS LOUIS SCHEFFER AND PIERRE VASQUEZ ASSAULTED IN PARIS.

*Pierre Vasquez, whose injuries were less serious, spoke about the attacks. He is convinced that the assaults were directly linked to their work: "This is the sort of thing you'd expect from a fascist regime." Continued on page ...*

The *police judiciaire* had opened an investigation. The simultaneous nature of the attacks and the initial witness statements caused confusion: two men who looked vaguely similar, and who had doubtless been chosen because of their resemblance. The

113

police were working on the theory that they were dealing with more than one assailant and a meticulously planned operation.

The media were baying for blood. They would not stand for one of their own being so savagely attacked. Vasquez, in a state of shock, had escaped with cuts and contusions. Scheffer was still in a coma and it was by no means certain that he would regain consciousness; the doctors offered no prognosis. The two reporters had been in the late stages of writing a book about a cold case dating back to 1974, one which implicated Jean-Jacques Susini*, a former Front National parliamentary candidate, an acquaintance of Pierre Lagaillarde* and General Salan*, a close friend of Jean-Marie Le Pen and, in 1961, co-founder of the O.A.S.* The case concerned the disappearance of Raymond Gorel, former treasurer of the *Organisation armée secrète*. Scheffer and Vasquez claimed to have uncovered new leads in the unsolved case. The book was scheduled to be published within weeks and M. Vasquez was insistent that there was no need to look elsewhere for reasons why they were attacked, it was proof that "the France of French Algeria has not yet been laid to rest".

1974? O.A.S.?

A forty-eight-hour fever. Pale and weak, Crozat spent two days traipsing from bed to toilet to empty himself. Eventually, having had no news from Roman, and not daring to listen to the radio or read the newspapers, he phoned Mireille. He showed up at the hotel in mid-afternoon and asked to rent a room by the hour like some junkie in withdrawal.

He sat on the bed, not even bothering to get undressed. The flower-patterned wallpaper was being peeled away in limp strips by the muggy July heat. Mireille tried to make him horny, but it was useless. Georges stared vacantly into space.

"What's eatin' you, *chéri*? What's got you all worked up, huh?"

She persuaded him to lie down and massaged his back, talking dirty to him in a throaty whisper, but Georges could not relax.

After much stroking and kneading, he allowed himself to be soothed, though he still had no desire to fuck. Wearing only bra and panties, Mireille was sitting on his legs and he liked the feel of her long nails digging into his aching muscles, the weight of her fat buttocks crushing his thighs.

"You got kids, Mireille?"

"What you wanna ask me that for, Georges? It ain't exactly romantic, *chéri*."

"No reason. Just asking."

"I got me three kids. All boys."

"You got a husband?"

Mireille stopped her massage.

"Come on, *doudou*, don't go spoilin' everything."

"Sorry, I didn't mean it like that. I just want to know if you're . . ."

"Don't you worry 'bout me, sugar. I'm here for you. You want to talk, that's fine by me, but no more questions."

She gave an embarrassed laugh and went back to her massage.

"Family is a good thing," murmured Georges.

"True. What about you, *chéri*, you got a family?"

Georges closed his eyes.

Mireille ran her sharp nails down his spine. Georges felt a jolt of electricity in his belly.

"Turn over, *chéri*, let's talk about somethin' else."

Mireille lifted her large buttocks, Georges turned onto his back. She gripped the old boxer between her thighs, began to grind her hips. He closed his eyes and let her carry on, getting excited at the idea of them as a pair of ageing lovers, with her

115

married to the game and him to his loneliness. Having paid for it spared him having to fake his passion. Behind his closed eyelids there was nothing now, no newspapers, no stink of rubbish bins.

Seedy as it was, the hotel room was preferable to reality: here he could close his eyes. As he headed back downstairs, he was thinking about work, about the Scheffer–Vasquez case which his perfunctory orgasm had blotted out for only an instant, about Toni Esperanza who would be waiting for him in the ring two weeks from now, about the detectives questioning the journalists' neighbours, about the woman who had looked him in the eye, about the horror he had seen on her face. He shuddered as he stepped out into the street.

Elbow leaning out of an open car window, smoking a cigarette, Roman was sitting in an unmarked police car opposite the hotel. This time he was alone, one hand on the steering wheel. Georges felt as though Roman knew everything, down to the exact time he would leave the hotel. He hunched his shoulders and crossed the street.

"Get in, Crozat, we need to talk."

Roman tossed the cigarette butt out of the window as he raced along the *périphérique*.

"You have a good time?"

Georges didn't answer.

"It's always good to get your rocks off. A little bedroom athletics, a little massage, people will tell a whore anything, they'll spill their guts. But go easy on the pillow talk, yeah? I wouldn't want you running your mouth off. What d'you say, Georges?"

"I don't come here to talk."

"I didn't think so, you're not exactly a chatterbox. She does it on the house?"

"She gives me a discount, I'm a regular."

There is barely space enough to slide a book between their shoulders.

"You tell her you're a cop? You should have – makes it easier to negotiate. But then, I'm forgetting, you're rolling in it these days, aren't you?"

Georges had razor blades in his mouth.

"O.K., well, we're not here to talk about your love life. You've seen the papers."

"Hmm."

Roman smiled.

"Vasquez can't come up with an e-fit, you were too fast for him. Scheffer is still in a coma and I'd be surprised if he remembers anything. The woman, the one who saw you at Scheffer's place, she says you're two metres tall with bloodshot eyes and hair coming out your ears! Jesus fuck, she thinks she saw a yeti!"

He laughed to himself, passed a speed camera doing a hundred and twenty an hour without even noticing the flash.

"A caveman! A fucking gorilla! Ha!" The laughter stopped dead. "You nearly screwed up the whole thing, Crozat."

"It was touch-and-go, having to do both at the same time."

"True, but that doesn't change the facts. When you work for me, you don't screw up."

Georges cleared his throat.

"I'm working for you?"

Roman stared at the road, weaving through the traffic.

"That's all you need to know. And if you get any bright ideas about fucking me over, just remember you've got more to lose than you think. Think about your friends down at Ring 14."

Roman took a cigarette from his pack and offered one to Georges.

"Sorry, I forgot you're a real athlete, Crozat, and smoking kills, am I right?"

He tossed the pack of Marlboro onto the dashboard and went on:

"It's just a little warning. Up to now I've been happy with your work and there's no reason that should change."

"I'm not going to fuck you over, there's no need for threats."

"I just want things between us to be clear."

"You sure we don't have to worry about our . . ."

Georges was about to say "colleagues", but the word wouldn't come.

"With . . . with the *police judiciaire*."

"Don't sweat it, if you get any flak I'll deal with it. Your job is to pay a little visit to whoever I tell you."

"Might be best if I lie low for a while."

"I've got one more job for you. After that, you can take a break."

"It's too risky."

"Don't go letting me down, Georges. If I smell trouble, I'll let you know. Meanwhile, you don't move an inch, you do as I say. I'll drop you at porte Saint-Cloud, that O.K.?"

Roman turned onto the slip road before he finished the question. As Georges stood on the pavement, Roman popped his head out the door and looked him straight in the eye.

"Don't worry about the newspapers, it's all bullshit, they've got nothing on you. Just stay cool, Crozat, and don't try to contact me."

Someone had been in his place. Above the fetid stink of the apartment he could smell tobacco. And not stale cigarette smoke, this was fresh.

He checked the rooms, opening drawers and cupboards, checked to make sure his gun was still there. Some things seemed to have been moved a couple of millimetres, enough for him to be suspicious but not enough for him to be certain. It hadn't been a search, just a casual visit by someone with a cigarette dangling from his lips. He opened the window to air the room. On the ledge there was a cigarette butt. His visitor was no fool, there were no signs of entry on the front door; the butt had been left there so he would see it. Another warning. Roman could get to him anywhere, at home, at work or in a seedy hotel on the other side of Paris; Roman, or someone else who worked for him.

The cigarette butt was a Camel.

Stay cool, Crozat.

Roman was a snake with a head at both ends, but as long as the police were still floundering, why throw such a godsend out the window?

The newspaper was still lying on the table with the picture of Scheffer in bandages. Georges decided to go to Ring 14, sweat it off, catch up with Paolo and Marco.

*

The Crozat–Esperanza bout was scheduled to take place in ten days at the sports centre in Fontenay-sous-Bois; the poster had set people talking in the world of amateur boxing. In the days that followed, the Vasquez–Scheffer story slipped from the front pages to the back pages. Vasquez had held a number of increasingly tetchy press conferences and eventually accused the police of not taking the investigation seriously. At which point, the media outlets prepared to champion his story dried up. The man who had attacked the still comatose Scheffer was still assumed to be a different assailant and had not been identified. Witnesses had seen a man of about forty with short hair emerging from the building on the rue Lacroix, but could not agree on a sufficient number of details to build an e-fit portrait.

Georges wondered whether Roman or his silent partners had enough clout to quash the investigation. Or maybe Georges' face, gnarled as a pollarded plane tree, made it impossible to build a recognisable e-fit.

All things considered, he was more worried about the upcoming fight.

He didn't know how to get out of the match; he wasn't doing enough training, Paolo was forever calling to hassle him, Marco was on his back when he swung by Ring 14 for an hour at the end of the day. He still went jogging every morning, but rarely worked the punchbag and practised his combinations in slow motion. He got breathless more quickly and his legs, though good for his age, were much too heavy to withstand a fight. If he still had the same power and technique, his stamina had long since left the building. His hand–eye coordination was slow, his muscles were slack. Paolo screamed at him through his voicemail.

"What the fuck are you playing at, Georges? People are starting to talk, they're saying you're not fit to fight, and I'm running out of arguments. For fuck's sake, the guys who've seen you in the ring are laughing at you, there's no-one out there who believes you can go a single round. Shit, Georges . . . where the hell are you?"

One way or another, ten days from now, no-one would be hassling him about his boxing career.

Georges put in a request for leave. Bergolio gave him a week, no questions asked.

"You look like shit, Crozat, I'm not sure a week will be enough. Is it true, this rumour that you've got a fight coming up?"

"Hmm."

"You O.K. with the commission these days? No more grief?"

"Yeah."

"You're going to get creamed."

"You want a ringside seat?"

Bergolio looked up from his paperwork and smiled.

"You sure you don't want to take a month off?"

Georges didn't tell Paolo he had taken a week's leave, he stopped going to training, he holed up in his apartment. He spent one night with Mireille, one night with a younger white girl, but he did not feel comfortable. Mireille was part of the half-hearted contract he had made with himself to carve out a new life after the last match, a pathetic existence, but one he could make the most of with no comeback. "Toni and me, we're going to sort everything out, the past and the future." He was starting to turn philosophical, spending all day sipping Löwenbräu in the kitchen, like so many boxers before him, broken by body blows and fear.

When the newspapers gave up on the story of the journalists, on the very first day they didn't mention the story, Georges found an envelope in his letterbox. Roman was greasing the wheels: he had added two crisp bills. Eight hundred smackers for just one guy. He wondered whether the Pakistani might be able to come up with one sad bastard a month; Roman seemed to be able to come up with an intellectual a week. This time the guy was an Arab. Brahim Bendjema, 220 bis rue des Pyrénées. A black-and-white photograph of a serious-looking man in a suit. Georges did not linger, studying the picture just long enough to be able to recognise the guy.

He put the cash, the note and the photo back into the envelope, laid it on the table in front of him and opened another beer. He drank, not bothering to turn the lights on, until he could scarcely make out the rectangle of paper, then he staggered to bed without getting undressed.

The next morning, he started the stake-out. His sports gear no longer fooled anyone. His washed-out face and his baggy track-suit made him look like a patient smoking a crafty cigarette outside a cancer unit.

The first time he saw Bendjema, he let him slip through his fingers. Having spent the morning and part of the afternoon waiting, he was not concentrating and didn't recognise him. Only when he saw the man coming back an hour later did he realise that Bendjema was seventy if he was a day. Though Georges found it difficult to work out how old Arabs were, the guy was at least twenty years older than in the photograph. Georges went home and brooded on this difficult dilemma. How could he beat up a guy that age without killing him?

He went back the following morning and tailed Bendjema through the streets. The man was tall – at least one metre eighty, even bowed as he was by his twisted spine – and had short grey hair. As he had the previous day, he came out of the building at 4.00 p.m. and walked as far as the rue Sorbier in Ménilmontant, where he sat on the terrace of a café called Le Lieu-dit and drank coffee and read *Le Monde*. The waiter clearly knew him and they chatted for a bit. An hour later, he was home again.

On day three, as soon as the old guy left, Georges managed to gain access to the building. The letterbox made no mention of a Madame Bendjema. The keypad entry system was active all day, but an ID card as a telephone repairman was enough to get him in. It was an opulent building with a gilded door, original par-quet floors and a concierge. He went up to the landing. Second floor, overlooking the street. Some mutt in the apartment across the landing started barking. Even when he went back down to the ground floor, he could still hear it. Dogs had always hated the smell of him.

On the fourth day, Bendjema spotted him. He had turned into the rue Orfila, Georges had counted to ten before following him. Bendjema was twenty metres away, standing on the pavement staring at him. The Wall headed back towards Pyrénées, zigzagging though the streets.

Arriving home feeling pathetic, he found a note from Paolo slipped under his door. His voicemail box was full, so the Portuguese had dropped by and left a short message full of spelling mistakes. The gist of the message, however, was the same: what the fuck are you up to?

On day five, at 4.00 p.m., he stationed himself in a bar on the rue Sorbier directly opposite Le Lieu-dit. True to his routine, ten minutes later the old man was sitting at a table on the terrace. From behind his newspaper, never moving his head, Bendjema scanned the street.

Georges watched for forty-five minutes and did not leave his post until the old man had left. Bendjema looked like a nice guy, he was well known in the neighbourhood and smiled at all the shopkeepers.

Bendjema's building was too risky, as was postponing the attack any longer. Georges decided to adopt the method he had used on Brieux, a lightning attack in the street. He retraced the route back to Pyrénées, scouting out possible locations. The car park entrance on the rue Orfila looked good. The automatic door was set back three metres from the street at the bottom of a steep concrete ramp. The place stank of piss and tramps; he would certainly not be disturbed, at least in the short time he needed.

He liked the idea that the old man knew what was going to happen. And that he did not change his routine. Georges went to bed after finishing off the last few cans of beer and half a bottle of sour wine. He dreamed he was stepping into the ring with

Esperanza, but Toni's face was that of an elderly Arab who knocked his teeth out.

The following morning, Georges rushed round to Ring 14.

Marco got on the telephone to Paolo.

"Hey, guess what? Georges has been here for the past hour sweating like a pig, ripping into punchbags and eating leather like a lunatic. Get your arse down here now."

Paolo showed up looking smug. Marco was full of himself. They had managed to get Georges back on track. Four days before the fight. Three hours' training. Georges wore out two young middleweights who had agreed to spar with him, fought twenty rounds on the rope, and lifted tons of weights. Paolo advised him to chill, that they had time, but Georges would not stop. He clenched his teeth, he didn't give a shit about the fight. He let the two ex-bruisers dream up their preposterous plans, but he didn't stop until he could no longer lift his arms.

He went home, pulled on a clean tracksuit, pulled the baseball cap down over his forehead and set off.

He lay in wait for Bendjema on the corner of the Bidassoa and Orfila. As soon as he saw the man, he stepped back, took a deep breath and started jogging, keeping his head down as he turned the corner. The old man was strolling down the street. Georges put on a burst of speed to intercept him by the underground car park. The street was deserted, the dark ramp leading underground was perfect. Don't hit him too hard, Georges, don't go killing the old man for fuck's sake, keep calm. The punishing training session had got his body under control, emptied his mind, drained his muscles, but still he was worried.

As he came to the car park, Bendjema stopped, stuffed his hands in his pockets and stood ramrod straight. As he ran, Georges glanced at him from under the peak of his baseball cap.

"What the fuck is he doing?"

Brahim Bendjema was staring at him.

Georges slowed.

The man was a bag of bones. Deep wrinkles encircled hollow eyes, his mouth was thin-lipped, his cheekbones prominent, his face expressionless, but his eyes were unwavering.

Bendjema's lips quivered.

"Who sent you, monsieur?"

Crozat was petrified. The old man's eyes misted over with a century of weariness.

"You don't know?" He moistened his lips. "If you like, I can explain. Ever since Alain Dulac phoned me several weeks ago, I knew that someone would come for me."

"Have you got a gun in your pocket?"

"I have more than that, monsieur, I have a war." Bendjema gave a faint smile.

"Forgive the allegory, it is one of the failings of age to want to condense the past into few words. When I am afraid, I choose my words with care. It is a matter of pride. Fear has always made me proud."

The old man took a careful step to one side, Georges watched him intently. Slowly, Bendjema took a hand from his pocket, gestured to a concrete step between two pillars in the entrance to the car park.

"We'll be more comfortable if we talk there, if you don't mind?"

Georges followed.

"I trust you'll forgive the disagreeable smell, but the choice of venue was yours."

\*

Georges locked himself in his apartment, reconnected the telephone and waited for news from Roman.

125

For two days, there was nothing. The phone rang a dozen times. Paolo and Marco.

On the morning of the third day, Georges went downstairs to check the post and found a new envelope. He ran back upstairs and locked himself in his apartment.

A name and an address, no photograph, no money, just a message on a card.

"You can do this one for free if you're not prepared to do the old man. Shift your arse."

The name seemed familiar.

It might be a trap, or maybe Roman was giving him a chance. There could be no question now of skipping the bout. He had to follow instructions.

Georges immediately went to the 11th *arrondissement* and, taking no trouble to hide, stationed himself outside 48 avenue Philippe-Auguste. For two hours he waited until a man arrived on a motorbike wearing a leather jacket and a helmet with a tinted visor. Beneath the leather, he was built like a brick shithouse. The guy took off the helmet, shook out his long hair, chained up the bike and turned around to give a passing girl the time to admire his body.

Georges was ready. With unusual speed, he made some mental calculations and then tore across the street. Roman or one of his henchmen was probably watching, he didn't even look around to check. He got his foot in the door before it closed and caught up with the biker in the stairwell. The guy turned when he heard the stairs creak.

The Pakistani smiled, happy to see Crozat though unsure why he was there.

"Sorry, Paki."

It was pointless asking questions. The Pakistani knew no more than he did; he had nothing to gain from this except a brief respite.

126

Georges spared the pretty-boy face, hitting just enough to stun him, then focused on the ribcage which was less dangerous than going for the stomach. His fists sank into the bouncer's flabby muscles.

Every punch was a lesson for Crozat. You don't walk out on Roman. The Pakistani had probably done nothing to deserve the beating; it was just another warning.

Imagine what could happen to you if you really piss me off.

"Stop, Georges! Fuck sake, stop, will you?"

Calmly, he continued pounding the Pakistani. The more disgusted he felt with himself, the more he felt the lesson was effective.

You're a complete arsehole, Georges, and your turn is coming.

The Pakistani tried to crawl up the stairs. Georges dragged him back.

Every punch will come back to you, every jab, every hook when the day of reckoning comes.

The Pakistani huddled into a ball against the wall. Georges kicked him in the kidneys. The Pakistani bawled.

"Shut up, shut the fuck up, arsehole! You're the one who got us into this shit, you hear me? You screwed up, so shut your fucking hole and take it like a man!"

He ended with a series of blows to the head. Blood spurted onto the stairs.

A neighbour screamed that he was calling the police. Georges stopped pounding and scarpered.

He waited all day, all evening, all night.

Every half-hour the telephone rang. He listened to the messages. Paolo and Marco.

No news from Roman.

He prepared himself. The old Arab guy had explained

everything. That you can never escape the snares you've laid behind you, that some day or other you will come and fall into a trap. That situations may have no meaning, but they always have a logic, and logic has no imagination. It's a boomerang.

The Pakistani had offered him five hundred notes to work some guy over and in return had taken a beating on the house. Georges had done everything he could to avoid stepping back into the ring; now he would go back with his tail between his legs, he needed it more than ever before.

There was no news from Roman. Had the good soldier Crozat atoned for his mistake?

He didn't give a shit. All that mattered was to get into the ring. As far as Georges was concerned, Toni Esperanza was the only accepted authority on his future.

Night dragged into day and nothing changed.

The telephone rang. On the other end of the line, Paolo was probably swearing at the overloaded answering machine.

The following day, just as the two coaches were about to kick it down, Georges opened the door, his sports bag slung over his shoulder.

"Let's go."

The two old-timers spent the drive yelling at him. He looked like death warmed up, they didn't know why they were even bothering to go to the bout, given it was a dead cert that Toni was going to knock his teeth so far down his throat he'd need to stick his toothbrush up his arse. Esperanza's trainer had phoned, there were rumours The Wall hadn't been training, that the bout was going to be a farce. For weeks, Marco and Paolo had been lying through their teeth to anyone and everyone, claiming Georges was training hard, that he was fighting fit. Georges had never seen Paolo so furious.

"Just look at yourself for fuck's sake, you're four, maybe five kilos overweight, you couldn't run a hundred metres and you stink of beer . . ."

"Don't sweat it . . ."

"Don't sweat . . . Are you taking the piss? The state you're in you couldn't go two rounds against me!"

"I'm ready."

"This is the fucking last time you'll see me in your corner, *caralho*, make no mistake. I hope Toni leaves you choking on your own blood, and don't come to me to patch you up! *Burro de merda!* What the fuck was with your little visit three days ago, why come down and bust your balls at Ring 14 and then chuck in the towel? Have you been running at least? Have you been lifting weights, or is that belly of yours all fat?"

The volley of insults continued all the way to Fontenay. When they got to the sports centre, Georges wasn't disappointed. The amateur boxing event had brought in five, maybe six hundred people. The heavyweight bouts listed last on the fight card would start at 9.00 p.m. In the ring, a couple of bantamweights were exchanging a flurry of punches, the crowd were keyed up. Kravine had a ringside seat.

Marco and Paolo dragged him to the dressing room.

Georges did some warm-ups, but he was so stiff, so heavy, that Paolo finally told him to save his strength.

He went for the weigh-in: 95.6 kilos – almost five kilos above his ideal weight. Esperanza weighed in at ninety-two. They dragged him back to the dressing room. Paolo smeared vaseline on Georges' face, his fury had turned to worry. Marco took over; tonight, he would be the coach.

"O.K., we know Toni, we know what he's like, he's an outside-fighter like you, but he's younger. I don't like to say it, but it's the truth. So he's going to go with long-range punches, but he can slug too, and he likes it. If he smells blood, if he has even a sniff that you're not on form, he'll go for blood. Given the state of you, you need to change your game. Toni doesn't react well to pressure, he needs to be in control. If you play it his way, the bout will go on for hours and he'll get you on a Majority Decision. So you have to go in hard, raw power is all you've got going for you tonight. You have to forget about safety and pile into him, got it?"

"Don't sweat it."

An official from the Boxing Commission knocked on the door, checked the hand tapes and the gloves, and left once the wrap was complete. Georges spent five minutes shadow-boxing, never lifting his feet, just to work up a sweat.

Paolo was preparing his corner kit; he hesitated, then added a large fistful of cotton swabs before closing it. Marco put the navy blue robe over Georges' shoulders.

"Let's go."

As he stepped out of the dressing room, the need to believe was a little stronger.

When Toni Esperanza took off his robe, Paolo's first thought was that he hadn't packed enough bandages. Georges' eyebrows would be gashed and spatter the walls. He had prepared for his bout against The Wall, he was solid muscle. One look at those abs, at those eyes like diamond drills, and it was obvious Esperanza had no intention of hanging around for Crozat's famous sixth round.

"This isn't going to be decided on points," Paolo muttered.

"No way," Marco said. "This is going to be the Guns of Navarone."

Georges slipped off his robe. Glistening with sweat, he might have looked the part to those at the back of the stadium. In Toni's

130

corner they were rubbing their hands. The Wall looked like he'd just got out of bed and forgotten to take a shower.

The two boxers moved into the centre of the ring, the referee made his speech and they touched gloves. Toni jogged back to his corner, Georges trudged back to his. He looked out at the stands. The crowd, whipped up to fever pitch, were shouting themselves hoarse. Kravine was chatting to the little band of officials clustered round him, pointedly not looking at the ring to show he didn't give a shit. But he had no fighters in this event. He had come to watch Georges.

"Georges! Get your arse over here!"

Arms dangling by his sides, Georges continued to stare out at the crowd.

He turned back to Paolo and Marco, who gave him their strategy again with both barrels: go in fast, hit hard, stop Toni before he got into his stride, none of his usual routine of taking the punches. Georges looked past them, smiling.

"Hey! You listening or what?"

He raised a glove towards the crowd. Roman had just sat down in the third row, ejecting some young lad from his seat. Face smeared with vaseline, The Wall gave him a smile, baring a gumshield covered in slobber. Roman stared back, expressionless.

The bell rang and the screams of the crowd rose an octave.

Georges dropped into a peek-a-boo guard: gloves up, elbows tucked in. For three minutes, he stood motionless, taking a hail of punches, doing nothing to block or dodge them. Having spent most of the round pounding on Georges' gloves, Toni started in on his stomach and his sides which The Wall had left exposed.

In the break between rounds, Marco tried to talk to him, but Georges wasn't listening. There were boos from the crowd, Esperanza and his team had no idea what the hell was going on.

Round two.

Georges kept his guard up and the dance began again. His only strategy was to stay right in front of Toni, shuffling without lifting his feet. Eventually, when his stomach had been pounded, he lowered his guard and began taking blows to his face. By the end of round two, he was bleeding and the crowd had turned against him.

First aid. Paolo did not say a word. Marco couldn't think what to say. Georges hadn't landed a single punch, he hadn't reacted. As the bell went, just before he put in his mouth-guard, he told them not to worry.

This time he made contact, thwarting the attack by getting Esperanza in a clinch.

"What's the matter, Toni? What's the matter, you fucking dago, you forgotten how to throw a punch? You know how much I got to throw this fight? The least you could fucking do is make it look good!"

Toni Esperanza blinked, the referee separated them and before Toni had time to put his guard up, Georges delivered a punch straight to the nose. Esperanza howled and the ref issued Georges with a warning. A dazed Toni screwed up the rest of the round, jabbing half-heartedly at Georges who was once again stock-still, hiding behind his gloves.

During the break, Toni's corner was in turmoil.

The fourth round was carnage, Georges' guard began to crumble and after every punch, every flurry, he piled on the taunts.

"Fuck's sake, I can't take a dive and make it look convincing if you keep throwing these pitty-pat punches, dipshit!"

At the next punch, Georges used his back to block the view of the referee and the judges, and threw a vicious right hook to Toni's kidney.

The crowd booed, the Spaniard flew into a rage. Georges let

his guard drop and he came away from the round with his eyes swollen and both eyebrows streaming blood. Marco and Paolo made no attempt to talk to him. To the opposing corner, their silence made it look as though this was all a plan, a dirty tactic to screw up the bout.

Round five. Georges' nose started to piss blood. After one particular punch, the referee inspected the damage. Georges told him he was fine and, for thirty seconds, looked as though he were actually boxing. He bobbed and weaved and landed two brutal jabs that Toni did not even see coming. At long last, the fight seemed to have started, the stadium erupted, then Georges went back to his role as a punchbag, dropped into a defensive stance. He took a left hook that had him seeing stars. On the ropes, Toni got him in a headlock.

"What the fuck are you doing, Georges? What is this shit?"

"I'm being paid to throw this fight, so throw a punch, you dumb fucking dago, you can't lose."

Totally bewildered, Esperanza glanced over at his trainer and Georges slammed a fist into his nose, hearing a dull crack. Toni danced around Georges, trying to get his bearings. The crowd weren't sure what to make of this farce, but Georges didn't care.

Esperanza unleashed a series of vicious combinations. Georges took the first two punches and, exhausted, dodged the third. He managed not to collapse, glanced over at the referee who was clearly considering stopping the match. He kept his guard up for the rest of round six.

"Georges, I can't keep patching you up. I don't know what the fuck you're playing at, but I'm telling you now if you don't finish this match in the next couple of rounds you're going to be carried out in a coma."

Paolo was increasingly worried, Georges was taking too many

blows to the head, he was starting to squint and Esperanza was showing no sign of fatigue.

Round seven. Georges boxed. Just enough to keep the flame alive. Esperanza was using all his muscle to tip the scales. The Wall was falling to pieces. He spent the whole round insulting Toni, calling him a shithead, a spic, a faggot, a ballerina.

At the bell, the referee came over to the blue corner and warned Crozat.

"If you don't stop this shit, this will be the last round."

It hardly mattered, it was a miracle that The Wall was still standing, he had taken as many punches in this match as in three bouts of thirteen rounds. His belly and his sides were no longer red but purple, his eyelids had swollen, leaving slits like razor cuts, his cheeks looked like putrid blood oranges about to explode. Paolo inserted a camphor-soaked cotton bud into Georges' nostrils, stretching them so that, for a minute at least, he could breathe more easily.

Marco wanted to stop the fight, Paolo whispered in Georges' ear.

"There's another way out of this, for Christ's sake, you don't need to get yourself killed, you can get through this."

"Don't sweat it."

Round eight.

The bell.

Legs still holding up. Gloves still on the ends of his arms.

Georges strode into the centre of the ring, he had decided to shake things up a little. Esperanza's nose was swollen, but next to Georges he still looked human. Half blind, Georges gave a brief object lesson in boxing. He bobbed and weaved, did a little fancy footwork, and every time he saw the slightest clink, he got under Esperanza's guard, delivering two powerful jabs that could be heard in the back row. Esperanza was reeling. The crowd were in hysterics. Kravine was on the edge of his seat and Roman, though he didn't move, was laughing, his mouth wide, his eyes lifeless. Georges goaded his opponent with little jabs at his gloves, little punches to the neck during the clinches, he humiliated Toni, treating him like a kid. At the end of his tether, with one minute to go before the end of round eight, Toni Esperanza abandoned any notion of strategy and waded in, determined to annihilate Georges even if it took every ounce of strength he had. His coach tried to shout over the noise.

"Chill, Toni, stay calm for fuck's sake! Don't let him get to you."

But Toni was no longer listening and Georges was smiling, smiling as he mocked him. Fucking dago queer, punch me, you fucking fairy, punch, for God's sake! Marco and Paolo had no idea what Georges was up to, but they knew he had Toni right where he wanted him, that his blubber had softened the blows, that he was still hanging in there, that he had managed to reserve what little strength he had. If he could get through this round, the two boxers would be on the same footing because Toni was using up all his strength pounding away at Georges' fatuous smile. He was throwing vicious jabs, punches that would have been lethal to an ordinary man, Georges thought, still smiling, but not a boxer. Be a man, Georges, you haven't won this yet. Try to be a man for once in your life. A real man who can take the blows.

Georges waited for the next combination, sensed it coming with the relish of an old boxer. God, how he loved these moments when the whole world was sucked into a funnel and landed on the ropes; when there was only him and his opponent, when every eye was trained on them, anticipating, not the next punch, but some mythic, dazzling, immediate future. These moments when he could stare into the face of some guy who understood him; they were here for the same reasons, working together towards a perfect ending.

Georges blocked the first jab, a counterpunch that look entirely normal, but he opened out his glove just enough, closed his eyes, relaxed every muscle, hoping it would not be too painful, and allowed the hook to connect.

Toni Esperanza paled; as his fist connected he was the first to feel Georges' defencelessness, his lack of resistance, the savagery with which his head snapped back. The crowd roared. Seeing Crozat fall to his knees, his broken body crumpling on the canvas, the roars suddenly stopped.

Paolo and Marco climbed between the ropes, Esperanza's team rushed over too.

Toni leaned over them, asking what was going on. The referee gestured towards the crowd. The paramedics rushed in with a stretcher. Two minutes later, Crozat's unconscious body was carried out of the Fontenay sports centre and Paolo was in the back of the ambulance, refusing to let go of Georges' hand.

# 8

In the shadow to the east, the green arms of the Chélif valley are flung wide. The river has swelled and now fills the riverbed. The snow-capped mountain ridges catch the first rays of sun. Verini is coming back from sentry duty, his machine gun gripped in his frozen gloved hands. The barn is waking up. From the piles of blankets in the fifteen beds lined up in rows comes a fanfare of snoring and coughing, of groans as eyes are opened. Verini refills the stove that has gone out, filling the firebox with paper and tinder. He douses the wood in methylated spirits, strikes a match. With the first lick of flame, there is a loud explosion as the stove and the flue that snakes around the barn rumble like a grenade going off.

The whole unit wakes with a start, every soldier grabs his gun, soot rains over the beds. Colona comes running, his breath making white plumes of vapour, clutching his machine gun. Black from head to foot, Verini had been sent sprawling on his arse two metres from the stove.

Colona is still buckling the belt of his uniform.

"You can add cleaning out the flue to the list of duties, you fucking idiots. And now that you're on your feet, you can get this shithole cleaned up."

Rabelais Sector D.O.P. starts the new mid-winter day with a bad joke and a hollow laugh. Out in the cells, the explosion may well have brought a glimmer of hope. In each cage, three shivering men huddled in filthy blankets share the four square metres. Every morning, Ahmed brings soup and checks that they all survived the night.

The cellar is the only place in the D.O.P. where the cold is not a problem. The detachment is at maximum capacity, there is too much work for Rubio alone so most of the time he is joined in the cellar by Paul and Henri. Every day now new prisoners arrive, guard duty is round the clock. The pitiful condition of the inmates is unavoidable. Their screams have obliterated the notion of silence. There are no longer any manoeuvres outside the camp. The D.O.P. needs every man to carry out this task. Two days ago, Casta got up in the middle of the night clutching his machine gun and wailed for five solid minutes in time to the man being tortured.

No-one stopped him.

The tall Kabyle is called Rachid. Perret offered to let him stay at the D.O.P. after he was caught and interrogated in September. For the past four months he has been working with the other Algerian auxiliaries. The influence he has managed to gain over them in a few short weeks is obvious. He is twenty-seven, educated and speaks perfect French; his silence is that of a man who has opinions; he has no time for the wisdom of slaves, that flagrant self-abasement that merely invites greater contempt. Giving Rachid an order amounts to asking a favour and in his silence is the possibility that he might refuse. His presence has shifted the balance between the soldiers and those who have been turned. Nothing has changed, but positions are clearer now; under his influence, the Algerian auxiliaries have gone back to being what they always were: prisoners in a political war. Rachid has intimidated the farm boys in the commando, the would-be Rubios who copy his manner, his way of talking. Not knowing how to react, they ignore the Kabyle.

Verini is still surprised at what has happened. How has this man managed to do such things? Almost without opening his mouth? But perhaps he is attaching too much importance to Rachid.

After the trauma of the interrogations and the torture, after the three weeks he spent in a cell, until Rachid was finally moved to the Algerians' barn, he did not say a word for a whole month. He watched. Then he got his bearings. He took on those chores that suited him and the Algerians acquiesced without a murmur. Ahmed was the only one whose privileges he did not question. Rachid quickly realised that Ahmed was untouchable. He drew closer to Colona and, with Ahmed, took on every little task that concerned him. He identified the cliques. Within a month, he had assessed the typology of this microcosm. And, with an almost imperceptible shift in his manner, a few well-judged glances, he managed to align himself with the three wayward conscripts. Before he even said a word, they knew Rachid understood; more than that, he thought as they did. In December, when he finally broke his silence, his voice seemed like one they already knew.

To the rest of the detachment, to the large majority of those who held no position, those who allowed themselves to be swept along by the tide of events, Rachid is coolly neutral.

Whenever he encounters Rubio, he looks down and lowers his head without bowing his shoulders, without bending his back so that he is still staring at him.

Of the three "draft dodgers", he has chosen Verini. As the weeks have passed, his influence over Verini has grown too.

Verini fraternises, he wants to make peace with the Algerian. He gets along pretty well with Ahmed, they can even share a joke, but Rachid wants to know what he thinks, what he believes. Their friendship is a precious thing and Rachid keeps it alive. It is always the Kabyle who chooses the time, the moment. Despite the mistrust, the pull of this relationship is powerful.

Rachid is from Bougie, a Mediterranean port city. When the uprising began, he was studying literature in Algiers, then left to join the *maquis*. He says nothing about his membership of the F.L.N. "Did you kill any French?" Verini asked once. Rachid did not speak to him for two weeks. Time enough for Verini to understand that this was the sort of question Perret or Rubio had asked him in the cellar.

Rachid is the big brother fighting in the *résistance* Verini always wished he had, while he represents the new Gestapo in this occupying army.

Rachid claims to be an advocate of negotiated peace, but his attitude belies his claim. He does not negotiate. He is on a mission. Verini has not managed to find out anything about his family.

Since Verini began to get to know him, this combatant who is neither a "rebel farmer" nor a fanatic who cuts the throats of children, he feels safe in Algeria. The cut-throats are no longer only on the French side ever since Rachid, in his calm, measured voice, has begun to talk about Algeria and the ancestral history of Kabylia.

Verini steps out of the barn and shakes the soot from his clothes. Christophe has unlocked the auxiliaries' quarters. Rachid is striding across the barnyard, swaddled in three layers of patched-up military jackets. Verini shakes out his beret and smiles. Rachid transfixes him with a look colder than the wintry air.

After the screaming and the silence, with Rachid, the Algerian war entered Rabelais Sector D.O.P. for a second time.

Winter departs the D.O.P. as suddenly as it arrived. The Algerian auxiliaries work in the garden, the quality of the food improves, the cramped conditions of the barn give way to the great outdoors, men are no longer living on top of one another, tensions ease. Colona keeps an eye out for trouble, his detached sense of justice preserves the crumbling consensus between them. Verini, Casta and Chapel have each earned an extra month of military service. At noon, the cellar is one of the only places on the Farm where it is cool. Under the corrugated iron roofs, it is the heat that now torments the prisoners in their cells. With the sun's return, the damage caused by the months of tension and horror and the changes undergone by the conscripts and the military regime are evident. They have been at the D.O.P. for eight gruelling; months they have no illusions now. Christophe, who represents the line of least resistance, has sought out the easiest refuge. He strides across the barnyard with Paul and Henri – who represent the line of greatest indifference – to help out with the interrogations. A team of twenty-year-old amateur soldiers have been transformed into experienced torturers. The executions continue, the interrogations are never-ending, the D.O.P. will not disappear at the wave of a magic wand, they are all here for at least another year. Like the Mediterranean crossing, the winter here has aged them, hibernation has left their cheeks gaunt, etched new wrinkles and hardened their faces, which have lost the last remaining fullness of adolescence. The faded uniforms, adjusting to their bodies, are now a part of them.

Verini has just finished a night on sentry duty. After breakfast, he watches four Arabs hoeing the vegetable garden. Rachid is among them. Standing in the shade of an orange tree, machine gun slung over his shoulders, Verini chats with the man.

The Kabyle talks about socialism, asks him about France, about conditions in the factory where he worked, the treatment of Algerian workers, the position taken by the union. Verini collects together his memories, finds his father's words to describe Nanterre. Back at home, he thought of the war as an Algerian matter, metropolitan France had little to do with Africa. Since arriving at the D.O.P., he has come to believe that the French government has little influence over the decisions being taken here. Aside from radio contact with the C.C.I., the detachment, being geographically isolated and militarily autonomous, seems to him to be run according to internal rules independent of any chain of command. Rachid smiles and explains that it is France that decides what goes on here.

"The orders come from on high, Perret takes his orders from France and the government ministers know exactly what is going on. You're naive, Private Verini."

"I am not naive, all I'm saying is that they can't control what the soldiers choose to do here."

"That's right, the D.O.P. is a kibbutz."

"A what?"

The sun is high, Verini is sitting leaning against the foot of the tree, Rachid is clumsily turning over the soil; he is no farmer, his hands are delicate, but he does his bit.

The Frenchman looks out at the landscape. It is a beautiful country, he thinks. When the war is over, Rachids and Verinis will be able to live there in peace. He is twenty-one and has an Algerian friend; he has had no news from Christine for months, he no longer writes, he feels some part of him belongs here in Algeria. He is not part of this war, he feels excluded. He closes his eyes and daydreams. The sun is mild, the Arabs swing their hoes rhythmically, he dozes off, thinking about her, about Adila, about the real journey, the one from which there is no return to

Nanterre ever. They have talked about it, she wants him to stay when it is all over.

He is woken by the sound of footsteps and a sharp metallic click.

Rachid is standing over him, aiming the M.A.T.-49 at his belly.

He feels sweat run down his back, his vision is blurred, his hands start to tremble.

Rachid is not trembling.

"You see? If I wanted to kill you, I would have done it by now."

Verini studies the man's face, looking for a sign that this is a practical joke. He struggles from his hazy dream in search of reality, he gives a faint smile that instantly fades, faced with the calm determination of Rachid. The Kabyle lowers the machine gun and hands it back to him. Verini gets to his feet.

The Kabyle turns away and goes back to his work. The other Arabs are frozen with fear.

\*

Casta floors the accelerator, eating up the five kilometres that separate them from the village; the six-cylinder arrives at the bridge over the river Chélif, so swollen with meltwater its metal arches are submerged. At the checkpoint on the far side of the bridge, a squaddie operates the breech of a machine gun mounted on the back of a jeep. A sergeant checks their pass. They are in civvies and carrying weapons, on a twelve-hour furlough from the D.O.P. Under his jacket, Verini is wearing his automatic pistol and he has two hand grenades in his pockets. The sergeant allows them to pass; his surliness is not an act. The Black Berets' reputation is appalling.

Casta drives like a maniac to the church. The large square in front of the church is deserted and the wedding party has already arrived. He parks the Citroën Traction at the bottom of the steps.

Best to avoid unforeseen consequences.

Colona has appointed two men to act as bodyguards at Rubio's wedding. His reputation in Orléansville means there is heightened concern about the possibility of an incident. And so the "draft dodgers" from the D.O.P. find themselves acting as G-men to an executioner. Plainly dressed, they mingle with the wedding party as unobtrusively as they can. Rubio's broad hands dangle limply from his sleeves; he is ill at ease in his black suit and grey tie. Freshly showered and shaven, he greets them with no more respect than he has shown them at the Farm.

"If there's ructions, we fire into the crowd."

Rubio draws a Baby Browning from his pocket.

He goes back to his chubby, radiant fiancée and they enter the church. They have no desire to see Rubio kiss his bride. Their M.A.T.-49s by their sides, they hang around outside in the oppressive heat keeping an eye on passing cars and pedestrians. The idea of taking a bullet to save Rubio's arse in the middle of this ceremony that has taken them away from the gruesome world of the D.O.P. seems comical. The whole thing is a farce played out against a blazing white set with them in the starring roles.

The bells ring out, the church doors open and the fifty guests stream out to form a guard of honour. Casta goes back to the truck and starts the engine leaving Verini at the top of the steps, ducking to avoid the rice being thrown. The couple are as handsome as they can be; a photographer immortalises the happy day. The night before, the bridegroom killed an elderly *fellaga* during an interrogation; maybe he was nervous, it being the night before his wedding. His wife is smiling.

The couple climb into the Citroën Traction. Rubio is thrilled to be driving through the town in this car, flanked by a pair of bodyguards. His wife is somewhat less comfortable in a car bristling with guns, with strange silent men who constantly glance around nervously.

The wedding reception takes place at the home of the bride's parents. The local rosé wine is flowing freely. Rubio knocks back a dozen Pernods in the space of an hour. It is a typically French spread, with a *méchoui* and some couscous in addition. Ties are loosened, voices are raised. The party is enlivened by Rubio's raucous laugh, his bride has been tipsy since her first glass of champagne. Casta and Verini eat standing at the entrance to the courtyard where the reception has been set up. The heat and the wine go to their heads. From one corner, a gramophone player splutters accordion music. "To the happy couple!" "Long live French Algeria!" "Death to the *fellagas!*" Dessert. Madame cuts the fairytale wedding cake before it melts in the sun. There is joy and happiness, but the belching laughter and the crude remarks are underscored by mute anxiety.

The *pieds-noirs* are deserting the area. The richest have already left and now the shopkeepers and the labourers are packing up and heading back to France. Cowards, traitors, good riddance to bad rubbish. Algeria is French, Africa belongs to those who work there, doesn't it? Then why is it taking so long to set things to rights? It's all the fault of the socialists, obviously, of Mollet's* government: France refuses to give the army the means to wipe out the terrorists. Everyone here knows what the *bougnoules* are really like, they know how they should be dealt with. "Isn't that right, Rubio? Dear God, what's the matter with the Arabs in this country?" Rubio, in shirtsleeves, is boxing with the youngsters. "We treat them well, the Muslims here, and are they satisfied?" the old men complain. "Well, what can you expect of people like that? The F.L.N. are scum, putting ideas in the head of the real workers."

Have a drink, Papi, the war won't last. It can't last.

The Bouchards are leaving.

Don't you worry, we're not leaving. Here, have a drink.

The dancing starts. As the party gets drunker, the more the idea that someone might toss a grenade into this crowd fades. Casta has started drinking. The garter. The apotheosis. The dirty stories, the bitterness, the fears and the catharsis of the sacrificed virgin, red in her white dress. The parade of gifts: exhausted, the poor thing opens, unwraps, thanks, kisses. Rubio laughs as he offers his beloved a gift, a pretty little package wrapped in white tissue paper. She opens it. Collapses onto the ground. Panic. It's the heat, quick – get some water, give her some air. But it's not the heat.

On the table, amid the folds of tissue paper, lie the cock and balls of the Arab he killed last night at the D.O.P. This is Rubio's gift to his wife, a pledge of love, of security. The women protest, the men don't know where to put themselves, the children rush to see and get a clout for their pains. Rubio lurches and shouts to the assembled party: "Yeah, them fucking socialists, they've got no balls!"

Casta reaches down and grabs his M.A.T., he is trembling from head to foot. Verini propels him out of the courtyard. Rubio can go fuck himself, let someone chuck a bomb and blow him to hell. They head off to drink in the bars on the rue d'Isly and end up in the brothel where the squaddies are having a wild time.

June 1958

Since mid-May, what with the Algiers Putsch*, the upheavals in the capital, the fear of a rift between the army and the government, there has been much to argue about up at the Farm. Coty has just called on de Gaulle. A new constitution is being drawn up. At the D.O.P., the torture continues.

The strange bond between Rachid and Verini grows stronger. The Frenchman clings to it, it is his bulwark against the horror

146

just as Adila is an emotional buffer against loneliness. Machismo has become a necessary veneer to ward off aggression: act tough in order to survive. Oblivious to the fact that this toughness is no longer just an act. Verini is increasingly brutal with the other conscripts, who are more brutish now that they have been plunged into this war. Disquiet has given way to routine, effort to expectation. The screams, like the faces of the prisoners, are now merely part of the landscape. The newly-wed Rubio works even harder than usual and, since the wedding reception, has been studiously avoiding Verini and Casta.

Pascal still imagines living with Adila, when she is no longer a whore, when there is no longer a war in Algeria.

But the war rages on, and on June 12, the supply truck does not arrive at the Farm. Verini is guarding the prisoners, he did not make the supply run today. He sees Roger running across the courtyard, then re-emerging from the farmhouse with Perret, Paul and two *gendarmes*. They set off in the jeep and the Citroën Traction, picking up four soldiers along the way. Half an hour later, they are back. In the back of the jeep is a body covered by a tarpaulin.

The first Frenchman to die at the D.O.P., Henri drove over a mine and *fellagas* hiding among the rocks opened fire as he leapt from the flaming truck.

Some lads from the 18th Artillery Regiment at Paul-Robert have been despatched as backup to patrol the sector and hunt down the *fellagas*. Henri's best friend Paul is devastated. He asks Colona when he plans to launch an operation to catch the bastards. The body is carried into the farmhouse. There is anger and a thirst for revenge. Casta, Chapel and Verini do not emerge unscathed. Chance has struck. Today it was Henri. Tomorrow it will be someone else. They are startled by the pale features of the corpse. He looks like a boy. They thought they had aged.

Two days later, a ceremony is organised for the dead man. The flag is raised, Perret makes a speech, the nation sends its condolences. Henri's parents will never know what it was their son did in Algeria: in his letters home he said everything was fine, and yet he died there.

In the week that follows, most of the conscripts go down into the cellar to lay into the Arabs picked up during searches and patrols. Verini and his friends hold out, they refuse to participate in this butchery and no-one forces them. But their position is becoming untenable, their neutrality an act of treachery. In his own way, Colona attempts to calm the situation, authorising extra rations of alcohol. A quarter-litre of red, one of white, one of rosé and one of rum. There are rumours that the booze, which simply serves to inflame things, is being adulterated with bromide to keep the men calm. Paul and the others knock back white wine with breakfast.

One evening, Paul unleashes a tirade of abuse against Verini, calling him a Communist, a traitor, a coward. Verini grabs a bottle and smashes it on the edge of the mess table. Paul lunges for his machine gun and the other conscripts intervene. The insults come thick and fast; Verini senses that this time he was prepared to kill. Both men are confined to barracks for a week. Verini is sent to the camp at Orléansville. He spends a week working in the mess kitchens; it is the best thing that could have happened to him. The punishment is not particularly disagreeable, but he is not allowed to leave the base and he misses Adila.

To the men in the commando unit, their failure to avenge the death of Henri is yet another defeat, one that has a lasting effect on morale. No-one ever sees the *fellagas*, no-one can track them down and still they kill. The cellar is the only place where they can do something about it.

Rachid has become withdrawn and no longer says a word. Is it his influence that has made the other Arabs so silent? They move now like shadows, offering no target for the resentment that is eating away at the commando unit. They have gone from being inconspicuous to being evanescent. Henri's death is a reminder of the impossible nature of their living cheek by jowl. The screams, which they no longer heard from force of habit, had once again become the toxic glue that binds them.

The orange trees are flowering.

August 1958

Adila is washing herself at the bidet. Verini is lying on the bed, smoking a cigarette. The gloom is filled with the sounds and smells of the bar downstairs.

Adila is beautiful. The young man cannot see beyond this. Just as in Nanterre, he loves – or believes he loves, it hardly matters – a girl his family would not approve of. He will not go back to France. Adila has discussed things with her family, her mother, a brother and two younger sisters. The couple have been invited to spend the weekend in Oran. Adila no longer charges him and pays the French madam's cut out of her own pocket. It is a fantasy world, of Prince Charming and the hooker with a heart of gold finding love in a brothel. It is a pipe dream, but even if they realised it they would not want to wake up.

Adila has suggested that, when the war is over, Verini could take over her husband's taxi business. She still has the Simca Versailles she bought for him. Verini will take his place.

He imagines driving the Simca through the streets of Oran.

They take their time, make plans for the future. She gives him money: his salary is not enough to cover his trips to town once or twice a week. Supply runs, prisoner transfers to the C.T.T., furloughs, he comes to Orléansville as often as he can, volunteers for every trip in spite of the dangers.

He ambles through the streets while waiting to go back. In the *souk*, he buys some light clothing and a *chèche*. Civilians mingle with soldiers and Verini imagines these same streets some time from now when there are no uniforms, no armoured cars, no boarded-up shops.

Chapel and Ahmed are waiting for him back at the base, sitting in the shade of the truck.

"How she is, my French woman in the brothel?"

"She talks about you all the time, she says she misses you."

Chapel gets to his feet.

"We have to wait a while. There's a jeep coming with us. Apparently Pradel finally got his transfer. Some other policeman is replacing him so we have to wait for him and head back together."

They wait. Sometime in mid-afternoon, a jeep arrives. Rubio, wearing civvies, is sitting in the back seat, another soldier from the commando is behind the wheel and in the passenger seat is a young, serious-faced policeman in plain clothes. One look at him and it is obvious things are not about to change in the cellar.

"I'd like to see that cop's face tomorrow after he's seen Rubio at work," Chapel cackles as the truck follows the cloud of dust raised by the jeep.

Verini, who is at the wheel, allows the gap between the cars to widen. The thought of the jeep going over a landmine with Rubio in the back seat does not bother him.

The following morning, the policeman's face is unchanged; he has put on his uniform, carefully placing the stripes indicating his rank as *sergent-chef*. He is strutting around the courtyard accompanied by the interpreter.

The men begin to miss Pradel and those fleeting appearances in the courtyard to smoke a cigarette. Though they never said a word to him, there was something reassuring about his pale, sickly face. The new one is called Thorez; only the three

"Commies" smile at the fact that he shares his name with the leader of the French Communist Party*.

The new police officer upsets the delicate equilibrium of the Farm. He is aggressive to the Algerian auxiliaries and within days of his arrival the atmosphere in the unit deteriorates. Colona is drunk more and more often and Thorez's influence over the conscripts increases. The Algerians are mocked and bullied. Rachid, the primary target of Thorez's paranoia and racism, shuts himself away and Verini no longer talks to him. Ahmed is anxious, worried by the silence of the Arabs.

Thorez makes no secret of the fact that he believes the Algerian auxiliaries pass messages to the outside, that they are spies in the pay of the F.L.N., that even within the D.O.P. they are plotting. The three "Nos" make no attempt to dissuade the others, the atmosphere is so tense that fights are regularly breaking out.

Then, one day, Colona reappears. Having spent a whole night almost sober, he goes to see Perret to demand an explanation. Thorez no longer visits the barns, but, in exchange, he seems to have been made head of operations. He now decides on manoeuvres and treks through the *djebel* with the commandos. Under his command, raids and arrests are more numerous, more savage. And still there are the screams that punish any momentary lapse of concentration.

August is drawing to a close. Verini gloomily celebrates his first year in Algeria. He has asked for leave. In the other branches of the armed forces, soldiers are entitled to a one-week furlough during their military service. At the D.O.P., no-one is granted a week's leave. Besides, it is not as though Verini wants to go back to France. Perret gives him three days and he tells his mates he is planning to go to Oran with Adila. Casta decides to apply for a furlough too, hoping to pay for a whore and go along for the ride with Verini. Sylvain is starting to resemble Colona; alcohol has left its mark on the young man's face; his moods and his behaviour have become worrying. It is something Verini and Philippe talk about from time to time, but what right have they to stop him drinking himself blind on cheap rum? They keep an eye out for him, try to steer him clear of the problems alcoholism is bound to create sooner or later. But that night they drink a toast, grateful for what little they have.

Casta is nodding off. Philippe throws him a lifeline.

"I gonna hit the sack. You coming, Sylvain, or you gonna sleep there?"

Verini sits on his own, sipping a beer and gazing up at the stars. Ahmed creeps up to him and whispers.

"Can I talk to you?"

"Sure. What's up?"

"Please. Not talk so loud."

Ahmed keeps glancing behind him, towards the Algerians' barn.

"It is problem. I am not happy and I am afraid."

"What? What are you talking about?"

"This thing, it is happening in the Arab barn."

"What? What's happening in the barn?"

"Pascal, I no want nobody die. Here we can wait until the war it is over, this I think. We do not make war here, you understand? I no want nobody die, but I do not know what I must do. I do not know, you understand?"

"What the fuck is going on? Who's going to die?"

"I know Rachid, he is your friend, Pascal, but Rachid, he want to start the war here. This is true, I swear it, and I do not like to betray my brothers, but I want no war. I want no war."

"What the hell are you on about?"

"For days and days Rachid, he talk to all the Arabs, he watch

152

me because he know I friends with you the French. I try to say before, but I can not. I no want nobody die. You are my friend, Pascal, yes? You understand what I say?"

"No. No, I don't fucking understand. What does Rachid want to do?"

"He make the others afraid, he is the leader now. He turn them against you, now they want to attack at night, to cut everyone's throats, take all the guns and go to join the *maquis*. This is what he want to do, Rachid, and the others, they say yes. This they will do soon, this week they say. And I do not know what I must do because I know they want kill me too, kill me because I say no, you understand? They want to make war here, kill everyone."

Verini stares at the door of the barn, but he is not thinking about the others, about the soldiers, about the Algerian; he is remembering Rachid standing over him holding his machine gun. He understands. He's been testing their reactions, planning this attack for months now, that Kabyle bastard who has been conning him. Pretending to be a moderate, talking about a negotiated solution when all the time his Algerian friend would slit his throat without a second thought.

He sits and thinks as Ahmed rocks on his heels, hands pressed to his lips, murmuring words in Arabic. Then Verini gets to his feet, tosses away the beer can and grabs Ahmed by the arm.

"We're going to see Colona."

Colona emerges from a haze of sleep and alcohol. Standing next to Ahmed, who is still praying, Verini explains what he has just been told. The *caporal* orders him to discreetly wake the commando unit.

Verini opens the padlock on the door to the Algerians' barn.

Paul and Casta grab Rachid from his bed and drag him outside. Paul is spouting insults, Casta tries to remain civil. Verini spits in Rachid's face.

"You fucking bastard!"

With his machine-gun butt, he splits Rachid's skull and the man crumples. They drag him to the farmhouse and down into the cellar. They wake the *lieutenant* and Rubio.

For two hours, Verini sits in the barnyard listening to the screams from the basement where the Kabyle is strapped to the metal bedstead wired to the mains and doused with water. The screaming stops and still he does not move.

The following morning, broken, bleeding and barely conscious, Rachid is tossed into the boot of the Citroën. Leaving the detachment under the command of Colona and Thorez, Lieutenant Perret leaves the farm accompanied by two *gendarmes*.

At lunch, Verini asks where Rachid has been taken.

"He confessed everything last night. Rubio nearly fucking killed him. When we caught him up there at the mountain pass, it was a set-up. The old man was in on it. The F.L.N. leadership in Algiers needed to know what was going on here at the D.O.P., they sent Rachid here, the A.L.N. set it up. All Rachid had to do was let himself be caught."

Colona slips a hand under his beret and scratches his bald pate.

"He's got balls, the *bougnoule*. And a dirty fucking clever trick. He gets to pick up serious intelligence, then all he has to do is escape or organise an attack here. He didn't say whether there were any moles in the detachment feeding information to the local *katibas*. Thorez is convinced there must be, but Rachid didn't give up any names."

"Where are they taking him?"

"He's a big fish, son. They'll take him to Algiers. The Villa des Roses or Villa Sésini*."

Verini regrets everything, he regrets having believed Rachid, having been his friend, he regrets having hit him and not having tried to say anything to him before the *gendarmes* dumped him in the boot of the car.

Colona offers him a shot of whisky.

"I feel it too, lad. That's human nature, that's war for you. Don't think too much about it, just remember the lesson. It's the same for that girlfriend of yours in the city, don't kid yourself."

For days, Verini says nothing, he wonders whether Rachid would have allowed someone to kill him, would have ordered it or done it himself. Of all the answers that have eluded him in the year he has been here, this is the most painful. He begins to drink heavily and finds himself, like so many others, trapped in the skin of a man others steer clear of, a man who is falling apart, a man filled with violence and rage.

January 1959

Winter has returned. Since Rachid's attempted coup, the Arabs in the barn are no longer the same. Verini no longer makes any attempt to remember their names or even their faces. Ahmed – despite, or perhaps because of his betrayal – has become suspect; he carries out his duties in silence, he no longer stays outside in the evenings. He is a danger to everyone. A traitor to his people's cause, he receives death threats from his brothers in whose eyes he can redeem himself only by another betrayal, this time of the French. Conscious of his position, he has withdrawn from life at the Farm and become one more invisible auxiliary. Even Verini obscurely resents him.

In December Verini and Sylvain visited Oran with Adila and another prostitute from the brothel.

Their weekend lasted the space of a single afternoon. Adila's father had died in a mining accident in 1953. Her mother was left to

155

look after her two younger sisters and a brother Verini's age who still lives at home. In Oran, any illusions they had were shattered. Adila's family were ashamed of her profession and her showing up there with another prostitute and two soldiers caused a scandal. There was a heated argument in Arabic, and Kacem, the brother, spat in the couscous his mother had prepared for the guests. Since Verini and Sylvain felt it would be inappropriate to say anything, the four of them caught a taxi back to Orléansville.

Reluctant to admit defeat, they had dinner at a restaurant. A bunch of soldiers made jokes about the girls, the restaurant owner gave them dirty looks. Sylvain was spoiling for a fight. They ended up spending the night in the brothel.

The following morning, Verini tries to convince himself that the plans they had made together were still realistic. He does not want to give up his dream of being with Adila. Especially as Sylvain will be demobbed from military service in two months. And Verini has long since done the calculations: Philippe will go home in April, leaving him four and a half months – including penalty days – to serve out at the commando unit. Alone.

With his demobilisation approaching, Casta is increasingly terrified of getting shot. In spite of black ice, he drives as fast as ever on the supply runs and more often than not he is drunk. Ahmed no longer wants to ride with him.

Rubio has not set foot outside the farm since graffiti was daubed on the wall of his house announcing his execution. In the meantime, his wife has left to stay with an aunt in Oran.

On January 26, suffering from chilblains and shivering from the cold, Thorez and six men return from a three-day operation in the *djebel* with their spoils. Having found a hideout in one of the caves, they set up an ambush, killed two *fellagas* and brought back two prisoners and about a hundred standard-issue blue Navy sweaters with epaulettes. But most importantly, they found a trunk containing more than a million and a half francs in cash. Four years' pay to a French worker. A fortune in Algeria.

During the night, Rubio forces the two prisoners to talk. Smugglers are soon to arrive at the cave and collect the money and the strange clothes.

An operation is quickly organised. Perret asks the 18th Artillery Regiment at Paul-Robert to send a second commando into the cave. To ensure that the money will not be left at the D.O.P. while half its men are in the mountains, the trunk must be despatched to 9th Infantry Division in Orléansville.

Casta and Verini, being the best drivers in the unit, are designated: Philippe Chapel volunteers to go with them. Colona agrees. All three are in civvies, Verini is at the wheel, the Citroën Traction leaves the D.O.P. on the morning of January 27. The other conscripts wave them off, laughing and suggesting they take a holiday in the sun with the million stashed in the boot. The peaks are capped with snow, the road iced over, all three are armed to the teeth, their black berets traded for woollen caps. The windscreen of the Traction is fogged with their breath. Pascal rolls down his window, glances outside, the bitter wind stings his eyes.

They are nervous. Has news of the raid on the cave reached the local *katibas*? The D.O.P. is under constant surveillance, the A.L.N. has never launched an attack to free the prisoners, but the Nationalists would do anything to recover their money. Like gangsters in their black sedan, clutching their machine guns, they laugh and joke. Verini drives as fast as he sensibly can, accelerating into the bend before the gorge.

Sylvain asks what he would do with a million and a half.

"Five hundred thou," Chapel pipes up from the back. "Equal shares."

Verini smiles, thinking of Adila, of where they could go with such a sum. Suddenly Philippe shouts:

"Look out!"

The Citroën, fast but heavy, goes into a skid.

Three kilometres away at the Farm, the first gunshots are heard.

"Where the fuck did that come from?"

"Sounds pretty far away."

"No, it's not that far. Shut up and listen!"

A burst of machine-gun fire echoes around the valley and fades. There is another burst, a few isolated shots, then the sound of an exploding grenade makes it clear where the noise is coming from.

"The gorge! It's coming from the fucking gully! It's them!"

"Caporal! The Commies have been ambushed!"

Two more grenades explode, there is a constant chatter of machine guns.

The jeep and the G.M.C. truck race down the dirt track with Thorez, Colona and Perret, and most of the commando unit, on board. They try to hear over the roar of the engines and the clank of the bodywork. A last gunshot.

"Fuck, that's it, they've stopped firing . . . I can't hear anything."

It takes them ten minutes to arrive on the scene.

The bonnet of the Citroën is open, the front of the car smashed into the rock face. The windscreen and the left-hand rear window are shattered, there are bullet holes in the bodywork. There is no-one to be seen. Colona leaps down from the jeep as it screeches to a halt.

"There they are! There they are, sir!"

Thirty metres from the mangled wreck of the Citroën, crouched on all fours and covered in mud, Chapel crawls out of the gorge and struggles to his feet. He waves his still-smoking machine gun above his head.

"Man down, we've got a man down!"

He plunges back into the ditch. By the time their comrades arrive, Philippe and Verini are dragging Casta across the gravel. The left sleeve of his uniform is ripped and blood seeps into the frozen ground.

Chapel and Verini are pale, their foreheads gashed and streaming blood. Casta is loaded onto the flatbed of the truck. His face green, pouring with sweat, he vomits, spits and whimpers over and over that he doesn't want to die. Verini is shaking like a leaf. Chapel clutches his weapon, shrieking hysterically.

"They attacked from both sides! They took the money, sir! They took the money!"

Thorez is ashen.

"We have to go after them, sir, we have to catch them! Verini, did you manage to hit them? Are any of them injured?"

Dazed, Verini cannot bring himself to speak.

Perret studies the overhanging rocks ten metres above their heads. If the *fellagas* were still there, they could wipe out the whole commando unit with three grenades.

"We'll deal with that later. Colona, round up the men, it's not safe to stay here. Get into the vehicles! Get in, for God's sake! Thorez, get back in the jeep. That's an order!"

They tend to Casta's wounds at the Farm before evacuating him by helicopter to Orléansville.

In the late afternoon, still badly shaken from their experience, Chapel and Verini report to the *lieutenant*.

"I was driving, sir, Chapel was riding shotgun and Casta was in the back. We were driving as fast as possible, but with the patches of black ice we couldn't go too fast. Philippe was the first to see them."

"Chapel?"

"I spotted a *fellaga* next to the gully, sir. I shouted and a split-second later there was a shot. The car went into a skid."

"Verini?"

"I don't know what happened. I think maybe the front tyre blew, sir, but I can't be sure. It's possible I panicked and swerved. I steered towards the rocks and then they started firing."

"How many were there?"

"I don't know, sir. I saw three, maybe four, high up on the rocks. Two or three in the ravine. Since I drove on a little way after the first shot, they were about twenty metres behind us. When the car hit the rock face, we fired from the windows, but we didn't really know where they were. Casta was the first out, he headed straight for the ravine and that's when he was hit."

"Chapel, how many did you see?"

"The same, sir. Three in the gully, four, maybe five among the rocks."

"Armaments?"

"Excuse me, sir?"

"What weapons did they have?"

Chapel glances at Verini, who shrugs.

"I'm not sure, sir, we didn't really see. They had rifles, and there were bursts of machine-gun fire."

"Grenades?"

Verini stands to attention.

"No, sir. We launched the grenades. I threw two and Chapel threw one. With the first one, I tried to aim for the rocks directly overhead, but it exploded over the road. The other two, we threw to cover ourselves, we weren't really aiming. They were firing from above and from the road off to our left. We fired blindly and we climbed down into the ravine, sir."

"Do you think you managed to kill or injure any of them?"

Again, the soldiers exchange a glance. Verini bows his head.

"They had the territorial advantage, sir, all we could do was retaliate, and mostly we were firing into the air. I doubt we managed to hit anyone, sir."

Perret scowls and lights a cigarette. The most impressive capture the commando unit has made in months and all they have left is a stock of Navy jumpers. The two squaddies stand to attention in front of his desk.

"I want you to write up a report and give it to Caporal-chef Colona. Dismissed!"

"Sir?"

"Verini?"

"How's Casta doing?"

"The surgeon from the 9th Infantry says he's fine. The bullet fractured the humerus and sheared through the triceps as it exited. There's no serious damage, but he won't be coming back here."

"Permission to visit him, sir?"

"You really want to make that drive again so soon?"

"We could do the supply run, sir, the day after tomorrow."

Perret looks down at his empty desk.

"As you wish. Talk to Colona."

Perret has not mentioned the money, but his silence is rebuke enough. Should they have done more, should they have risked their lives to save a fistful of money in a war that costs hundreds of millions every day?

"Fuck him," Verini says as they walk past the cells beneath whose corrugated iron roofs, decked with wet snow, some fifteen Arabs are freezing to death.

That night they tell the same story, and the following morning they write up the report together, then wait for permission to visit Casta at the infirmary in Orléansville. The Corsican will get to go home early.

July 1959

One month to go, in the same summer heat he suffered when he first arrived. Pascal watches sweat trickle the length of his arm to his elbow as the Arabs pick oranges. The beads of sweat drop from his tanned skin and fall, small black circles that evaporate on the dusty steel of his semi-automatic. He is thinking about Rachid.

Since April, he has been on his own. Casta kept in touch at first when he got back to France. Demobbed after three weeks convalescing in a military hospital in France, he went back to Corsica. Those few letters he sent to Verini and Philippe were difficult. Difficult to write, probably, and certainly to read. Because all three of them knew. There was no point hoping that "everything's fine there", to say that "everything's fine here". Yet still Verini and Chapel pretended, because they wanted to believe that, when their turn came, France would be fun, that Algeria would be forgotten.

Then, in May, only Verini remained behind to receive letters from his friends. And now it was an ordeal to read about Philippe in Paris "gradually going back to work" at his father's restaurant. About Sylvain going back to work at the garage. Gradually. The word terrified Verini. As though going home would be an interminable period of convalescence. Into his last letter, received in June, Philippe had slipped a thousand-franc note: "Buy a round and raise three glasses to us." Verini saved the banknote and wrote back: "We'll meet up and have a drink together when I get back." There have been no letters since. It's just as well. Now he has to get by on his own. In June he also got a letter from his uncle. It had been months since he had had news from his family. Months since he had written to them. His father still hasn't written. Once or twice maybe he scribbled a signature at the bottom of a letter from his mother, but Pascal doesn't remember. Christine, too, only wrote a few times. Is it possible he received more letters than he remembers? Is it just that he never replied, that he threw them away and forgot he read them?

Colona is his only support. But Colona is not his friend.

His last refuge is Adila. The taxi company, the end of the war, but now they only talk reluctantly about such things; they no longer believe.

Though summer here is easier to bear than winter, the long days drag and intensify the sense of time running in a loop. The fragrant orange grove, the sweeping scenery: Verini no longer smells or sees these things. In addition to the terror that he might be killed in the few weeks he has left, there are the daily fears he has to contend with. The sentry duties, the supply runs, the prisoner transfers, keeping an eye on Paul who is desperate to find the slightest excuse to provoke a fight.

Verini is in the brothel. He is waiting at the bar until Adila is free. After he sees her, he'll spend the night at the Hôtel du Grand Chélif where soldiers get a special rate. A night alone in a clean room, this is the only way he has found to relax since his friends left. Tonight, he's not even really interested in the sex, already he can picture himself lying on the bed in the hotel room. From the bar, he studies the room. The soldiers who have been here for months, the ones he recognises, and those who have just arrived and have not yet learned to hide their fears. Verini decides to leave, to forget about going upstairs and head over to the hotel. He does not want to stay; he drains his glass. He feels a shoulder

163

press against his. Paul, his fair complexion flushed with drink. Next to him, Rubio. The interpreter's eyes, two black marbles set deep in hollow sockets, are streaked with bloodshot veins. He reeks of alcohol. Verini steps aside and asks for his bill. Busy at the far end of the bar, the madam cannot hear. Verini does not want to shout any louder. Paul cradles a glass of Pernod between mottled hands swollen with the booze and the heat. Slumped over the bar, the farm boy from Touraine who became a butcher in Algeria is staring into the cloudy liquid. The two butchers of the D.O.P., brimming with hatred, far from the chain of command and the rules of the detachment. This is the first time Verini has seen Rubio at the brothel. His wife is in Oran. He has not set foot outside the Farm, outside the cellar, for weeks.

Paul is carrying a gun. Rubio, who is taller than him, is standing ramrod straight and his head, which towers over the farm boy, seems to be the seat of Paul's thoughts. In his pocket is the Baby Browning he always keeps with him. Verini came in civvies and is unarmed.

He leans over the bar and calls again to the madam.

"You not going to have a drink with us, Verini?"

Paul does not give Verini time to answer.

"You come to see that *bougnoule* bitch of yours? Don't stay too long, I like fucking that whore of yours myself."

No-one would intervene, not the Arab bouncers or the pimps upstairs. Rubio has turned towards the tables, glass in hand, leaning against the bar. Everyone knows who he is. No-one here would move a muscle.

Verini raises his hand and signals to the manageress.

"Stay here with us, Verini, have a drink."

Paul has grabbed his arm.

"Get your hands off me."

164

Rubio stares straight ahead, stupefied, his eyes blazing. Paul releases his grip.

"What's her first name, that whore of yours?"

Paul now rolls his *rs* with the same hoarse drawl as Rubio the *pied-noir*.

The manageress comes over.

"What can I do for you, handsome?"

"Give handsome here a Pernod," Paul says.

"Nothing. Just the bill."

"He'll have a drink with his mates, he'll raise a glass to Henri. Isn't that right, Verini? You'll drink to Henri."

"How much do I owe you?"

The manageress hesitates. Rubio doesn't seem to hear them. The madam glances from him to Paul and then Verini.

"It's on the house. In honour of your friend Henri. Is he being demobbed?"

Paul is bent over his glass.

"He's dead. We're going to raise a glass to Henri. With Verini here."

"I don't want anything. Just the bill."

"You buy this round, you old trout."

Rubio scans the room, his eyes moving from face to face, and every eye he catches suddenly looks away. Paul has started to quiver. The manageress sets three glasses on the bar and pours the shots. No-one touches them. Paul is muttering loudly between clenched teeth, his forehead touching the rim of his glass.

"I fucking wish you were the one who copped it, Verini, down in the ravine with Casta and Chapel, your little queer buddies."

Rubio does not move.

"I'm going to take your whore from you, Verini."

The conversations around them have trailed off. Verini picks up his glass, his hand is shaking. He brings it to his lips, then stops and sets it down without drinking. The madam is signalling towards the door. Behind him he can hear chairs scraping.

"I'm gonna fuck that *bougnoule* bitch of yours, Verini."

His head now resting on the bar, Paul looks as though he is praying.

Verini turns towards the door. He takes one step, then another, walks past Rubio. The interpreter's voice is slurred.

"Don't turn back, Verini."

Rubio says the words without looking down at him.

Verini keeps walking. He can no longer hear what Paul is saying to his glass. Conversations start up again. Verini pauses in the doorway. He turns back. Rubio is still staring straight ahead, still holding a half-full glass. Next to him, bent over the bar, engrossed in his tirade of abuse, Paul continues to rant.

Verini looks at the stairs. A couple of johns are just coming down the steps. From behind the bar, the madam shoots him a look that says get the fuck out. Verini takes a step, then another, he walks past Rubio again, not bothering to look at Paul's stooped back, he puts a hand on the banister and goes upstairs.

By the time he reaches the door, his back is slick with sweat. He knocks. Adila calls out that she is not ready.

"It's Pascal."

She opens the door, she is washing herself in between clients, wearing a cotton *djellaba* which is wet under the arms, across her breasts, between her thighs. Her brown skin marbled by the ridges of the damp fabric makes him want to throw up.

"What's the matter? You're sweating. Come in, I'm nearly finished."

Verini does not let her touch him, does not respond to her questions. He does not get undressed but spends half an hour

166

lying on the bed chain-smoking cigarettes. Adila talks about him being demobbed in August, tells him she has had the Versailles taken to the garage for a mechanic to look it over. Verini says nothing. There is a knock at the door, three short raps to indicate his time is up. Adila could let him stay a little longer, but Verini gets up, says goodbye and goes out into the corridor. He passes the doors to the other bedrooms, goes down the stairs and stops at the bar.

"How much do I owe you?"

The manageress gives him the bill.

"Listen, handsome, if you want to get that pretty face smashed in I don't give a damn, but your carry-on is going to cause trouble for Adila. I don't want to see your face in here again."

Verini scans the room, Paul and Rubio are no longer there.

"What about Rubio, is he barred too?"

The manageress says nothing and deals with the bill.

Verini leaves without saying goodnight.

The streets are empty, cats hiss and dogs raise their hackles as he passes, stubbornly defending some bone they've recovered from the gutter. The streets leading from the brothel to the centre of town are dirty and smell of piss and shit, of spices and overflowing dustbins. As he comes to the rue d'Isly, he passes three soldiers patrolling in a jeep. The young recruit behind the wheel waves to him. Verini walks along the street past graffiti scrawls, a clumsily boarded shop-window with the words "For Sale" daubed on the planks.

He can see the hotel, the light of the reception desk, he can hear the muffled clatter of pebbles stirred up by the river Chélif, and above it, the murmuring water. The nightwatchman gets him to sign the register, name, rank, regimental number, then gives him the room key. It is a modern hotel, the cleanest in town, and usually the most expensive. Since the war it has been standing empty so the owner, for more modest prices, has changed it so soldiers can use it as sleeping quarters. The sheets are changed every other day. Verini gets undressed, stands by the window smoking a cigarette and listens to the river. A man is staggering along the pavement towards the hotel. Another soldier planning to spend the night here. The street is deserted.

The sheets have clearly been used, but Verini manages to get to sleep despite the smell of the last soldier to use the room, the reek of dust and sweat and a subtle whiff of a bad night's sleep.

August 1959

Verini is leaning in the shade of one of the cell walls. Through the row of breeze blocks at eye level, he can see into the cell. An Algerian is sitting on the ground, back to the wall, knees drawn up to his chest. Another is lying on the straw mattress, the hood of his *djellaba* pulled over his face. He does not bother to shoo the flies that land at the corners of his eyes to drink. His mouth is open and flies are lapping at the white salt from the spittle that has dried on his lips. The corrugated iron roof creaks and buckles in the heat, the silence is broken only by the drone of flies circling amid the stench of blood and shit.

He unhooks the water canteen from his belt, slips it through the breeze blocks and shakes it. The man sitting by the wall hesitates, he swallows with difficulty, his throat making a dry sound like a belch. He gets to his feet with little difficulty, despite his gauntness, despite the exhaustion and the beating he took last night. Standing in the cell, he looks at the soldier; he does not look into his eyes, but stares at a point somewhere in the middle of Verini's face.

"Go on, take it. Drink."

The Arab does not move. As though the flask might be a bomb, might be salt to slake his thirst, or some electrified contraption.

Verini opens the canteen, takes a long swig, swallows and holds it out again. He shakes it and a few drops of water spill out, falling on the dirt floor with a soft plop. The prisoner watches the falling drops, looks up, holds out his hand, still staring at a point just below the soldier's green eyes. He is waiting for the moment when they crinkle with laughter and the hand jerks away.

"Go on, take it!"

With his index finger, the Arab grazes the canvas that covers the canteen. It is still there. It has not been snatched away. The soldier is not laughing. The Arab's lips, split from the blows he has suffered, chapped from the heat, are stuck together. How old is he? Fifty? Less? He swallows and again his throat make a hollow sound, he opens his hand and takes the flask, draws it towards him, his eyes never leaving Verini.

"I'm not going to kill you, for fuck's sake! Go on, drink!"

The Algerian cannot believe it. To be offered water in the Rabelais Sector of the D.O.P. should mean that he is about to die, or will die soon. He drinks and water streams down his chin, dissolving a black stain that mingles with the water drops and turns blood red. He drinks little, looks again at the soldier, wipes his chin, drawing a thin trickle of blood through his stubble and across his cheek.

"Your friend, give him some water."

Verini gestures to the man lying on the straw mattress.

The Arab who is standing takes another gulp, runs his tongue over lips that have been softened by the water.

"He is not my friend."

"So what? Give him something to drink."

"He is my enemy, he killed my herd."

"I don't give a shit, now let him have a drink."

"In the name of Allah, I would give water to my enemy. But he is dead, soldier. He died while you were watching."

*

A night on guard duty. Over time, Pascal's perch on the roof has become as dangerous as standing sentry by the wall. But he is reluctant to change his habits, he clings to them like *grigris*. Three weeks until he leaves for Algiers. Colona has told him. There is talk of relocating the D.O.P., abandoning the Farm. Verini will not serve out his days confined to barracks here. This is a comfort and a worry. Where will he be sent to serve out his five weeks' punishment? Verini drums his fingers nervously on the butt of his machine gun. It is a clear night, the moon half full, there are stars above the Farm, meteorites trace secret lines across the milky sky. In the cellar, in pidgin French, a man screams that he does not know anything. Verini stretches, takes a date from his pocket which he chews, sucks, biting on the pit, focusing on the noise it makes between his teeth. A clatter of pebbles makes him look down. The trees cast long shadows. He sees a pair of feet in dusty leather sandals half hidden by a tree trunk. He does not move, stops his chewing noise and aims his machine gun at the body he cannot quite make out a few metres away. Another scream from the cellar. A foot shuffles on the stones, steps into the moonlight, hesitates and stops. A hand on the tree trunk, its skin the same colour as the bark of the orange tree. The chirrup of cicadas grows louder. Verini listens, trying to work out how many there are. The insects are drowned out by the sound of Rubio's voice bellowing in Arabic coming from the bricked-up basement window. There is a loud scream, the result of a sudden electrical jolt. At length there is silence. Verini concentrates intently on the shadows, on the night sounds. He is sweating. He thinks he hears a whisper of voices next to the tree. Can he hear sobbing? The figure, bathed almost entirely in moonlight, is leaning towards the farmhouse wall. He can see the outline of a face turned towards the basement window. He hears Arabic words interrupted now and then by racking sobs. Whoever is down there is listening to what Verini is trying his best not to hear. A desperate howl comes from the torture room, pleading for mercy. From his screams and the length of time the man has been in the cellar, Verini knows that either the man has confessed everything he knows, or he knows nothing. Rubio and Paul go on torturing him. Perret is no longer there and no-one now takes notes or listens to what he has to say. He shrieks, the sound muffled as his teeth clench under the force of the electric shock. The figure below steps out of the shadows, stumbles over the stones and cannot manage to suppress a cry: "*Baba!*"

Verini gives a start, the roof tiles rattle. The weeping teenage boy looks up, sees the soldier on the roof of the shack and dashes off through the orange grove. Verini listens to the boy flee and, trembling, aims his gun through the leaves, unable to do anything.

*

Paul climbs into the back of the jeep, his head lolling on his chest. Colona is in the passenger seat, there is a new recruit behind the wheel.

Over dinner, Martin, the radio operator who hangs out in the cellar, gives them the low-down: Paul flipped out. The interrogation had only just started and the guy was saying he didn't know anything, same as always, so they lit him up, a few low-voltage shocks. The guy spits on the ground, starts swearing at them and shouting something in Arabic. Paul takes out his M.A.S.-36, aims it at the head of the *bougnoule*. Just to frighten him, scare him shitless, the usual routine. Then Paul puts a bullet through the guy's

171

head, just like that, in cold blood, before he has a chance to say anything. No shit, Rubio and Perret got blood and brains all over their boots.

Paul is transferred to another commando unit in the 22nd Infantry Regiment at Ténès. If Perret hadn't been there, Rubio would probably have hushed up the murder. How often has that happened before now? This is what Verini in wondering, though he is not sorry to see Paul go.

Rubio was on the job, he didn't come up to say goodbye to his disciple. Paul's departure elicited a few half-hearted waves, but the farm boy did not wave back.

When he goes home to his farm in the arse-end of nowhere, who will Paul be able to tell about the two years he spent here? The power over life and death he wielded at the D.O.P. This virus that will eat away at him to the end of his days. Verini fervently hopes that on some sweltering summer morning that reminds him of the *djebel*, Paul will pick up his rifle, and take a long hard look at himself in a barn. Or maybe in a cellar. But then again, maybe one day, while knocking a pig unconscious, he will feel an uncontrollable urge to swing the hammer again, and again, and again, and he will listen as the animal howls, remember other howls of pain and be unable to understand the difference.

Verini understands now what it is about Rubio that scares him. If there is a possibility that Paul will one day blow his brains out, with the same puzzled look in his eyes he must have had when he executed the Arab, Rubio will never suffer any qualms, any regrets, will never question his actions. A line that Paul probably crossed when he fired in cold blood, when he squeezed the trigger and wondered what it might feel like to put a bullet through his own skull.

Verini completes his two-year service without ever having

been down to the cellar. He tells himself this over and over, it is his only defence against the terrible sense of doom that descends on him now he is close to leaving the D.O.P.

While he has even one minute left to spend here on Algerian soil, he cannot relax. It takes less than a minute to die.

*

Colona has opened a bottle of whisky, Ahmed is basting the lamb on the spit over the coals. Verini is afraid that the smell of the *méchoui*, a clear sign of celebration, will attract A.L.N. bomb makers, that the dirt track he will take for the last time tomorrow will be pitted with mines.

Colona pours him another shot.

"It'll be fine, lad, a month from now you'll have forgotten all this. You've done your time, it's over."

But nothing in the old soldier's blotchy face suggests forgetfulness.

A new conscript arrived two weeks ago; he takes photographs. He is pale, cannot sleep, has trouble with the heat and constantly clings to his camera. Click! He photographs Ahmed tending to the *méchoui*; he is not smiling. He frames a shot of Colona and Verini clinking glasses; they too look tense.

"Thanks."

Colona pats him on the back.

"What are you talking about? Thank you, son, for leaving here in one piece."

"Me, Casta and Chapel, we owe you. If we'd had a different senior officer, we might have been forced to do things we didn't want to do. That's down to you, that's all I wanted to say."

"You got yourselves through this shit by yourselves. Just like you did the ambush in the ravine. You're shrewd bastards."

Colona winks at him and downs another shot. Thinking about the ravine and about leaving tomorrow brings Verini out in a cold sweat; he tries to smile.

"Cheers! I'll keep in touch."

This time Colona chuckles, stares deep into Verini's eyes and seems to find something there that satisfies him.

"You're a good lad. For a Communist."

Verini laughs too, he is surprised by the sound of his laughter. Further off, Ahmed has been listening and Verini knows he must go over and talk to the old Algerian to spare himself the bitterest regret. He walks over, but he cannot find the words. He is leaving; Ahmed will die here.

The old Arab serves a portion of *méchoui* to Colona, who salutes and goes off to eat in the privacy of his hut. The rest is divided up between the soldiers. They tease Verini, talk about the girls he'll meet in Paris, about the new Citroën DS 9 none of them have seen yet, about all the things they miss that he will have in abundance. He doesn't mention the five weeks' extra time he has to serve. He thinks about this, it is what separates him from the others: after two years, it is the only difference between him and them. But tonight, they drink his health, they make the most of his good fortune, of his nervous, anxious joy. Tonight even Roger, the last of the pack that tagged along after Rubio, is like a kid at a leaving party. It is impossible to see the combination of youth and horror in his face, he looks just like the others. The new recruit takes more and more photographs; he looks healthier in the glow of the firelight; he is probably thinking that things are not so bad.

The Algerian auxiliaries have been locked up for the night, the house is calm, silent. Verini looks around for Ahmed but cannot see him. He downs his rations of red wine, white wine, rum, and opens a can of beer. Heads grow heavy, voices trail off, silence falls over the group and those on guard duty get ready.

Verini gets to his feet and goes to piss.

Rubio is leaning against the courtyard wall a few metres from the fire, the flickering flames dance across his face.

"So that it, then, you're on your way home?"

Verini does not respond, he walks past, unzips his fly and turns towards the wall.

"Though you've still got your five weeks. You obviously didn't understand last time, Verini. Fuck off and don't come back."

Verini goes back to the fire and sits for a moment on his own after the others have left, then he goes to bed. Some few minutes later, the screams begin. This is Rubio's goodbye.

Colona shakes his hand.

"I had a quiet word with the *lieutenant* and he'll see what he can do, they might let you off the extra time in Algiers, or cut it short. They did it for Chapel."

"I don't know how to thank you, *chef*."

"Just don't step on a mine today."

Verini wheels round, taking in the yard used by the soldiers, the one next to the farmhouse, the prisoners' cells, Rubio smoking a cigarette by the whitewashed wall.

"You're the only person I'm going to miss, *chef*. And the only person I felt like killing in this country is over there."

"Don't worry, he's gutted to see you going home."

"I somehow don't think he'll miss me."

"Neither do I. But when this shit's over and we head home with our tails between our legs, Rubio's life won't be worth a rabbit fart. The army won't take him, he's a loose cannon. He asked Perret to put in a good word so he could get a job in France with the police or the C.R.S. As far as Rubio's concerned, Algeria is finished. He'll be thrown out of his own country, if he doesn't die first."

"I hope he does."

"Don't think about it anymore, Verini, you've got a train to catch."

"You seen Ahmed?"

"I haven't had my coffee yet this morning."

"Tell him I said goodbye."

The *caporal* looks up past the farmhouse towards the summit of *djebel* Tazamout.

"I have to say, son, I'll be surprised if I get to talk to him any-time soon."

The jeep starts up, Colona is laughing fit to burst.

"Don't get caught up in an ambush today, Verini!"

Verini turns back.

He watches the Farm grow more and more distant. For the last time. He can hardly believe it. Leaving that place alive, he feels indestructible, then, as the road flashes past, he feels ashamed.

At the station the train is already waiting. He tosses his knap-sack into a cattle truck that stinks of manure. His machine gun and his M.A.S. were handed in to the 9th Infantry who issued him with an ancient Galand revolver for the duration of the journey, the same model he used back in Frileuse.

In Algiers, at the headquarters of the C.C.I., an officer at recep-tion checks his papers, runs a finger down the list of names and directs him to an office. A wave of heat and dizziness makes him stop in the doorway. He takes a deep breath, tugs at the sleeves of his uniform and knocks.

He is ushered in without a word by a *capitaine*, his chest bedecked with medals, who takes his papers and picks up a file. Verini stands to attention.

"And what do you plan to do when you're demobilised, Verini?"

He does not reply; the officer repeats the question. Verini hesi-tates, feeling his throat tighten.

"Set up as a taxi driver in Orléansville, sir."

The officer looks up from the file.

"I'm sorry?"

Verini looks past the man's head, through the window, to the hills of the white city where the war does not exist.

"Are you pulling my leg? Have you any idea what will happen if you set foot in Orléansville with no gun and no uniform?"

He blinks.

"No, sir. What will happen to me?"

"What do you think will happen? Within twenty-four hours you'll be found with rocks in your belly."

"Why, sir?"

The officer hesitates a moment, his eyes flash with anger.

"Because you fought against the rebels, because you're known there."

"There's a lot of French people living in Orléansville, sir, lots of people who are opposed to the F.L.N., and they haven't been killed. Why should it happen to me? I'm just an ordinary Frenchman."

The officer looks at him as he stands to attention, trembling slightly, staring just above his head.

"Look at me."

Verini loses something of his self-assurance and looks down.

"What exactly are you trying to get me to say, *soldat*?"

Sweat leaking from every pore, his throat clotted with words, with insults, Verini mutters:

"I just don't see why I can't go back there, sir."

The uniform is suffocating. He has the same feeling he did in Frileuse, of making some terrible blunder and being unable to stop himself. The *capitaine* looks down at the papers and signs them with a curt gesture. His voice is strained; above his collar his carotid artery is pulsing visibly.

"Private Verini, I should tell you that in view of your service record, Lieutenant Perret recommended I send you home immediately, but since you seem determined to remain in French Algeria, you will serve out your five weeks' punishment in Algiers."

He rubber-stamps Verini's file and hands it to him.

"Hand this in at the reception desk and they'll direct you to your quarters.

The file in his hands trembles.

"I still don't understand why I . . ."

The captain leaps to his feet.

"Shut your mouth and get out of here, or I'll have you arrested!"

Verini holds the man's gaze for a moment, tears welling in his eyes.

He manages to salute and to leave without yelling.

For the past three weeks, Verini has been stationed in a barracks in the centre of town. Every day, a truck drops him and five other conscripts outside the High Court – the Tribunal d'Hussein-Dey – where he stands guard.

The other soldiers live in constant fear of being attacked. Verini, numbed, feels no fear here in the city.

He does not talk about what he did up there, in the Farm. He stands guard, he salutes the officers who have dealings with the court. He looks at the passing girls. In the evenings, he can go out for a drink or something to eat.

The time he spends in Algiers is useful. It is a stepping stone between the D.O.P. and France, a transition for which he is grateful as the day of his departure looms. He is sleeping better. As he stands to attention in the blazing sun, he thinks about Adila, and though he feels guilty that he did not say goodbye, perhaps it is better this way. The war is over for him. He has escaped. He thinks about her, believes that one way or another she too will come through this. Pascal has decided he should not worry about other people, there is nothing he can do for them. He has bought some books and he spends his evenings in the barracks reading. He buys newspapers, to find column inches censored or blank. His fellow soldiers in the barracks are less ignorant, better informed than those at the Farm.

The ship casts off in three days. He spends his last hours standing on the steps in front of the courthouse where lawyers – French and Algerian – are pressing charges against the army and against certain officers. Behind his back, complaints denouncing torture are piling up.

He visits the city. Up in the hills of El Biar, he strolls past the Villa des Roses but the sentries move him on. In the district of Belcourt, he walks straight past the infamous Villa Sésini without being troubled by anyone.

His kitbag packed, no lighter and no heavier that it was when he arrived, he heads down to the rue d'Isly – perhaps because it reminds him of Orléansville – to a café where a few young French people stand around a jukebox listening to *yéyé*. Standing at the bar, he thinks of Battaza in Nanterre, celebrating his send-off to the Navy. Verini drinks a few beers. Suddenly he flinches, feeling something pressed into his back. He knows it is the barrel of a gun; he does not turn but raises his hands to his shoulders, holding them away from his body. He is scheduled to depart tomorrow morning.

But it takes less than a minute to die.

No-one around him notices anything. He feels someone's breath on the back of his neck, he tenses his abdominal muscles and prepares to turn round. His every muscle is tensed. The ragged breathing behind him explodes in a muffled laugh.

179

"Stay calm, Verini."

The pressure of the gun barrel against his back grows fainter and quickly disappears. He feels himself pale, feels a cold chill run along his spine and sweat trickle between his shoulder blades. He turns round.

"If I'd wanted to kill you, I would have done it by now."

The pistol disappears into Rachid's pocket, and seeing the rage in Verini's eyes the Kabyle takes a step back. He stands up straight and arrogantly stares Verini in the eye.

"They tell me you're leaving tomorrow. Why don't we drink a toast to friendship, *soldat*?"

Verini says nothing and stalks out of the bar.

The *Kairouan* casts off.

On the deck, overlooking the deserted quay, the cheers of a thousand soldiers join the blast of the foghorn. Hatred, joy, wild energy, grief. Some of them hide away and cry. Below, Arabs are unloading trucks, wheeling handcarts, while others doze on crates waiting for the next shipment.

Verini is walking towards the stern when a sailor stops him and says he cannot go any further. Verini says nothing. The sailor hesitates, stands aside and lets him pass. The *Kairouan* comes about. Verini looks for a figure on the docks. There is no-one. He stands there smoking until the coastline has disappeared beyond the horizon. Pascal Verini does not remember the promise he made to himself that, on the voyage home, he would shout himself hoarse.

II

# 1

Centimetre by centimetre, Paolo's flabby ageing arse was sliding off the fake leather armchair; he woke just as he was about to fall, and gripped the armrests. The blanket lay in a ball at his feet, the sun was already up.

Shuffling towards the small window, he stretched and listened as his shoulders and his neck cracked. Outside, the sprawling suburb was grey, the sky leaden, the sallow sun unable to pierce the cloud. But for the evidence of the few trees in the small park, it might have been a winter's day and not a summer morning. He opened the window to air the room and the breeze brought up a whiff of the socks he had been wearing for the past five days.

"Hey, Porkchop!"

Paolo started and turned round.

"Jesus Christ! So you're awake, big man? You're not going to pass out on us again?"

Georges shook his head and grimaced.

"What the hell am I doing here?"

Paolo hurried over to the bed and put a gnarled arthritic hand on Georges' shoulder.

"Don't try to move. The doc said it'll take a while for you to get back on your feet, but you're out of danger. You were in a coma for three days and you've been drifting in and out for the last couple. Three times you ripped out the tubes and the wires and you've been swearing at everyone."

"So, what happened?"

"You gave us a hell of a scare, Georges."

"What happened?"

"You don't remember?"

Georges frowned.

"If I remembered, why the fuck would I be asking you, dip-shit?" He lifted his arms, stared at the tubes snaking from his veins, then slowly brought his hands to his face and felt the bandages. He touched the surgical collar.

"What the fuck is this thing? Jesus Christ, I can't feel anything, Paolo."

"Don't panic, you're not paralysed. Like I said, you'll be fine. You just need to stay calm."

"Calm? I don't understand, where am I?"

"Fontenay hospital. You really don't remember anything?"

Panting like a bull, The Wall sat up in the bed and groaned in pain.

"The last thing I remember was the Pakistani talking to me about some shit down at Ring 14. I can't even remember what it was about."

"Paki? Jesus, Georges, you haven't set foot in Ring 14 for ten days, and I haven't seen the Pakistani there for weeks . . . Don't tell me you don't remember the bout with Toni?"

"I don't remember anything. Toni?"

"Esperanza."

Georges stared at Paolo in disbelief.

"What bout, what are you talking about? Toni put me in hospital?"

"Stop fooling around, Georges. Don't tell me you don't remember. Are you taking the piss or what?"

The heart-rate monitor went into overdrive, Georges shifted restlessly. With one hand, he ripped the sensors off his chest and the furious beeping stopped.

"I genuinely don't remember, Paolo. But something's not right. I don't know what it is, but I've got to get out of here."

Paolo tried to stop him, tried desperately to catch his panicked eyes.

"Has it got something to do with the old Arab guy holed up at your place?"

"Sorry? What Arab guy?"

"Don't get stressed, big man, lie back, you're not well."

A nurse raced into the room. Georges stared at her, still clutching the wires.

"What on earth are you doing? Are you insane?"

Georges felt his body go limp; he fell back on the bed and vomited bile.

The mallet struck just below the kneecap. His foot jerked. The doctor shone a pencil torch into his eyes and got him to follow the light, had him spread his arms wide, close his eyes and wiggle each finger. He felt Georges' head with his fingertips. Georges did not flinch, even when the doctor's fingers triggered an electric shock that jolted through his jaw, his forehead and the left side of his face.

"You have fractures to the nose and the jaw, and two cracked ribs. You're also suffering from whiplash. Most worrying are the fractures to your skull. You're lucky you have such a hard head. We'll need to keep you under observation for a couple of days."

"I don't remember what happened."

"Don't worry, that's normal. It should all come back to you over the next few weeks. What's the last thing you remember?"

Paolo answered for him.

"I've been working it out and it must be at least two or three weeks before the boxing match."

The doctor cupped his chin in his hand and gave a thoughtful "Hmm".

"On the subject of boxing, I . . ."

"It's O.K., Doc, I'll explain it to him."

The doctor took his leave, adding that he would be back in the afternoon to run more tests.

Shoulders slumped, sitting on the edge of the bed, Georges thought for a moment.

"What was he going to say?"

"Lie back down, you look like shit."

"Come on, Paolo, stop dicking around. What *about* boxing?"

Paolo padded over to the window and the grey suburb fuelled his resolve.

"This is the end, Georges. Another blow to the head and you could find yourself being fitted for a wooden suit."

Georges balled his fists.

"All this from a bout I don't even remember? This whole thing is bullshit, Paolo. I can't believe it. Tell me exactly what happened."

"You were asking for it, Georges."

"What are you talking about?"

"You goaded Toni for eight rounds straight, got him on edge, taunting him and talking shit. Then when you had him wound up, you let down your guard, you spread your arms and you let him deck you. You got yourself annihilated deliberately."

Paolo turned back to Crozat, who was moving his lips soundlessly, like a fish out of water.

"What the fuck have you been doing, Georges? Who's the Arab guy holed up in your apartment? And who was that cop at the bout?"

"You're saying I deliberately let Toni put me in hospital?"

Georges struggled out of bed, tottered and then ripped out his tubes and catheters, spraying drops of blood across the sheets. He pulled off the sensors that had just been replaced and vented his anger on the heart-rate monitor, shaking it until the machine was spitting sparks.

"I can't fucking remember!"

"Georges, stop it . . . Please, get back into bed . . ."

"Who is this Arab guy? We have to go back to my place. We have to talk to him."

"Are you off your head? You can hardly stand up."

Two nurses came racing in this time. Seeing Crozat's beet-red face as he choked in the neck brace, the hospital gown at his feet, one of them immediately ran back to get help, leaving her colleague to block his path, feet apart, arms outstretched, trying to get the boxer to calm down.

Georges shouted that he wanted his clothes. Paolo went to the wardrobe and took out a sports bag.

They stumbled out of the hospital room with the nurse still trailing behind, insisting Georges could not leave just like that. He gave a roar that rooted her to the spot, telling her that she and her payment slips and her discharge forms could all go fuck themselves.

Before climbing into the Citroën AX, Georges leaned on the bonnet and threw up.

Paolo careened out of the car park as though he were leaving a burning bank and two dead bodies behind him. Once they were on the motorway, he tossed a box of tissues onto Georges' lap.

"Clean yourself up, your nose is pissing blood. You're making a big mistake, we should have stayed at the hospital."

"Tell me what the fuck is going on!"

Paolo eased his foot off the accelerator.

"The second day you were in hospital, I went round yours to pick up some things for you. The old man was sitting on the landing outside your apartment. He was in a terrible state. He was filthy and he clearly hadn't eaten for days. He told me you were supposed to meet him, that he had been waiting for two days. What did you want me to do? I could hardly leave him there shivering like a tramp."

A wad of Kleenex now stuffed into his nostril, Georges pounded a fist on the dashboard and bit his lip.

"Jesus fuck! I still don't get it. What's he look like, this guy? Didn't he say who he was?"

"No, he didn't say anything, just that you were supposed to meet him. You were in a coma, the doctors didn't know if you were going to make it. I wasn't about to ask any questions. Has this got to do with whatever shit you've been involved in recently?"

"What? You're not listening to me, Paolo: I've got no idea who this guy is, I don't remember . . . anything. All I've got are images of random strangers with their faces bashed in, some fucking envelope and the Pakistani."

"Don't get so worked up, if you'd told me what you were up to, we wouldn't be in this mess."

"How much do you know?"

"I don't know anything! You didn't fucking tell me anything!"

They parked the car in a loading bay on the rue Copreaux. Georges looked at each step as he climbed, feeling the heft of his weight, reassured by the familiar creak of the stairs.

Paolo slipped the key into the lock.

Hardly had they stepped inside than there came a commotion in the kitchen, the sound of a chair being overturned, of crockery smashing. A stooped figure in a grey raincoat flitted past like a ghost heading for the bedroom. Paolo gave a start. They crept towards the bedroom door. Cowering behind the bed, arms extended across the blankets, an elderly man with sparse grey stubble was aiming Georges' Taurus at them. They quickly retreated and took cover behind the wall.

"What the fuck is going on?"

"I don't know."

"What's his name?"

"Don't remember . . ."

Georges stared stupidly at Paolo who shrugged.

"What? I don't remember his name."

From the room came a tremulous voice.

"Monsieur Crozat? Is that you? Tell me it's you."

Georges tugged at his neck brace to ease the pressure on his jugular.

"Yeah, it's me. Who the hell are you?"

"It's me. We had arranged to meet. I've been waiting here almost a week."

"But who are you?"

The voice seemed to hesitate.

"Monsieur Bendjema. Brahim Bendjema. We were supposed to meet."

"O.K., alright, we were supposed to meet."

"Who's that with you?"

Paolo laughed.

"I'm the guy who let you in the other day."

"He's a friend, now drop the gun."

A few seconds later they heard the clatter of the Taurus on the floor.

"We're coming in. Don't do anything stupid."

Pouring with sweat, Georges stepped into the room. Bendjema smiled when he saw the boxer.

Nothing. No memory. Who was this guy? Georges felt dizzy and reached out towards the bed. He took another step and felt his knees give out. The Wall slumped to the floor. Paolo rushed in.

"His head! Shit, shit, shit . . . Did he bang his head?"

Bendjema watched as the old man struggled, hesitated, then helped to lift Georges onto the bed.

When Georges opened his eyes, the Arab was sitting next to him holding a glass of water in one hand and a small blue oval pill in the other.

"Take this, it will make you feel better."

"What is it?"

"A little pick-me-up. They haven't killed me, so I don't think they'll do any damage to a healthy, strapping man like you. And they won't aggravate the head injury. Your friend told me what happened."

Georges propped himself up on one elbow and swallowed the pill.

"I ache all over."

"It should help with the pain too."

Leaning in the doorway, Paolo watched the scene.

"You alright, champ?"

"I'm starving. Was I out long?"

"About an hour. I'll go make something to eat, then I'll leave you to it. I'm guessing you have stuff to talk about."

Georges studied the old man sitting by his bed. Bendjema was in a terrible state, he was all skin and bone, and his filthy hair was plastered to his head. Who was this guy?

The pasta shells swimming in melted butter skittered away as he speared them with a fork. Paolo made to leave, and begged Georges to be careful. He was clearly not referring to his head injury, but looking straight at Bendjema who smiled at him by

190

way of goodbye. Paolo did not leave until he had made Georges promise to call him later.

Crozat sat stuffing his face while the old man sitting opposite did not even touch his food.

"I will not be able to stay here long. Now that you're out of hospital, they are bound to coming looking for us."

Georges stopped chewing and looked up, his chin greasy with butter.

"They?"

"I'm in danger, Monsieur Crozat. I got away from them by the skin of my teeth before hiding out in your building. Now I understand why they did not come here, it's because you were in the hospital."

"I don't remember anything. I don't understand any of this."

"I think you may be in danger too. Does the name Alain Dulac mean anything to you?"

"No."

"Martin Brieux? Vasquez? Scheffer?"

"Nope. Who are they?"

"You were paid to beat them up. Scheffer is still in hospital. I was next on your list."

The fork bounced off the plate before falling on the floor.

"You were working for a policeman. You told me that the day we met, the day you came for me. You said his name was Roman. Do you remember?"

"Roman?"

"You have forgotten him too?"

"Fuck. I don't know what exactly I've done, but that's one name I haven't forgotten. A vicious little shit. You're saying I was working for Roman? Are you kidding me? I wouldn't have anything to do with a guy like him. Paolo said there was a cop at the bout . . . a match against . . ."

"I think he's looking for you. You told me you had a way to get him off your back, something about the boxing match. We arranged to meet afterwards . . ."

Bendjema smiled.

"I think it may have worked all too well. You've got yourself an amnesty."

"An amnesty?"

"Amnesia. But these things you can't remember, they haven't gone away. You were supposed to come and find me after the match. I waited for you, but then I noticed two men watching my building. I managed to get away, to get as far as here. I hid outside all night, trying to work out if your building was being watched. In the morning, I came upstairs. I hid out in the old toilet on the landing until your friend found me."

"How did you know my address?"

"You gave it to me, Georges. You have to believe me. Roman isn't going to let this go. As soon as he finds out you've left the hospital, he'll come looking for you."

Georges looked down at his plaster cast, his hunger had disappeared.

"Quit it with this crap," he said without much conviction. "Roman's a thug. I've nothing to do with him, so why would he come looking for me? I don't know who the hell you are, but this whole thing is bullshit. I don't know why you've made up this story, but I'm a cop, I work out of the *commissariat in* the 14th *arrondissement*, I pound the beat and on the weekends I box. I've taken a bit of a drubbing and I need to rest."

Georges got up and paced up and down the kitchen like an animal in a cage, his face burning with questions.

"Get the fuck out, I don't owe you anything."

Now it was Brahim Bendjema's turn to get to his feet; he reached over to the sideboard and opened out the newspaper.

The front page had a large photograph of Scheffer in hospital, with an inset picture of Vasquez. Bendjema read out the description of the man in the tracksuit and baseball cap seen leaving the scene of the two assaults.

He tossed the copy of *Le Parisien* onto the table.

"The man in the baseball cap, that's you they're talking about. That's what you were wearing when you came for me. My colleague Alain Dulac gave me the same description. There's no room for doubt."

Georges felt suddenly winded and slumped heavily onto a chair.

"I remember an envelope in my letterbox, I remember opening an envelope. And I remember faces. That guy, there, he's one of the faces."

He pointed a shaky finger at the picture of Vasquez.

"What the fuck have I done? Why would I do something like that?"

Georges looked quizzically at the old man; he could find nothing else to say.

"Did you check your letterbox when you got back from the hospital?"

Georges trudged down to the lobby of the building and then climbed the stairs again as fast as he could, clinging to the banister, his head pounding. Back in the apartment, he tossed a white envelope onto the table: there was no name, no address.

Unable to move, Georges glanced from the white rectangle to the old man. Bendjema picked up the envelope, opened it, took out a card and read aloud:

"The Pakistani doesn't clear your debt. You still need to deal with the old man."

"I'm assuming 'the old man' means me." Bendjema looked amused. "Who is the Pakistani?"

"Some guy who trains at my gym. All I can remember is talking to him. I don't even remember what it was about, that must have been . . . I don't know, weeks ago. Did Roman write the note?"

"It's not signed, but I suppose so."

Bendjema put down the card and said carefully, "We made a deal, Monsieur Crozat, even if you can't remember it now."

Georges grabbed the old man.

"I don't fucking owe you anything, I don't know you, this whole thing is bullshit! I'm a cop, I don't go around beating up random guys, I'm a boxer! A boxer, you got that?"

"You're hurting me. Please, calm down."

Georges let the man go.

"Who are you? Why did Roman want you roughed up? Why did I . . . why did I agree to meet you?"

"You were going to help me, Georges. In return for a favour."

Crozat shuddered, feeling a scream welling in his throat, he clapped a hand over his mouth and the scream emerged as a shrill whistle. His head was exploding and his nose was streaming blood again.

"Amnesia?" he spluttered. "I didn't have anything to forget, I didn't have anything to hide, I was . . . I was just me, Crozat."

Bendjema laid a hand on his shoulder.

"Your memory will come back. There's more I can tell you, but right now it's not safe for us to stay here."

"I was going to help you? Help you to do what?"

"To go back to Algeria, like we agreed." Bendjema smoothed his rumpled raincoat, stared into the boxer's puffy eyes and saw a jumble of questions.

"Listen, I know what's happened to you. Your friend already explained it to you, and I haven't made any of this up. You woke up in hospital; and you don't remember how you got there. I'm

194

the only person who can help you understand what happened. Take all the time you need to sort your head out, but you can't do it here."

Standing in the kitchen with his sports bag slung over one shoulder, Georges tried to make sense of things. The one clear memory he had, the last thing he could remember, was his bout with the black kid, Gabin, he remembered winning. What the fuck had he been doing since?

He took another of the old man's pills, turned on his heel and suddenly noticed his answering machine.

"The answering machine."

Bendjema was getting impatient.

"What about it?"

"There might be messages. What do I do?"

"It's your apartment, listen to them. But hurry up."

"I can't . . ."

Bendjema walked over and pressed PLAY.

"Hey, Georges, it's Marco. I don't know what the hell you were playing at with Toni, it's none of my business, but if you hadn't wound up in hospital I'd say it was a pretty underhand trick. Give me a call when they let you out. And take care of yourself for fuck's sake, you gave us a fright."

"Hey, Crozat. Good bout. But don't think this is over. When you're back on your feet, if you breathe a word of any of this, you're a dead man."

"*Chéri* . . . ? *Chéri*, it's Mireille. There's been a lot of problems, *doudou*, some cop, he came by the hotel looking for you, he beat up Romolo pretty bad and he scared me. He was asking what you tol' me. I didn't tell him nothin', *doudou*, but you got me in some real bad shit. I didn't say nothin', I swear I didn't, but I can't be havin' you comin' back here."

Georges had shuddered as he heard Roman's voice, and his eyes flew wide as he listened to Mireille's message.

"I don't know that woman, I've no idea who she is . . ."

"Seems you've forgotten a few things rather more pleasant than our policeman friend."

"Jesus, let's get the fuck out of here."

*

The small rental car sped along the A6. Georges studied the landscape nervously with the curiosity of a man revisiting his memories. The black hole had plunged him into a state of enforced recollection, a state heightened by the fact that he was sitting next to this elderly stranger who claimed to know him.

The pills kept him alert and in a state of low-level anxiety while the chemical cotton wool alleviated the general ache in his body. The messages on the answering machine. Had he ever had any dealings with Roman? Bendjema insisted he was working for him. For the money? He had woken up in hospital remembering winning a boxing match, only to be told his career was over and that he had become a vicious thug. Had he done it for this woman, Mireille?

Georges in *love*? Even the word sounded absurd. The explanation appealed to him, though it did not change anything. This Mireille was probably a whore like all the others – the ones he could remember – and from the way she kept repeating that she hadn't said anything, she had obviously dumped him.

And boxing?

The end of his career. Paolo said he had deliberately let himself be K.O.'d. It was the most ridiculous thing he'd ever heard. If it hadn't come from Paolo, he would never have believed it.

Bendjema was dozing. Georges felt an urge to wake him up.

No-one had suggested that they were friends, but that was the impression he got from the old man.

Acquaintances, maybe, unless Bendjema was lying. Jesus Christ, with no memory, how am I going to know what the truth is?

Probably best to be cagey with the old guy, listen to what he's got to say. Pounding fucking headache, I can't think.

Georges slowed down, took the next slip road and pulled up in front of a line of shops in a service station. Bendjema opened his eyes, waking from his doze with a start.

"Where are we?"

"Coming into Auxerre, I think. I need to get something to eat."

"I'm worried that we're not exactly inconspicuous. I need to get some clean clothes and you . . ."

"What?"

"I don't know how we could make you less conspicuous."

Georges looked down at the tracksuit and could think of nothing to say.

"I could take off the neck brace."

"That might be a start. At least while you're in public. Are you in pain?"

"I'm used to it."

"You haven't forgotten everything, then?"

"I haven't forgotten anything. Apart from the stuff you've been telling me."

The Algerian laid a hand on his wrist and Georges placed his on the old man's chest.

"This guy who came looking for you . . . me . . . if you're bullshitting me, if you're fucking me around, you'll get to see him again and sooner than you think."

Bendjema smiled, his wizened old hand gently patting the boxer's arm.

197

The old man bought a T-shirt, a navy blue cotton jumper and a sleeveless grey jacket with lots of pockets; Georges bought himself a baseball cap bearing the initials of Bourgogne Regional Council.

While the old man was in the toilets cleaning up his stained trousers, Georges studied the sandwiches, nose pressed to the labels, reading the list of ingredients. In the end he got a mixed salad, a couple of shrink-wrapped apples and a black coffee.

The old man commented on the frugal nature of the meal.

"I need to watch my weight. Now, you should be eating more fat. You can't weigh more than sixty-three kilos. Given your height, I'm surprised you can stand."

"Oh, I can stand, don't worry about me."

"Yeah, you look tough and wiry."

"It's the first time anyone's ever compared me to a boxer. It's funny, at my age."

He stirred his coffee, smiling down at the plastic cup.

"But I suppose you're right. I learned how to take the punches."

"You have to know how to throw them too. Things have to balance out."

Bendjema looked up and studied the boxer's ruined face, wondering whether this was the sign of a balanced equation.

Georges bowed his head.

"You got a good memory? I mean, at your age, do you still remember everything?"

"I'm a historian, memory is my business."

"What are you planning to do in Algeria? Hide out?"

"If you like. I'm going home."

"So that was the deal? Are you going to tell me what I'm supposed to do?"

"That was the deal, Georges."

Georges bit into an apple, keeping the sliver in his mouth and forgetting to chew.

Bendjema consulted a road map.

"We're going to make a little detour. I'll give you directions."

"What is this shit? I'm not your flunkey. You drive, I need to get some rest."

"I never learned to drive. If you're tired, I can give you another pill. It'll help you stay awake. And besides, this was always part of the plan. You might not remember it, but we agreed to make this detour."

"Shit, so all you needed was a driver, yeah?"

While Georges manoeuvred out of the car park with some difficulty, Bendjema took another pill.

"Listen, you are being on the level, yeah? Roman really is on our tail?"

"The danger is very real, Georges, we have to be careful."

"Damn. I'm finding it hard to believe you. I mean, me, working for that . . . that . . . Roman is a thug and a killer, the guy's connected – shit, he's got connections like you wouldn't believe. If you asked me to work with him right now, I'd be out the fucking door. It's not like I was a different person two weeks ago, so why would I have agreed to do it then?"

"I can tell you what I know, maybe that will help you understand."

"So you're going to tell me my life story?"

"I'm a historian."

"It can't be that complicated."

The old man smiled.

"Scheffer and Vasquez were working on a book about something that happened during the tail end of the war in Algeria and about the last diehard supporters of French Algeria. Alain Dulac, who is also a journalist and a historian, was working with them. So was Brieux. It may all be ancient history, but a lot of the people in this story are still alive, some are still in politics, others are businessmen. Old men who would like to die without having someone hurl stones at their coffin. Men whose careers started out during the Algerian war. Archives are being unsealed and, over time, more and more evidence has been piling up. My work is a part of it. I'm working on my own book and Scheffer and Vasquez have been using some of my research about a particular place and period. To be completely honest, I don't know who is pulling Roman's strings. People in powerful positions who may now be retired but still wield the sort of influence that would allow them to call on the services of a corrupt cop. You're just the last link in the chain. If they were found out, he wouldn't hesitate to kill. These are ruthless old men determined to protect their reputations and their secrets. They've ended up believing their own mythology and they'll defend their version of the reality tooth and nail. Especially now that a new political generation has come to power. People who had nothing to do with the colonial period. Very soon, their amnesties and their protection won't do them much good. You were one of a long line of people sent to shut me up. I don't know why you agreed to take the job. When you tracked me down, you seemed to have doubts. I managed to dissuade you, but you were ready to follow through."

Georges accelerated.

"You've been bullshitting me. You can't do anything about Roman, you don't know anything."

"I know someone in Marseille who can help you, someone well informed. Otherwise, if you take my testimony to an honest policeman, you might be able to sort things out. I can identify the men who came after me."

"You really think it's as simple as that? If I was the one who beat these guys up, then I'll be the one to get it in the neck. It'll be my head in the noose. What the hell am I saying? It's like I'm talking about myself in the third person."

"Nothing is simple. But right now, you haven't murdered anyone."

Georges swerved away from the hard shoulder.

"What the fuck are you talking about? I don't fucking know, do I? I don't know whether I've . . . whether I've killed someone. Or maybe you know something I don't? Just tell me what the hell you know."

"Calm down and keep your eyes on the road, please."

"Fuck the road! Has someone been killed? Is that what you're saying?"

"Scheffer . . ."

"What about Scheffer?"

"The doctors are pretty vague. He's still in a coma. They're not sure whether he'll pull through and what state he'll be in if he does. The papers have played it down, but it looks unlikely that he'll regain consciousness."

The car was doing 150 k.p.h., and Georges did a last-minute lane change to avoid a Dutch caravan crawling towards the sea.

"You're saying he's going to snuff it?"

"No-one knows, Georges. But you don't have much choice. If we can't track down the people behind this, at least we can expose Roman. The answers are in Marseille, for both of us."

The rental car skidded to a stop outside a toilet in a lay-by, Georges leapt out and managed to stagger as far as a sink where he vomited loudly. A terrified boy scuttled away from the urinal, pissing on his trainers in the process.

Georges swilled out his mouth and splashed water on his face, his ragged breathing made his ribs hurt, he felt as though he had a red hot poker stabbing into his brain. He pounded his head against the mirror to calm the pain. Bendjema came into the toilets and asked him to stop. He didn't hear; he hammered on the mirror with his fists, smearing the broken glass with blood, oblivious to his fractured fingers. The old man tried to stop him and Georges grabbed him by the throat and slammed him against a cubicle door.

"I'll kill you, you fucking *bougnoule*, I'll put a bullet in your head. This is all your fault, you got that? This is all your fucking fau—"

The barrel of the Taurus digging into his chin shut him up. Georges cursed himself. The sports bag, the car, his gun.

"Let me go or I'll blow your head off. Put me down right now."

The boxer put Bendjema down. Still gripping the pistol, the old man jabbed it harder, forcing Georges' head back.

Tough and wiry.

"You don't ever lay a hand on me again, you got that, Georges? You never lay a finger on me."

Georges blinked. The old man's eyes were steady.

"Now step back. I'll be outside when you've calmed down.

Georges let out a long breath, then gulped lungfuls of oxygen until his hands finally stopped shaking.

Memories: his burst of anger had triggered a series of flashes, he had seen himself standing in front of an apartment door, in a street lined with leylandii, seen himself crouching in a small shed that stank of rubbish bins, seen himself running down the streets, hands streaked up to the wrists with blood.

You're not right in the head, you're completely out of it. This old guy is ill, you don't know what you're doing, you're not thinking straight. You're crazy, your brain is shot to shit. You need to get a grip, you've got people coming for you. Maybe it's Roman, maybe it's not, but you know it's fucking true, it's all you've been able to think about since you woke up in hospital. You don't need to know who it is, you know you need to keep running. You know that.

Georges watched the shards of mirror tumble into the sink, ran the tap and washed his hands and face.

As he came out of the toilets, a little group of bystanders scattered. The Algerian was waiting for him in the car. He got behind the wheel and the two men sat in silence for a moment.

"Where's my gun?"

"I'll hang on to it for the moment. Later, we'll see. Now, drive."

Georges rubbed his chin. The gun barrel had ripped away a piece of skin.

"So, tell me, how old are you?"

"I'm seventy-eight. But don't be fooled by appearances. I'm more fragile than I look."

Georges gave a faint smile that froze as he remembered Scheffer.

# 2

They turned off the motorway a few kilometres outside Lyons. It was 7.00 p.m. For the next fifty kilometres, the old man directed them along a warren of narrow, winding roads. New green shoots were growing in the yellow fields of mown hay. The route led them away from the main roads and down into the Loire valley as the sun set.

They had hardly said a word for three hours. Georges drove slowly, his tiredness catching up with him, keeping an eye on the bulge of the Taurus in Bendjema's pocket. The old man seemed more nervous. He was constantly checking a small, battered notebook filled with spidery writing and tracing the route they were following on the map.

They stopped at a crossroads in a village named Saint-Jodard. On one side of the road was a huge stone building. A convent. Through the wrought-iron gate, Georges saw a nun in a white wimple crossing the courtyard, oblivious to their presence.

"Turn right, Georges."

The road twisted and turned sharply before reaching another crossroads where a narrow path plunged steeply down towards the Loire, the tarmac overrun with weeds. The steep hill afforded a sweeping view of the windswept mountains. On the left, just as the road became a dirt track, an old house with a red-tiled roof towered over the surrounding landscape, shimmering in the last light from the setting sun.

"I think this is it."

Georges parked the car in front of a wooden gate that had been dismantled and sanded down ready to be repainted. Bendjema opened the passenger door.

"Wait for me here."

"Hey!"

"What?"

"The gun. I'm still a cop. You're not going in there with my service revolver."

Bendjema took the gun from his pocket, checked the safety catch and handed it back. He smoothed his jacket, ran a hand over his grey eyebrows and stepped into the garden.

He headed towards the recently renovated house which was comprised of three wings flanking a large tiled patio. The exterior walls were not yet finished. Near a small well, a pile of cut stones lay next to some freshly dug foundations marked out with string. It looked as though renovations had been going on for some time, the work almost completed but never finished. A breeze from the valley rustled in a thicket of bamboo. Georges got out of the car and stretched, took a few steps and relaxed.

Bendjema had disappeared into the courtyard.

*

The Arab walked towards a large picture window that had obviously replaced an ancient barn door. Inside was a jumble of salvaged objects, a bed, an old sofa, dressers and tables covered with dustsheets. The interiors were also being refurbished. Bendjema headed towards the front of the house.

He listened for a sound before knocking on the main door.

The house was silent. He leaned on the door and pressed his forehead against the glass. The room was a kitchen. In the middle was a rustic table on which were heaps of opened letters. Leaning against the wall next to a rickety chair was a hunting rifle. Opposite, to his right, were two closed doors. Bendjema hesitated, then turned the handle. A smell of cold, stale food and condiments. On the extractor hood above the cooker was a glossy black-and-white photograph now smeared with grease: on the deck of a yacht, a man of about forty glares at the camera, his hand gripping one of the shrouds. Bendjema carefully picked up the hunting rifle, quietly checked to see whether it was loaded, then went on with his inspection. A saucepan and a plate soaking in the sink, a shelf lined with cookbooks, and everywhere little details evoking the sea: a thin wire in front of the jars of spices – to stop them from falling if the ship pitched and rolled? – a storm lantern above the table; a cork float attached to the car keys hanging from a nail; a framed drawing of sailor's knots bearing the dedication "Happy Birthday, Captain", and signed "Jeannot". A creak of wood came from behind the door at the far end of the room. Brahim retreated slowly, never taking his eyes off the door which he had in the sights of the shotgun. He reached the main door, stepped outside and closed it behind him; only then did he notice a small brass bell hanging on the wall. He pulled the cord and took another step back, lowering the weapon and concealing it behind his leg.

The reflections on the glass panes of the door made it impossible to make out the figure coming towards him. A man turned the handle and opened the door. Greying hair, dark at the roots, barefoot, his fingers scrabbled in his thick beard. Behind the narrow slits of his wrinkled lids, his eyes had taken cover from the light. He brought up a hand to shade them.

"What is it?"

The elderly Arab stood motionless in the shadow of the house while the man's eyes adjusted to the light.

"Hello."

The man blinked and that part of his face not covered by his beard changed colour. He glowered, took a step back into the kitchen, retreating from the Arab, bumped into the table and stumbled back as far as the chair, groping the empty space where the shotgun should have been.

The man hesitated for a moment, clenched his fists and decided to brazen it out. He strode towards Bendjema, his sagging features contorted with rage. Bendjema did not retreat, he simply raised the shotgun, jamming the barrels into the man's chest, but still he kept coming, forcing Bendjema to step back.

"Go away! Get the hell out of here!"

"I could hav—"

"Shut up!"

Jabbing the weapon with all his strength, Bendjema finally managed to stop his adversary.

"Calm down, or this is going to end badly."

The bearded man gave a start and suddenly stood, frozen.

Georges had crept up behind him and was pressing the barrel of the Taurus against the back of his neck. The Wall glanced nervously at Bendjema, trying to work out what he should do next. The man with the beard stared evenly at Bendjema and said slowly:

"Tell the guy behind me to put down his weapon. You hear me, Kabyle? Tell him to drop it."

"Put the gun down, Georges."

"Fuck him. Police. On your knees, hands on your head."

"Do what he says, Georges. I'll deal with this."

Crozat hesitated, eased the pressure.

Bendjema's eyes never left the bearded man as he lowered the shotgun, the barrels pointing at the ground.

"Now what do we do?"

"Put your pistol back in its holster. We're going to talk."

"You and your friend can get the hell out of here," the man said again.

"We're just going to talk. It won't take long."

"You're dead. I killed you. You were dead, you can stay dead. Now fuck off." He looked from Bendjema to the man in the neck brace.

"Go, or I really will call the police."

He stepped back into the house and closed the door, his shadow melted into the reflection on the glass before disappearing. Georges lowered his arm and stared at the .38 in his trembling hand.

"Shit. That's the first time I've ever put a gun to someone's head. He didn't even blink." He looked up at Bendjema. "Who is this guy? You said we were going to see some friend of yours."

"It was my way of presenting the matter. I didn't want to worry you."

Georges wasn't really surprised. Being friends with Bendjema was never how it seemed at first.

"So what do we do? Do we go?"

"I'll handle it."

The old man drew up a teak chair bleached grey by the sun and rain. He sat facing the main door, broke open the shotgun and laid it in his lap.

Georges tried to formulate a question but gave up. He wandered off into the garden, sat next to the foundations on a pile of stones which lay waiting for the mason. It occurred to him that the foundations were precisely the dimensions of a man's grave. Georges might not have fitted, but Bendjema could have stretched out comfortably. Georges pushed up the peak of the baseball cap and, still gripping the .38, glanced at the front of the house.

The elderly Arab sat motionless, staring at the door. Was the other old man sitting inside staring back?

After about fifteen minutes, the stones beneath his buttocks grew cold and Georges got up and walked around. When he came to the thicket of bamboo, he turned. Bendjema had not moved a muscle. In the gathering dusk, the sky above the house flushed pink. The yellow stalks of bamboo were shot through with green veins. The small pointed leaves were quivering, though he could not feel a breath of wind on his face. It had never occurred to him that such things could grow in France, he associated them with the tropics. Georges listened to the rustle of leaves, then turned back to the house, slipping the revolver into his pocket.

The chair was empty.

The Arab had gone into the house.

Georges waited nervously for a gunshot, for a scream from inside the house, waited long enough so that he could be sure the two old men were not ripping each other apart, then he walked along the lawn and stared up at the sky dusting the scene with red and orange.

The hole in his memory was reassuring, a gaping void he could fearlessly skirt around so long as he did not set foot inside. In the meantime, he could fill this void with whatever he chose. With a landscape, with the smell of fields. Above his head, the little forest of bamboo snared the setting sun in its fronds. He dozed off.

He woke in darkness to a pounding panic, rolled onto one side, his fists raised to ward off a jab to his face from André Gabin.

But there was nothing but darkness and a scattering of early stars. He sat up, waited for the pounding in his head to subside, then turned towards the glow from the kitchen. He walked to the house and pressed his face against the glass.

On opposite sides of the kitchen table, the two old men sat facing each other, their heads bowed. The shotgun lay next to Bendjema, who was talking while the other man listened. Georges knocked at the door. The man with the beard did not react, Bendjema turned and beckoned him to come in.

The Wall stood in the doorway. The man with the beard got to his feet, took an already-open bottle of red wine and filled a glass which he drained in a single gulp.

The Algerian also got to his feet, taking the shotgun, and tugged Georges by the arm.

"Let's go next door."

Georges woke at dawn, bathed in sweat, lying on a battered sofa under a threadbare blanket. The sunlight from the picture window hit him full in the face. The room was filled with bric-a-brac from the 1960s which lay gathering dust among the electric sockets and light switches that dangled from the walls. Bendjema's bed, more fitting than a sofa to a man of his advanced years, was empty and neatly made. The pain in Georges' skull killed his first thoughts stone dead. His right arm and leg were numb. He waited for a few minutes for feeling to return, then, weak, nauseous, grubby and in a sorry state, he shuffled out of the barn dragging his foot.

The two old men were once more ensconced on opposite sides of the kitchen table. There was no shotgun. In front of the man with the beard was an ashtray overflowing with cigarette butts. Had they even slept?

"Good morning."

Bendjema turned his head.

"You don't look too good, Georges. How are you feeling?"

"I wouldn't mind washing my face, if it's not too much to ask."

The bearded man gestured to the door on the right.

The bathroom was upstairs. Georges quickly freshened up and washed the neck brace, which was brown with dirt and sweat inside. He wrung it out as best he could and put it on again. The coolness of the damp foam rubber was pleasant.

In the kitchen, the Arab was now alone. He pushed a bowl of coffee across the table.

"Is there no solid food?"

"I don't know."

"Listen, you can't expect me to live off fresh air. Neither of us has eaten since lunchtime yesterday and I'm not long out of a coma."

"So you're worried about your figure . . . Have a look in the fridge if you like."

"D'you think he'll mind, the other guy?"

Bendjema smiled and lowered his head.

"Help yourself. We're sorting things out."

"Yeah, really? Then what's he doing out there with his can of petrol?"

In the middle of the garden, the man with the beard doused a pile of papers, flicked open a Zippo, sparked the flint and tossed the lighter onto the pile. The can had obviously contained heating oil, thought Georges as the fire slowly caught. If it was petrol, the whole thing would have blown up in his face.

He opened the fridge and stuck his head inside. Bendjema wandered out of the house.

Munching some bread and cheese, his free hand gripping the butt of the Taurus in the pocket of his tracksuit, the boxer went out to join the two old men.

The flames were consuming several thick bundles of typed pages and, on top of the pile, a small yellowed book with a photograph stapled to the cover that had just begun to blister, a portrait of the guy on the yacht in the picture in the kitchen, though here he looked a lot younger. Was it his amnesia that had him staring so intently at a burning pile of papers that had nothing to do with him?

The wind whipped the flames towards them and the three men stepped back; the man with the beard lit a cigarette, then looked at Bendjema.

"So now that you've told me your story, what do you plan to do?"

"I'm going back to Algeria." Bendjema hesitated. "Fancy coming with me?"

A mouthful of smoke went down the wrong way and the bearded man spluttered and coughed.

"You're insane, Rachid. You really think I ever want to set foot in that country again?"

"What did you just call him?"

The bearded man turned as though noticing the heavyweight for the first time, but though he was looking at Georges, his words were addressed to the Algerian.

"So is he going to Algeria with you?"

"Monsieur Crozat is coming with me as far as Marseille. I was planning to suggest that you accompany us."

"What did he call you? 'Rachid'? But that's not . . ."

"How did you manage to get this meathead involved in this affair?"

"Hey! What the fuck is going on here? What's your real name?"

The old sailor picked up the petrol canister and headed back to the house. He went into the west wing, an airy workshop with large picture windows.

"What's your real name?"

"Rachid Amokrane."

"So you have been fucking me around. And who's he?"

"Verini. Pascal Verini. We knew each other back in Algeria."

"If you don't tell me what's going on right now, I'll walk out of here, I'll call Roman and I'll grass you up to clear my debt. And give me another pill, my head's exploding."

In the *atelier*, Pascal Verini picked up a mallet and a chisel. He began working on a large hunk of stripped wood set on a workbench.

"What's that stuff burning?"

"Memories, I suppose. Of the war. Let's go back inside and get you something to eat, you look pale."

As the elderly Kabyle fried some diced vegetables, Crozat listened to the story of Rachid and Pascal. The pill had eased his headache, but the more he listened, the more everything in his mind became confused again. He had no idea that something like the D.O.P. had existed.

"More or less everyone knows there was torture. But the fact that it was official and systematically organised isn't something you find in school history books. The French anti-insurrectionary experts had long, lucrative careers afterwards. Some were employed by the Americans to help train the Green Berets who would later be sent to Vietnam. Some took posts with the military juntas in South America – General Aussaresses*, for example, did a stint at Fort Bragg before going to Brazil to train the secret police. In fact, that bastard more or less invented the methods of torture that the French later exported."

"What about you, how did you get away after this guy Verini clubbed you with a rifle butt?"

"How do you think I survived, Georges? The fact that I'm still alive means that after a few weeks I turned traitor, I worked for the other side. And though it didn't change anything, I did my best in the few weeks I managed to hold out at the Villa Sésini."

"The villa what?"

"A torture centre in Algiers run by General Massu's paras."

"And after the war?"

"I was one of the traitors allowed to leave Algeria. I was even given a new identity."

From the workshop, the sound of mallet blows alternates with the roar of an electric saw biting into wood.

"What about him? What did he do after the war?"

"He hasn't told me."

"Yeah, he looks as hard-headed as you do. So where's his wife?"

Bendjema stopped stirring the vegetables.

"He's got a wife?"

"You didn't notice the cosmetics and the make-up in the bathroom? The bedroom upstairs with the family photos?"

"I didn't know, and he didn't say."

"And Roman? Is this whole thing linked to something that happened fifty years ago?"

There was no point continuing; the Kabyle could no longer hear, he was off somewhere far away.

Georges went outside for some fresh air. In the workshop, Verini was pounding the chunk of wood like a lunatic, sweat streaming down his face and dripping from his beard. Georges wandered over to the window, then went inside. No reaction. He stood and watched, fascinated by the way the chisel gouged the wood, moving along the grain and suddenly sending up showers of splinters. It seemed futile, hopeless, given the size of the log, and yet a shape had already begun to appear, rough-hewn and lacking detail, but recognisable. A crudely formed head and one shoulder. Verini stopped and looked up at the hulking brute with his tracksuit, his neck brace, his head wrapped in filthy bandages, who was staring, spellbound, at the rough shape.

"What do you want?"

"Me? Nothing. I just came to have a look."

"Don't trust Rachid. He's a liar."

"What? Oh, Bendjema . . . Yeah, I know. He's dodgy."

Georges smiled, unaccountably pleased by this flicker of complicity between him and the old sailor. Verini picked up his mallet and went back to work, only to hit his thumb with the hammer. He blew on it and shook his hand.

"You're police, aren't you?"

"Yeah. In the 14th in Paris. You know the area?"

"I lived in the 14th for a while, I like the area."

"Yeah, it's not bad."

"But I don't like cops."

The Wall packed away his smile, tugged the visor of his baseball cap and made to leave. In the doorway, he had a change of heart and turned back.

"Your friend Rachid, or Bendjema, or whatever you want to call him, he's going to die if he doesn't make it to Marseille. That doesn't bother you, after everything you went through in Algeria?"

"He said we're friends? Bullshit. I don't owe him anything. And if you're dumb enough to follow him, that's your business."

Georges opened his mouth, pulled his cap further down and turned on his heel. Behind him, Verini gave a start and called after him.

"Hey, what did you call him? 'Bendjema'?"

The policeman was too far away to hear. Verini picked up his chisel and returned to his work, only to hit his thumb again. The thumbnail split and the wound began to bleed.

When Verini came into the kitchen, his hand dripping blood, Georges was tucking into a vaguely oriental stir fry. Bendjema, stiff as a poker, was picking at his food with a fork.

215

"You just get on a boat and disappear?"

The Algerian nodded.

"We drop you off in Marseille, you board the ship and I never hear from you again?"

Another silent nod. Georges wiped his mouth with the back of his hand.

"What about Roman? What do we do about Roman?"

"What is he talking about?"

Rachid cleared his throat.

"It's possible we're being followed by a police officer."

"What?"

"Yeah," Georges chipped in. "A killer."

"Georges doesn't remember much. He took a bad knock during a boxing match."

Verini faltered.

"What the hell is going on here? You show up at my house, you tell me your life story, you whine about your guilt, you stir up old memories, and why? Because you're in the shit. And if that wasn't bad enough, you bring the police to my house."

"You owe me this, Pascal."

"Fuck off."

Rachid smiled, brought a hand up and parted his hair to reveal a mark.

"I still have the scar, you know. From the rifle butt. Directly beneath it, there's a tumour. I, too, will forget, just a little before I die. At first I found it funny, ironic even, that the tumour was right there, under the scar. I decided I wanted to see you again. This isn't about friendship. It's about finishing something we started fifty years ago."

Georges stopped chewing and, suddenly worried, was staring at Bendjema.

"Don't let him fool you," Verini said. "Rachid has conned more

people than you think. When I first met him, he was only working for one side, but even then he was twisted." Verini turned to
Rachid. "I'm guessing things haven't changed for the better since
you started working for the French . . ."

"It's true, though," Georges interrupted. "I've seen the pills he
takes for his headaches."

"So what? It's all bullshit, he's no more sick than I am."

"There's still a price on my head in Algeria." Rachid flushed
crimson. "But it hardly matters since I'm going home to die. I
refuse to allow you to—"

"Get off your high horse, Rachid. I haven't changed my mind.
I want to make sure you get on the boat. And if what you're saying is true, so much the better. Whether it's a bullet or a tumour,
it works just as well for me. We'll check the timetables before we
set off. I don't want to be hanging around waiting. It takes about
four hours to get to Marseille, an hour to get you aboard. If I
don't drag things out, I should be back here by tonight. And if
this story of yours isn't bullshit, if there is some guy following
you, I don't want you here any longer than necessary. Once we
get to Marseille, you're on your own."

Verini pushed open a door and went into a large, cluttered
room with a camp bed in one corner. The room served both as
study and library. A large window looked out onto the fields and
the hill sloping steeply towards the Loire. At the bottom of the
valley was a grove of poplar trees.

Rachid was shocked by the view. Verini's house was eerily
similar to the Farm at the D.O.P.: remote, surrounded by fields,
with a courtyard and a barn and a dizzying view over a river valley, even the alignment of the building was the same.

Pascal had picked up the phone, Rachid told Georges he was
going to shower.

Upstairs, the Kabyle first entered the bedroom Crozat had

talked about. He studied the family photographs: two children and several grandchildren. From one of the pictures Verini, cradling a baby, beamed happily.

This was his wife's room, to judge from the decor and the clothes in the wardrobe. They had separate rooms.

Rachid undressed in front of the mirror without so much as a glance at his aged body, marbled with scars, and stepped into the shower. He turned the water on and gently massaged his skull at precisely the point where the tumour, though he could not feel it, had already grown to the point that it was inoperable.

\*

The shave did him good and he looked better. In spite of the heat he pulled on his jumper to hide his arms. He went into the study. The window was open and Verini was leaning against the frame, gazing at the view and smoking a Gauloise. The midday heat rushed in, swelling like a balloon into the coolness of the room. Outside, the garden was an expanse of carefully mown lawn; in the middle, a hollow some metres in diameter formed a sort of pond in which reeds grew.

"The next ship sails tomorrow morning at eleven. There was one berth left, so I made a reservation in your name and paid the deposit by credit card. You owe me two hundred euros."

"In my name?"

Pascal walked over to the overstuffed bookcase, took down a large-format book and tossed it onto the desk. The cover was a photograph of a village whose houses had been all but razed to the ground by burning napalm. The title, in red: *Forgetting and Rebuilding*. An old edition from the 1970s. Above the title was Bendjema's name.

Rachid picked up the book and examined it.

"It was my first book."

"I've read all the others."

"I thought you didn't want to remember . . ."

Verini went out into the kitchen.

"What did you think, Rachid? That we would pick up the conversation where we left off fifty years ago? As though time . . ."

". . . had not passed? It hasn't passed for me."

"I've done my rebuilding, you can deal with your hang-ups about being a traitor, we're not going to found a two-man club of Algerian war veterans."

"What were you burning this morning?"

"Rough drafts of manuscripts. I've been keeping them for years, I decided now was a good time to get rid of them. Oh, and my military record. That was the one thing I kept . . . Shit, I don't want to have this conversation with you, Rachid. And don't start up with that bullshit about betrayal. If the paras managed to turn you, it wasn't because you were friends with a nice little French boy. It's because you wanted to save your own skin."

"You think I didn't have the courage to die? Whether you believe it or not, I hoped there would be a peace in which you and I could be friends."

Verini uncorked a bottle of wine and poured himself a glass.

"You always were one for speeches. Well, don't try shifting the blame onto me. You did what you could, or what you wanted, it had nothing to do with me."

Rachid picked up a glass from the draining board and filled it. Verini smiled through his beard.

"Not a Muslim?"

"No, a socialist."

Verini raised his bushy eyebrows and gestured towards the door with his glass.

"And him? What's he?"

Crozat was lying in the sunshine, his arms spread wide, his head buried in the thicket of bamboo.

"An amnesiac."

"Not everyone can be so lucky."

Rachid raised his glass towards the ceiling.

"To amnesia."

He took a sip and licked his chapped lips.

"You don't think we were friends?"

It was Verini's turn to drink.

"I don't remember now what we were."

He turned towards Rachid.

"Young?"

"When I came home, I worked in the factory in Nanterre with my old man for a year. Then I decided to leave. I replied to an ad, a shipping company in Le Havre was hiring sailors to work on cargo ships. I went for an interview. Before I got there, I went to a barber. The minute he opened his cut-throat razor, I ran out into the street screaming, covered in shaving foam. I didn't get the job. I don't know if it was because I hadn't shaved, but I didn't get it. I went back to Paris, but I never again set foot in Nanterre. My old man and his buddies from his unit used to talk about Algeria, about the bastards torturing people over there; they'd talk about it in front of me like I wasn't even there. I don't know what I would have said, but no-one in my family ever asked the question. I left Nanterre and never went back. I haven't had any news from them in fifty years, I have never got in touch with them either. My folks must be dead by now, but I don't know when they died. I don't know what became of my little brother and my little sister. I burned my bridges and I don't regret it. It's possible to live without a family. Friends are enough. I stayed in

220

hotel rooms in Saint-Germain. I ate in cafés, I did some odd jobs, some wheeling and dealing. In '68 I was a photographer, self-taught, I did freelance work for the papers. But I ditched the camera. Me and Mohamed, a friend I met in the local café, we started going to the student demonstrations and beating the shit out of cops whenever we could. He was the son of an *harki* and drank like a fish."

"You were a revolutionary?"

"A revolutionary?" Verini gave a dry laugh. "No, we had a gun and we were looking for this guy we wanted to kill."

"Who?"

"An officer in the C.R.S."

Rachid smiled.

"Did you ever find him?"

"Not the guy we were looking for. After the riots, a girlfriend suggested something. She knew some people in the *Mouvance autonome*, a left-wing group looking for guys who knew how to handle a gun, how to use explosives. An old man who hung out in one of the bars I used to go to convinced me that it wasn't for me, that fighting for what I thought was my freedom simply meant relinquishing it to someone else, that I'd end up being conned. I listened to him. I nearly did it, but in the end I listened to him. I left Paris. A friend of mine had gone to stay with some girl in Brittany, so I called him. I settled near the gulf of Morbihan and set about refurbishing a sailing boat – one of the old *sinagots* that smugglers used during the war. The *sinagot* is perfect for navigating the shallow waters of the gulf. Anyway, that was my first boat. I've been a sailor ever since. Until recently, when my health started to give out. When I was no longer fit to go to sea, I couldn't bear to have to look at it. So we moved here."

"You and your wife?"

"I've done all sorts of jobs, I've been a dishwasher on the Côte d'Azur, a blacksmith, a deep-sea fisherman, we've renovated a dozen houses, moved at least twenty times. It's pretty obvious I was running from something. But I loved it too, starting new lives, learning new things."

He sipped his wine and, as he set the glass down, he stared at Rachid.

"But the dreams, the nightmares, they followed me everywhere."

Verini drained his glass and poured another.

"And then they stopped. I don't remember exactly when or how. It was fifteen years ago maybe. The guilt began to fade and with it the thirst for revenge, that nearly did for me. I swear, Rachid, by the time you showed up here I barely thought about Algeria. The only reason that I didn't throw you out is because there's nothing now that can turn back the clock. Even standing here with you. I'm more afraid of ghosts. For a very long time my anger got the better of my freedom, that was the way I was, and more than once it landed me in jail. There were certain words, certain faces that made me see red, certain cafés I wanted to burn to the ground the moment I set foot in them. Maybe if I hadn't ended up in so many fights, I might have wound up in a bank waving a gun. But I remember what the old Commie once told me: that sort of freedom is bullshit. I was better off at sea. My wife made things easier. And the kids. I did everything I could not to be like my old man. I'm not even sure what that means, but it must have worked because my kids still talk to me. When I had my first grandchild, I felt – I don't know – as though everything could be washed away. That even if one day someone told this kid that his grandfather had fought in Algeria, it wouldn't ruin his life. Here was something that, like my children, was part of me. A child that existed only because I had stayed alive. It took a long time for me to admit that my life . . . It sounds stupid, but in a way I thought my life was a dream. The dream of a corpse rotting far away in the dust, a man with his throat cut lying at the bottom of a ravine."

Verini turned away, struggling to remain dry-eyed.

"I lived selfishly, heedlessly, I thought that society, that the state, owed me something. Only when I stopped believing that did I make any headway. That's probably when the nightmares stopped. But it's not an absolution."

The words were muffled now, whispered between clenched teeth.

"I hope the bastards who volunteered to go down into that cellar and the men who gave the orders still wake up at night. I've never talked about this to anyone, not to my friends, not to my family, no-one knows. No-one I know has ever heard of you or of the D.O.P. I put it all in the book I tried to write. A book that's now a pile of ashes. If my wife had been here when you showed up yesterday, I would have denied everything. I would have denied knowing you. Anger has become an old man's solitude, his peace. And I'll take it with me to my grave. That's why I want to be sure you get on that ship. Don't kid yourself. And when my wife comes home, I won't even mention you were here. I don't bear the weight of other people's mistakes any more, or even the mistakes of the man I was when I was twenty, who should probably have joined the *maquis* with you. Those mistakes, they're part of my childhood. At your age, you know what that means. At the age of twenty, even with my little Commie family, I chose to save myself, that's all. Just like you did. No worse and no better than any other man. But the sins of others are no longer mine."

Rachid was listening, just as he had done long ago. Supremely detached, like a chess player. Verini didn't care. He was talking to himself, talking to the walls; Rachid, whether friend or enemy, was of no importance.

The Kabyle crossed his fingers on the table and looked out at Georges, still sprawled on the lawn.

"You know that Ahmed died just after you left? He joined the *maquis* the day you left the Farm. His body was found by the roadside five hundred metres from the D.O.P. a week later. He was executed by the F.L.N."

"Why are you telling me this?"

"I don't know. Maybe I'm wondering why we had more choices than he did, why we managed to survive."

"We didn't have the same choices. Ahmed . . . The poor old bastard. I remember thinking he was old, but he would have been, what, forty-five, fifty? Ahmed had nothing to sell like you did, he had nowhere to go like I did."

"So what does that make him? A traitor to the war or a hero to humanity?"

"Stop busting my balls, Rachid. Your dialectics stink of rotting corpses. I've said what I had to say, if you don't like it, too bad."

Verini got to his feet. He crossed the courtyard and went into his workshop. The hammer blows began again.

# 3

Georges sat up as the sun was beginning to wane. He had spent his afternoon nap boxing. Against men who were not boxers. Vasquez, Scheffer and the others. The men did not defend themselves and Georges kept throwing punches. They stood firm, their faces bloody, they never crumpled. Outside the ring, the stadium was empty.

He turned towards the road, unsure whether he was still dreaming. A procession of women was marching down the little road and taking the dirt track towards the river. They were saying the rosary. Some distance behind, two young monks brought up the rear. The grey habits and white wimples were flushed by the setting sun. The women were smiling, their light, quick steps dictated by the steepness of the hill. One of them glanced briefly at Crozat and looked away, losing the rhythm of her stride and stepping on the heel of the nun in front of her. Georges watched until they disappeared behind the house.

The grass rustled.

"They're novices with the Contemplative Sisters of St John. They spend two years at the Priory of Saint-Jodard. Afterwards they go on missions, mostly to Africa. Do you feel you have a vocation?"

"What?"

"They're pretty, aren't they? There are Brothers too."

"Religion's not really my thing."

Verini ran a hand over his chest and his sleeves, brushing away the slivers of wood, then wiped the sawdust from his face.

"They don't all last. Some of them go over the wall and never come back."

Georges struggled to his feet, feeling dizzy.

"Fuck . . . I'm sleeping all the time, but I'm not feeling any better."

"What happened to you?"

"Boxing match. Some guy put me in a coma. But it's not just that. Apparently, I let him do it."

Verini looked at Crozat.

"You just stood there and let yourself be beaten to a pulp?"

"Yeah, that's how I reacted when they told me. I don't remember it."

"Rachid has made something to eat."

"I'll come up now."

"They won't be back for at least an hour."

"What?"

By now it was dark, they had wolfed down the food in silence and Georges got up from the table clutching his head.

"I'm going to lie down."

Bendjema's pills no longer had any effect.

"Take two."

"I can't sleep if I take those things, I'd be better off getting some rest."

Left on their own, the two old men were ill at ease. Verini had had a few too many.

"I'm going to head off too. We need to set off by five tomorrow morning. You should get some sleep."

"I don't sleep much anymore."

"Neither do I, but I don't want to sit here and listen to you ranting and raving about the Farm."

"We won't get another chance. Don't you want to—"

"You're the one who wants to talk. I don't need to. You made a mistake, Rachid, we were never friends and that's not likely to change now. Get that into your head."

"That's got nothing to do with it. If we can't talk to each other about this, who can we talk to?"

"There's been too much talk already, if we carry on we'll start believing in our own fantasies. Goodnight."

"Why did you read my books? Why did you try to write one of your own?"

Verini closed the study door behind him.

Rachid waited for a moment, smiled to himself, then went out onto the terrace and sat at the patio table. Few stars were visible; a south-westerly had blown up trailing clouds with it. The old Kabyle ran his fingers over the scar on his head. The skin still felt raw and he flinched as though from an electric shock. Exhaustion had made him hypersensitive.

The walls surrounding the courtyard, cloaked now in darkness, quickly began to look like those at the Farm, and Rachid turned towards the garden, allowing his memories to overlay what he could see. The barred gate, the dirt road, the main door to the white farmhouse, the cell block, the second courtyard and the entrance to the cellar there, where the clump of bamboo swayed in the breeze. On the very spot where Crozat the amnesiac had slept.

Rachid Amokrane trembled at the power of these memories. His old bones had never let him forget. It would take a tumour to do that, to kill the brain and at the same time this body, crisscrossed with scars impossible to erase.

227

A crouching figure darted across the garden. From the prisoners' cells to the white farmhouse.

It looked like a children's game, like a kid scampering away to hide. Following the logic of his imagination, Rachid looked to see what had flushed out the shadowy figure. He stared into the gloom. Who was this man? Lieutenant Perret? A sentry or a *gendarme*? Then he saw himself, sitting at the table under the lantern that hung above the door. There was no-one here but him. The shadow was playing with him.

Was running away because of him.

Rachid got up and listened intently, suppressing a smile.

The wind. The cicadas.

Then he felt a wave of fear crushing his chest, burning his ears, as adrenaline coursed through him. He retreated as far as the house and stood looking at the garden. Leaning in the doorway, panicked, he tried to reason with himself. Perhaps, caught up in his memories of the Farm, he had simply imagined it. He was at Verini's house, in France, far from Orléansville and the *djebel*. He was losing his grip, what he could see was being replaced by the very images he was trying to dispel: the Farm, Rubio dashing across Verini's garden. Was this the onset of hallucinations, of madness?

He listened in silence, tried to reason it away, then gave up.

He had seen someone.

He went indoors, turning off the outside light and then the kitchen light; he stepped back from the door and stood at one of the windows. The teak patio table, the courtyard, the walls, the windows of the workshop reflecting the moon.

Nothing moved.

Rachid went into the study and Verini immediately sat bolt upright in bed.

"What the hell are you doing?"

"There's someone in your garden. Where's the shotgun?"

"What? What are you talking about?"

Verini's voice was slurred from the wine, he turned on the bedside lamp.

"Turn it off! Turn it off now!"

Rachid rushed over and switched off the lamp.

"There's someone in the garden," he whispered. "I saw him."

"You're paranoid."

"Were you expecting someone?"

"Do I look like I'm expecting someone?"

"Where's your shotgun?"

"Give it a rest. There are stray cats and dogs out there. There's nothing else, now go to bed."

The Kabyle slinked along the wall as far as the window and leaned out. Verini groaned, got out of bed and groped his way as far as the kitchen. He switched on the light and turned towards the window. Rachid's paranoia is contagious, he thought. He hesitated, walked over to the door, opened it, stepped out onto the terrace in his bare feet and waited. Nothing. He went back inside and pulled a bottle of wine from the rack. The door banged, making him jump. Georges shambled in, wearing a T-shirt and rubbing his face.

"Shit . . . caught my foot in the mat."

"You could give some warning before barging in."

Verini smiled and proffered the bottle. Crozat declined.

"Pounding headache, can't sleep. Too hot."

He noticed Bendjema in the study staring out at the darkness.

"What's going on?"

"He thinks there's someone in the garden."

Georges froze.

"Don't you start too. There's no-one there, he's just being paranoid."

Seeing the look of panic on the face of the hulking boxer, Verini changed his mind.

"Oh, for Christ's sake, quit it with this bullshit."

"You don't know Roman."

"Neither do you, you can't remember."

"I still remember who he is. If someone's sent him after us, it wouldn't have taken any him longer to get here than it took us."

With one hand Georges ripped off the neck brace while with the other he fumbled at his hip.

"You looking for your gun?" Verini laughed.

"Shit, it's in my jacket, in the barn."

Verini pretended to aim the wine bottle.

"Go ahead, I'll cover you."

"Turn off the light," Rachid shouted.

Verini snorted. "You're mad, the pair of you."

Crozat switched off the lights. Rachid came and joined them in the kitchen, they could hear his fretful breathing in the darkness.

"I'm going to get my gun. Don't stand in front of the windows."

Verini slammed his glass down on the table.

"Jesus, I'm sick of this shit. Go and get your gun if you want. We'll switch off the house lights, then turn on the spotlights in the garden. That way maybe you'll give up this nonsense and go back to bed."

The was a long gust of wind as Georges scuttled out. Verini tripped over a pile of books and knocked over some curios before making it to his desk. Rachid heard him open a cupboard and pad back into the kitchen; he unhooked the storm lantern, set it on the ground and struck a match. The faint, flickering glow lit up one square metre of terracotta floor tiles. Pascal opened the rifle and checked both barrels were still loaded.

230

Almost immediately, Georges came back, closing the door behind him, and took a deep breath.

"I got it!"

He crouched down and checked his pistol in the glow of the lamp. Rachid took shelter behind the desk, Verini stood by the main door and Georges by the window.

"O.K., on the count of three, flip the switch on the left." Verini chuckled. "God, we'll be in a sorry state in the morning after playing Cowboys and Indians all night." He counted to three and they flipped the switches. The garden and the terrace were immediately bathed in light.

Pascal blinked and gave a mocking smile. Rachid whipped his head round, scanning the house, then threw himself on the floor.

In the courtyard, a crouching figure next to the table stopped, as though frozen by a flashbulb.

On the other side, in the middle of the lawn, another man stood frozen, one foot hovering, scarcely two metres from Georges on the other side of the window.

Both men were armed with revolvers and fired simultaneously. One bullet punched a neat hole in the double-glazed window and lodged in a dresser, the second shattered one of the glass panes in the front door. Georges stupidly tried to open the window before returning fire. But the guy had already bolted. The other man had upended the garden table and taken shelter behind the teak tabletop. Verini fell to his knees, poked the shotgun through the shattered pane of glass and fired both barrels at the sky, filling the kitchen with smoke. The twin gunshots in the confined space left him half dazed.

Outside, the crouching man scuttled out of range of the spotlights. Georges slipped his arm out the window and blindly fired two shots. A reed slowly snapped, bending until it touched the surface of the pond.

The two men had disappeared. Inside, no-one moved until they heard the distant sound of a car starting and roaring away.

"Who were they?"

Sitting at the kitchen table, the shotgun in his lap, Verini tried to stop his hands from trembling.

Rachid was ashen.

"The two men who followed me in Paris. That was them."

Georges had also recognised one of them.

"The one I saw was Roman's driver, so the other guy had to be Roman."

Verini swallowed painfully.

"How did they know we were here?"

Georges strapped on his brace again, his neck was stiff and painful.

"Paolo knew you were hiding out at my place," he said to Bendjema. "But he didn't know we were coming here. So who did know?"

"Dulac. He helped me find Verini's address."

"Roman must have got to him, that's the only possible explanation."

Verini resisted the temptation to pour himself another glass of wine.

"What do we do now?"

"Roman doesn't know I'm going to Marseille. So we stick to the plan."

"Are you fucking crazy?" Georges roared. "You think they've gone home? Maybe they weren't expecting a welcome party, but this isn't over. They'll be on to us the minute we get to the village."

"The path," Verini said. "We can take the dirt track that leads down to the river and pick up the main road just past the bridge. It's dry at the moment, so its driveable."

"The car!"

"What about the car?"

"They saw the car, they'll know the model and the number plate. They're police for fuck's sake, and we just shot at them. They can have roadblocks set up from here to Belgium if they want to."

Verini winced as he got to his feet, he rubbed his knees.

"I've got some land down by the river, and there's a truck."

Georges ran to the barn to collect his belongings, Verini tossed some clothes and a washbag into a rucksack. He peeled off his sweat-soaked T-shirt, then froze, one hand clutching his chest. He grabbed an inhaler from the nightstand and took two quick blasts. He sat down on the bed and waited for the pains to subside.

From the doorway, Rachid was staring at the long pink scar running down his chest. Verini and the old Kabyle exchanged a look.

"Dodgy ticker. I had a bypass ten years ago."

Rachid looked down.

"Are you still coming with us, even after what's just happened?"

"If I had any hesitations, I don't now. I'm now going to stay here and wait for those sick bastards to come back. I'll drop you in Marseille and then take a holiday."

He pulled on a clean shirt. Rachid smiled, as though in apology, or as though he were proud of him.

"That C.R.S. officer you were looking for in '68, I know where he is. But you wouldn't have found him. He'd left Paris by then, he had been transferred to Tours."

"What are you talking about?"

"Rubio's not dead. He's living in Marseille."

Verini fell back on the bed, colour draining from his face, and Rachid was afraid he might die right there.

"You fucker! That's why you came looking for . . ."

Georges barged in.

They've slashed the car tyres, so we would have had to walk anyway. What's going on here?"

*

Crozat led the way, carrying the storm lantern, and Rachid followed in his shadow, trying not to sprain his ankle on the rocky ground. The hill became steeper, they could hear the murmur of the river and the breeze was cooler. The smell of silt drifted between the trees masking the smell of timber. When they came to the fork, Pascal indicated the right-hand path.

"It's about two hundred metres down here. Slow down a bit, I can't keep up."

They followed a rusted wire fence some two metres high, passed several padlocked garages and lock-ups they could barely make out, not daring to shine the lantern past their feet. Eventually they stopped in front of a gate which Verini opened. The lock-up was closed and the van, an ancient Renault Trafic, was parked in the tall grass down two bare, rutted tyre tracks.

Verini slipped the key into a lock thick with rust and opened the driver's door. The interior light picked out the dust-covered dashboard strewn with shells, feathers and old road maps. He slid across the passenger seat and opened the other door.

"As the youngest, you get to do the driving."

The old men squeezed together onto the passenger seat and Georges climbed behind the wheel.

"It's a diesel. Don't try to start her cold, she's done four hundred thousand kilometres."

He waited a long moment until the glowplug indicator light went out, then turned the ignition. The Trafic started first time.

"Turn right as you go out and head down as far as the bridge where you cross the Loire. We're about fifteen kilometres from the main road, after that five minutes to reach the motorway to Saint-Etienne."

"Four hours to Marseille, is that what you said?"

"Maybe five in this old truck, or even six. But we have time to spare."

Georges turned off the track onto the bridge.

Twenty-five minutes later, they came to the motorway and it was clear that no-one would be able to fall asleep at the wheel. The engine couldn't have been any louder had it been sitting in their laps.

"Right, you know how to drive. I'm going to get some sleep."

Verini clambered into the back of the camper van, lifted the back of one of the seats and hooked it to the roof, then stood on a low table and hoisted himself onto a makeshift bunk. The van was kitted out like a ship's cabin.

Rachid offered Georges a couple of pills and he swallowed them dry.

"I'll get some rest too, if you don't mind, Georges."

"Sure. Listen, don't think we're out of the woods yet. Roman will have the name of your mate and the number plate of his van."

From the back, they heard Verini's voice.

"It's in my wife's name."

"That's hardly going to make it difficult to figure out!"

"We're not actually married."

Rachid climbed into the back and Georges concentrated on the ribbon of tarmac, keeping the right wheel on the hard shoulder and the speedometer needle at 110 k.p.h. It seemed sensible.

Rachid made up the second berth and struggled to climb up.

"There are blankets in the cabinet above your head."

The Kabyle rolled a duvet over his legs and for several minutes the whine of the engine served as silence. When he spoke, Rachid's voice was so low it was barely audible.

"What?"

"Your wife. Does she still live with you?"

"We've got a little place on the Atlantic coast. She spends a lot of her time there."

"So you're the one living inland?"

"Now that I can't sail anymore, I prefer not to have the sea right under my nose."

"Pascal, I don't intend to board that ship without seeing Rubio first."

For a while, Verini took refuge in the roar of the engine.

"So that was your plan from the beginning. Still as twisted as ever, Rachid. But you do what you've got to do, I'll be there to see you off. That's all."

"I wasn't lying, I really don't have much time left. The tumour is inoperable."

"So? You think that gives you the right to go and torture another old man? Rebuilding and forgetting! You're no better than the men you condemn."

"Don't give me that, Verini. Are you telling me you don't want to find out what became of Rubio?"

There was a moment's silence before Pascal answered.

"The bastard . . . I can still remember the vicious fucker's voice."

He gasped for breath.

"Night after night I heard it in my dreams. I don't want to see him again."

"I had nightmares too. I dream about what happened to me. They've never stopped."

236

Verini thought for a moment.

"I'm not going to wind up in jail on account of that piece of shit. I won't have you getting me involved in your revenge. This is your business, it's not mine anymore."

Rachid gave a nervous laugh.

"Stop trying to convince me that you're over it. I know you, Verini. You make me laugh with your family photos and that house you've never finished. You haven't come to terms with things, you're still hiding away, nothing's changed. You never finished your book, no-one knows your story except me, your kids have no idea who you really are, and the way you crow about having grandchildren is pathetic. If you think your secrets will die with you, you're more naive now than you were at twenty. You'll take this to your grave, just like the rest of us."

Verini turned his back and pulled the blanket over his shoulders.

"You can quit the act, it won't work. Maybe it's not perfect, but at least I have a family. And friends. I don't need to go recruiting war veterans. The same men whose throats you were prepared to cut."

"I don't have children because the paras crushed my balls between two planks."

At these last words, Georges, who had slowed down to listen to the conversation, floored the accelerator.

Bendjema's pills glued his eyelids to his eyebrows, he drove for three hours solid without blinking and without realising how much time had passed.

As the sky began to blaze, he swore and turned off the motorway. The van pulled to a halt in a shriek of brakes in a rest area lined with trees and picnic tables.

Rachid was still sleeping like a log, but Verini, being a former sailor, woke as soon as the van stopped.

"She's overheating. Every fucking light on the dashboard is blinking."

"Shit! You've been pushing her too hard."

"Sorry?"

The air was fresh, scorched pure by a red, bloated sun. The iridescent dawn broke over the parched shrubs and the waxen-leafed eucalyptus trees. In the middle of the lay-by, hands on his hips, Georges stood bathing himself in the light.

"You need a deckchair?"

"What?"

Verini had interrupted him just as a thought was taking shape. A vague impression that, ever since he had been unable to remember things, time had been a series of sunrises and sunsets with nothing in between.

Having peered under the van, the old sailor gripped the bumper and hoisted himself upright.

"Shit. She's leaking. The radiator hose must have burst."

He popped the bonnet open. There was a twenty-centimetre crack in the rubber hose. Hand on his forehead, Georges stared at the complex workings of the engine.

"You got tools?"

"They're not much use without a replacement hose."

Parked a little further away in the lay-by was another camper van, a Mercedes. It was the only other vehicle in sight, and the bodywork was liberally adorned with graffiti. Georges eyed the paintwork suspiciously.

"You think maybe there's someone in there?"

On the van, in the middle of the hand-painted swirls, was a logo: *L'Institut Bancal.* Verini banged on the side door. They heard noises from inside but it was the back doors that opened. A bleary-eyed young guy with a moustache hacked and cleared his throat before asking what was happening.

"We broke down. A burst radiator hose."

Through the half-open door, Verini could see a motley pile of objects, including a fine collection of stuffed animals wearing sequinned caps. They obviously did street theatre. It took a minute for the guy with the moustache to wake up. Behind him, on a mattress strewn with props and scenery, another figure began to stir and a girl's voice, worried, asked what was going on.

The guy with the moustache pushed back a lock of his hair, closed the door and, after some muffled sounds, opened it again. He had pulled on some clothes and stepped out, unfurling a tall, lanky frame that looked as though it would scarcely fit inside this shambles.

"So what did you say was the problem?"

"We've burst a radiator hose."

He glanced from the Trafic, with its bonnet up, to the old man with the beard, and lastly the tall guy covered in bandages and wearing a neck brace.

"Yeah? We got some bits and pieces, yeah, I'm pretty sure we can sort you out. Thing is, I don't know where it is . . ." He jerked his chin towards the van. "In there somewhere."

"It's a thick radiator hose."

"O.K., I'll go have a look."

"If it's a smaller piece, I can probably cobble something together."

As they walked back to the van, Rachid got out and stretched himself.

"What's happening?"

Verini grabbed a toolbox from the back of the van and set about removing the damaged radiator hose. Rachid and Crozat sat at one of the picnic tables and watched the goings-on around the Mercedes van. The young man with the moustache had opened the sliding door, only to have a pyramid of unlabelled tins of food fall out on top of him and clatter across the car park.

He did not seem particularly bothered by this and carried on extracting strange objects, tools and wooden army crates, then he crouched down, rocking back on the heels of his oversized crocodile-skin shoes. He tossed various bits of junk machinery over his shoulder.

Verini, hands covered in engine grease, strolled over to him carrying the burst radiator hose. Crozat and Bendjema watched them rummaging and comparing, delving through piles of props: toy guns, stuffed animals, shooting targets, clay pigeons and pieces of plywood painted with wild animals from whose bellies streamed crimson entrails made of wool and fabric. Into the midst of this shambles a girl with a pink boa appeared, her eyes still puffy with sleep. Lastly, a second young man emerged from the van, taller and thinner than the first, but battling with the same mane of unkempt blond hair.

A minivan full of kids with bicycles strapped to the roof drove into the rest area, slowed, then drove away again. The roar of traffic from the motorway was growing louder, the shadows of the trees began to shrink and the heat was blistering.

While Verini and the man with the moustache examined the engine, the girl and the lanky beanpole unearthed a camping-gas cooker, some grubby bowls and the wherewithal to make breakfast.

Georges hung back and watched while Rachid went to chat with the troupe.

"It's, like, a modern take on a puppet show."

"Really?"

"There's a bunch of other shit. We play music and stuff. What about you guys, where are you headed?"

"Marseille."

The strange members of the troupe regarded the two old men and Georges with almost equal curiosity.

240

"What are you planning to do there?"

Rachid hesitated.

"I'm taking a boat, they're just coming along for the ride."

The hose had been replaced. Verini collected water from the washbasin and topped up the radiator.

"Thanks, it should hold out now. Do you need help loading your stuff back into the van?"

"Don't sweat it, this is a good opportunity for us to have a clear-out. We set off before dawn this morning and we're supposed to be performing in Valence tonight."

"Valence? Shit."

"Something wrong?"

"I thought we'd been on the road longer. We're running a bit behind schedule."

The whole group sat down to eat and, as the young people gradually woke up, the old men began to tire. But Rachid seemed happy. He bombarded the troupe with questions.

"So what's it called, this show you do?"

"*Clay-Pigeon Shooting is Fun!* It's about war, and the puppets are all animals who were victims of roadkill. It's set in a hospital. Lucio plays an old guy who's convalescing, Mélanie is a nurse, and I'm the *legionnaire*."

"Did you write it yourselves?"

Gaël, the man with the moustache, nodded. He looked at the two old men. The one with the beard looked sullen, the elderly Arab was smiling shyly.

"Why did you decide on a play about war?"

Gaël let his hair fall over his face, then tossed it back with a quick jerk.

"My dad served in Algeria. He never talked about it, but I wanted to try and do something. He refuses to see the show. Actually, nobody much comes to see it."

Verini got to his feet, left the table and went back to his van. Georges, who hadn't uttered a word, took this as an opportunity to slope off, and lay down on the dry grass under a tree.

Rachid smiled in apology for his companion's abrupt departure.

"We fought in Algeria too, Pascal and me. He doesn't like to talk about it."

"I thought as much."

"Really?"

"It's your age and . . . Well, mostly it's the eyes, they remind me of my father's eyes."

"What do you mean?"

"I don't know. It's like all you want out of life is something that can make you smile because otherwise the pain is too great. My father smiles like that sometimes. It lights up his face, because it seems to come from a place where laughter doesn't exist. You're taking a boat back to Algeria?"

Rachid smiled.

"Yes."

"So who are they?"

"Verini, the one hiding out in the van, was a guard at the torture camp where I was held prisoner. The one lying on the grass is . . . an ex-boxer. He took a bad beating and he's forgotten some things he wishes he hadn't done. It bothers him that he doesn't understand why he did them, because he's forgotten that too."

\*

When at last they drove away, the performers from l'Institut Bancal had not even started sorting out their van; the three of them were sprawled on the grass watching clouds scud along the Rhône valley. A few metres away, the entrails of the gaping

Mercedes van lay scattered among the fleet of cars that had invaded the rest area.

It was 1.00 p.m. and it hardly mattered how fast they were driving towards Marseille.

Rachid felt calm, probably because he had stood his ground against the tumour that would one day eat away his memory, spending several hours telling the youngsters his story. Words had always been his life and Verini could tell that the old Kabyle was keyed up and furious making plans.

"Are you happy now? Which version did you give them? Rachid the hero of the revolutionary war or the wise old man who forgives? You think they'll turn your story into a puppet show and immortalise you forever?"

"Who said I forgive anything?"

"So, did you tell them you plan to kill a man before you set sail for Algiers?"

"What?" Crozat whipped round.

"Keep your eyes on the road, Georges."

"What the fuck are you on about now?"

"Stop trying to outsmart everyone, Rachid. You got him involved in your plans, the least you can do is tell him before we get there."

Georges was beginning to panic, his face a rictus of anger.

"Right, don't piss me about. What the hell is happening? Don't tell me this is something else I've forgotten. Who are you planning to whack? Was this always part of the plan?" Rachid took his time and, seeing him struggle for words, Verini smiled.

"I think I know who's been pulling Roman's strings."

Crozat took the bait, hook, line and sinker.

"Who?"

Try as he might, Verini could not but listen.

243

"A former officer in the C.R.S. who became the head of security for the Front National. You're a cop, Georges, you must have heard of the *Département protection sécurité*. The D.P.S. is – or was – much more than the 'security branch' of the Front National. It was a full-blown paramilitary organisation with a thousand members and a special squad called 'the ghosts' tasked with infiltrating the military and community organisations, and stirring up trouble in the *banlieue* where the F.N. didn't have control. Most of them are ex-soldiers and former policemen. Bernard Courcelle*, the leader until 1999, was a former military intelligence officer, a friend of Bruno Gollnisch*. In the army, Courcelle had been responsible for gathering intelligence on mercenary groups and arms dealers. After he was demobbed, he had a string of jobs before becoming head of the D.P.S. There is evidence of mercenaries being involved in attempted coups in former African colonies. The D.P.S. might have been set up for political purposes, but the mercenary wing made money through little sidelines like arms trafficking. In 1999, the government set up a committee to investigate the D.P.S. but their report was never published. The Front National dismissed Courcelle and denied everything. Courcelle worked in the Republic of the Congo for a while as chief of President Sassou Nguesso's guard before taking over as head of security for the oil industry infrastructures in Pointe-Noire. I know it sounds like I've wandered off the subject, but all of this is relevant to the story.

"A lot of the veterans of Algeria found a new home in the D.P.S. The man Roman is working for – assuming it is Rubio – is a link in the story. Pascal and I know him of old. Rubio was a *pied-noir*, a boxer like you, he began his career working for the D.O.P. in a farm a few kilometres outside Orléansville. He was an interpreter, and the most ruthless of the torturers. I found out that he retired from the Front National in 2000, but for thirty years he was part of a tradition of right-wing militants that can trace its roots back to the wars in Indochina and Algeria. A man of his experience probably appealed to Le Pen, who volunteered to serve in Algeria, and is known to have worked at the notorious Villa Sésini. Rubio would be eighty now. He's living out his days near Marseille. The book I've almost finished writing traces the careers of a number of key figures who served in French Algeria. But mostly it's the story of Rubio . . ." Rachid paused, he looked tense. "I'm going back to Algeria because I refuse to be buried in the same soil as Rubio. I like the thought that I can go home while he has no choice but to stay and be buried here, in his country of exile. But before I take the boat, I'd like to pay him a visit."

Crozat was spellbound; the hairs on his arms were standing on end.

"What about Roman, will he be there?"

"If Rubio is the man behind things, he'll definitely be there."

"How do you know?"

"Because I left a little message for Rubio telling him that I'm coming to see him. I also told him you're coming, Pascal."

Verini started from his seat and grabbed Rachid by the throat. Georges triggered the hazard warning lights, pulled up on the hard shoulder and separated the old men.

# 4

Eyelids drooping, arms numb, Georges Crozat was hunched over the wheel, exhausted. The two old men had not opened their mouths since the fight. Verini was dozing – or pretending to – in the bunk at the back while Bendjema, in the passenger seat, did not utter a word. Georges shook himself and surveyed the scenery, unable to remember what he had been doing for the past four hours. He had been driving, obviously, but where had the time gone, what had become of all the road they had covered? Frantically he tried to remember what he had been thinking about during his mental blank. A blink of the eye into which a whole section of his life vanished while he waited for another sunset. The Mediterranean light sent shooting pains along his optic nerve.

"Where exactly are we going?"

Just opening his mouth made him wince. The fracture to his jaw woke up as he did.

His notebook in hand, Bendjema gave him directions. They turned off the A7 into Aix-en-Provence.

"We should stop. I'm exhausted. You got any more pills?"

Rachid took the blister strip from his pocket. It was almost empty. He gave a pill to Crozat and kept one for himself.

Georges ripped off the bandage drooping from his eyebrow and glanced in the rear-view mirror: his face was less swollen. But if physically he seemed to be looking better, inside he felt completely destroyed. Paolo's warning echoed in his head: "Another blow to the head and you could find yourself being fitted for a wooden suit." Roman was a heavyweight and he knew how to throw a punch. Georges tried to remember. Roman training at Ring 14, the way he dodged and weaved . . . He felt the way he did on a night before a fight and wondered who had set up this bout. The Wall turned towards Bendjema who was leafing through pages in his notebook.

Verini reappeared, leaning over the passenger seat. The two old men did not so much as acknowledge each other: the van suddenly felt too small for the fear and bitterness of these three men.

"Where are we going?"

Rachid did not look up from his notes.

"Somewhere near Cassis, on the coast, it's a rocky peninsula. We'll park up there and wait until dark. What are you planning to do?"

He was speaking to Verini.

Verini did not answer and disappeared into the back of the van. The cabin filled with the smell of Gauloise, Georges wound down the window. Rachid smiled between gritted teeth.

"He'll come with us."

The old Kabyle was spoiling for a massacre. In the ring, the worst thing you could see was a guy with that look on his face. Verini had one of his coughing fits. When it finally stopped, Rachid turned back to him.

"You O.K.?"

Verini said nothing. Rachid settled back in his seat and stared at the road.

"During interrogations, Rubio always had a knife in his hand. He'd wave it in front of my face while I was strapped down and he was asking me questions. He'd press the tip of the knife lightly against my stomach or my throat, like it was a fingertip. From time to time, he'd unexpectedly slash at me as he passed. Little cuts to keep me awake."

"Why are you telling me this?"

"To put fire in your belly. You know there was a time when Verini used to go round looking for Rubio in order to kill him. Don't think he doesn't want to kill him still, he's just afraid of ending up in prison. That's the only thing that's stopping him."

At 6.00 p.m. the Renault turned onto a dusty dirt track that wound its way up the steep scrubland of Port-Miou peninsula. The sky was the same colour as the sea and the white line of waves breaking on the rocky coast extended as far as the eye could see. Strong gusts from the *mistral* rocked the camper van. At Bendjema's signal, Georges cut the engine. The road overlooked a narrow blue inlet where a few motorboats came and went. On the far side of the cove, on a spit of land barely a kilometre wide, a winding road connected a series of lavish modern villas set in gardens with swimming pools and surrounded by trees and roughcast walls. The *mistral* made the brutal heat bearable. Rachid got out of the van and stretched slowly, his eyes fixed on the far end of the peninsula and the houses overhanging the sea.

Georges got out and followed the old man's gaze.

"Is that where we're going?"

"It's one of the last houses, I'm not sure which one."

Verini slid open the side door of the van and came to join them, carrying a pair of binoculars. He raised them to his eyes.

In the gardens and around the azure swimming pools he could see children playing, families having an aperitif. He spotted a villa where the pool was covered with a tarpaulin and the garden deserted. Was this Rubio's house? He handed the binoculars to Rachid, indicating the villa in question. Though there was no-one in the garden, the shutters on the windows were open.

"Maybe. We'll have to wait till it gets dark and then check out the area. I know the house is number 3, but it's impossible to see from here. We'll have to scout out the area to be sure."

"I'm not going. If Georges wants to go with you, that's his business. Take the van if you want."

Verini settled himself in the van out of the sun and the wind, he unpacked the shopping he had bought in one of the service stations, opened his knife and made himself a sandwich. Crozat went over to join him and the two men ate in silence.

Rachid crouched down. Sitting back on his heels, the old Arab did not take his eyes off the house.

At 7.00 p.m. a small car pulled up outside the gates of the villa. A woman emerged wearing a long dress and carrying a small black briefcase, pressed a button on the intercom or entered a keycode. She walked across the garden, opened the door with a set of keys from her pocket, and disappeared into the house.

Verini was brooding silently, Georges took off his neck brace to make it easier to breathe and to eat.

"Why don't you want to go with him?"

"What?"

"You're going to let him go in there alone?"

"I've more reason not to go than you have to go with him. That whole story he's been spinning might be a lie. Roman and Rubio have probably never even heard of each other. But Rachid needs some muscle. If you do go, you'll find out for yourself. Rachid knows you beat up those journalists. If you don't go, he'll turn you in. You've walked into a trap. Rachid is a cunning bastard. He wants revenge and he's determined to have it, that's all he cares about. Don't kid yourself."

"Maybe. But even if that's true, you're talking bullshit. You've got more reasons to go than I have."

Verini opened a can of beer, took a long swig and wiped his beard.

"Well, well, looks like your brain is starting to function again. The thing is, it was different for me than it was for him. This is all about ego. That's what Rachid's like. You don't go through what he went through and come out alive, you don't switch sides as often as he's done unless you're a seriously tough bastard. But he's not going to drag me into this. I refuse to get involved in his little scheme. When he's settled his score with Rubio, he'll be off to Algeria, but you'll be left with one more fuck-up on your hands. You'll be left to carry the can."

"He's going to die there."

"And I plan to die at home."

Verini took another long draught and, staring at the man sitting next to him, shook his head angrily.

"For a guy who goes around beating up old men he doesn't even know, you worry too much about that old man. You don't owe him anything."

Jaws clenched, The Wall pounded his fist against his head until he could no longer stand the pain from the fractures in his skull.

"I've got no choice. There's this guy, Scheffer, who's dying in hospital. I might not remember doing it, but I put him there. I have to see this thing through to the end. I've got no choice."

Taking his can of beer, Verini stepped out into the wind and looked at Rachid, staring through the binoculars, motionless as a lizard in the *djebel* sun.

"Yeah. Maybe. Scheffer, did you say?"

At 8.00 p.m. Rachid got to his feet. The woman with the briefcase had came out of the house. He had seen a red sticker on her windscreen. A doctor, maybe, or a nurse.

The *mistral* and the cool of evening meant the gardens began to empty. A few kids were still splashing in swimming pools and

Rachid watched for a moment. In Port-Miou, the sailing boats lay at anchor, families piled back into their cars and drove away.

Shortly afterwards, the streetlights in Cassis flickered on and the sun set behind the rocky inlets. Rachid was increasingly convinced this was the right villa, the sort of place an old man might live out his days, never going out, no children to play in the garden.

Verini came over.

"Does his wife live with him?"

"She died a few years ago. He's alone."

"You'll find nothing over there. Nothing but an old man who's half senile just like us."

"He's expecting us."

"He probably doesn't even remember you. You're off your head, Rachid. You should go back to Algeria while you've still got half a brain and make the most of it."

Rachid pulled his gun from his pocket. It was not Georges' pistol, but an M.A.S.-50, the very model Verini had had in Algeria.

"What the hell are you doing with that?"

"A souvenir. You see, I didn't have a military record to hang on to."

"Rachid, you're making a mistake. Why go and kill him now? You've known where he is for ages, why didn't you do it before now? You claim I don't have the balls to go, but you've been waiting until you're on your deathbed to make up your mind. It's juvenile, it's . . ."

Rachid aimed the 9mm at his chest.

"You're right. Before I die, I need to do something that means something."

"Put down the pistol."

"Are you scared I'll put a bullet through your heart? Your heart's already fucked. And you're going to die without ever having done anything, with only memories for company."

"Put it down, there's no point. You've written books, that's

251

worth much more than the death of some old man. Finish your book about Rubio, and let it be. That's the best thing you can do."

Rachid stuffed the gun back in his pocket.

"If you don't want to help, stay out of it. Where's Georges?"

"He went for a walk about an hour ago."

"Shit. We have to get going, what the fuck is he doing, that moron?"

Verini looked at Rachid in disgust.

"You're a complete jerk."

But Rachid wasn't listening. He peered through the binoculars and then suddenly swore. In the setting sun, walking past the roughcast walls, he could see Georges strolling past Rubio's house.

"What the hell does he think he's doing?"

His features swollen and his face more bruised than normal, Georges turned to face the hill, then crossed the road and walked past the gate to the villa. Twenty metres further on, he turned back towards the hill and gave a thumbs-up. He kept walking and Rachid lost sight of him in the dense foliage.

"He's going to be spotted, with that face of his and that ridiculous neck brace. The guy really is as dumb as he looks."

"So this story about the other cop, Roman, is that bullshit? Did you set things up so Crozat would come with you? Did he even do the things you've said he did, or did you make the whole thing up?"

"He beat up four men and he'd been paid to attack me too. The accident during the boxing match might have left him dazed, but he's a dangerous man who was working for vicious bastards just like Rubio. The sort of men you despise, the sort you've been running from all your life, the sort of men who sent you to Algeria. Don't trust Crozat."

Verini was no longer listening.

*

252

Breathless from his climb, the boxer reappeared on the rocky outcrop where the two men were waiting.

"His name's on the letterbox. It's the right house, and there are lights on inside. I didn't notice anybody watching."

Rachid said nothing. His anger evaporated the moment he heard they had the right address.

Seeing him nervously checking his M.A.S.-50, Georges turn to Verini. The sailor nodded.

"You sure you know what you're doing? You really want to commit murder? If Roman isn't there, and it doesn't look like he is, then I'm having nothing to do with your 'execution'. We don't know for sure that Roman is working with Rubio. I can't get myself . . ."

Verini looked down at his shoes. Rachid was already opening the passenger door.

"If you walk away now, Georges, I'll turn you in to your colleagues. Just think about Scheffer."

"Yeah, yeah, I know, your friend here said you'd say that. I don't give a fuck. You see, I took his advice, I bought the paper while I was in the village. He's obviously been following the news. I might be a bit slow, but when people talk, I listen."

He pulled a copy of *Libération* from the pocket of his tracksuit bottoms. He showed Bendjema an article on page five. Vasquez and Scheffer had held a press conference the night before to announce that publication of their book would not be postponed as a result of the attacks they had suffered. Scheffer had pulled through and had been released from hospital some days earlier.

"You've been fucking me around, and I told you not to do that. And don't think that gun of yours would stop me beating the shit out of you. The only reason I won't is because I don't know how to beat up an old man without killing him. So, here's the deal: I'll track down Roman without you, because there's no way he's waiting for me by the poolside . . ."

He touched the peak of his cap as though in salute.

"Of the new memories I've been making since I got out of hospital, you'll be the first I plan to forget."

Rachid did not say a word. He got out of the van, checked his weapon, looked at the two men and then stalked off.

Verini and Crozat watched the old Kabyle walk down the hill in the half-light, gripping his pistol.

Half an hour passed and still the two men paced, constantly looking down towards the villa. Georges was ashen, the tension in his body reawakened the searing pain in his ribs and in his head. He ranted and raved to himself, forcing himself to remember, calling himself a fuckwit, muttering "Why, why, why?" The greater his anger, the more the vivid images flashed through his mind, the faces of Dulac and Brieux, waking up in hospital, the yawning abyss, the white envelopes. He tried to rip open the envelopes, but this was where his memory stopped. He wanted to open the white envelopes, convinced that inside he would find himself, together with a solution to this clusterfuck.

Verini paced behind him, tension clutching at his chest. The pain in his left arm had come back, just as it had when Rachid first mentioned Rubio. That sick bastard Rubio was hiding inside the house he could not tear his eyes away from. He cursed Rachid under his breath and then suddenly he remembered Rubio looming in the doorway of the white farmhouse. Rubio in the brothel. Rubio leaning against the barn wall as the flames flickered over his face.

*Don't turn back, Verini.*

Verini chugged another beer to stop his hands from trembling.

Rachid's madness, his memories, his mangled brain had infected them both.

"We can't let him do it!" Georges let out a strangled roar.

Verini hesitated.

"What we can't do is hang around here! I'm not spending my last days in prison for this."

Georges kicked at the ground.

"I'm a cop, I'm still a fucking cop! I can't just let him kill someone. And neither can you."

"It's not just someone, it's Rubio."

"So now you're happy for him to be killed as long as Bendjema does it for you?"

Crozat looked down the hill at the streetlights on the road running along the peninsula, the lighted windows of the villas, the headland and the last few houses before the rocks. He ripped off his neck brace.

"It's probably too late to do anything. Aw, fuck it! I'm taking the van."

Verini tossed his beer can into the scrubland.

"Wait up."

The old sailor angrily fetched a canteen of water from the van, splashed water on the number plate on the front of the Trafic and smeared it with fistfuls of soil. The mud made the numbers indecipherable.

"For fuck's sake," Georges roared, "move your arse!"

Verini daubed the rear number plate, tossed away the canteen and jumped into the back seat. He grabbed his bag of toiletries, dug out the G.T.N. inhaler and took three deep puffs. While Georges sped down the road, he lifted one of the seats and retrieved the shotgun. The barrels felt strangely hot to him. In fact, his hands were cold.

They passed two young boys on mopeds heading to the bars in

Cassis, they slowed as they passed the lighted houses hidden behind the whitewashed walls. Verini wished he was still seeing them from the safety of the hill a kilometre away. Gripping the shotgun in his lap, the ex-soldier broke out in a sweat and felt the same surge of fear he had once felt on the supply runs from Orléansville. Crozat parked the car fifty metres from the villa.

"What do we do when we get in there?"

Verini did not have the faintest idea. Georges persisted, choking back his own fear.

"What do we do if Bendjema's already killed the guy?"

"We get the hell out, what else can we do?"

"And if he hasn't done it yet?"

A shudder ran through Verini's old bones. Despite his best efforts his voice sounded shrill in his ears.

"I don't know. Nothing. We try to stop Rachid?"

The Wall looked doubtful, needlessly checked his Taurus. Verini rummaged in the pocket of the door and pulled on a pair of leather gardening gloves.

"What are you doing?"

"I've been inside. I've no intention of leaving my fingerprints all over the place."

Georges stared down at his bare hands.

"What about me? I'm a policeman, so my prints are in my personnel file."

Verini dug out a pair of moth-eaten wool gloves with holes in the fingers. Crozat slipped them on and Verini covered the holes with some insulating tape he found in the toolbox.

Verini slipped the stock of the shotgun under his jacket, letting the barrels hang down by his side. They walked along the pavement, a carpet of pine needles deadening the sound of their footsteps. The *mistral* dropped to a breeze as night drew in, Verini recognised the familiar smells of the sea.

He walked on, intent on saving Rubio's skin. The mere thought maddened him. When they came to the villa, he grabbed Georges by the arm.

"Give me a minute, I need to catch my breath."

They ducked behind the wall, checking both sides of the road and the neighbouring gates.

"We have to go now, for Christ's sake, your buddy's been in there too long already."

Verini flushed and, taking the rifle from under his jacket, elbowed Georges out of the way and went in front.

"There are no buddies of mine in that house."

Seeing Verini dash into the garden with the shotgun primed and ready, Georges could not help but wonder whether he was planning to go in all guns blazing.

Crozat ran after him.

A large hallway, an empty coat stand, a mirror hanging on the wall and, beneath it, an old-fashioned rotary dial telephone on a high stool.

In the doorway to the living room, Verini stopped dead.

On that day long ago, he had stood off to one side. Far enough away to avoid the rice being thrown. The steps in front of the church had been thronged. In the photograph, his left shoulder cropped off, Pascal Verini is looking towards the bride and groom who, like the rest of the wedding party, have their backs to him. Rubio and his wife. Orléansville. 1958. At the foot of the steps, out of the picture, Casta must be waiting in the car, staring with the same murderous hatred at Rubio on the happiest day of his life.

The reception.

The little package wrapped in white tissue.

The screams from the cellar.

*Soldat de deuxième-classe* Verini at the age of twenty hanging on Rubio's living room wall.

Crozat managed to catch him before he collapsed on the tiled floor. The old man's face was grey, under the thick beard his lips were quivering.

The living room was spacious, large windows overlooked the garden, the swimming pool covered by a tarpaulin scattered with pine needles. The lights were too white, the house strangely empty, more sparsely furnished than might have been expected from outside. Table mats, ornaments, a flowery three-piece suite, a hammered brass tray on a low table and on it, a teapot and a set of the ornate glasses traditionally used for mint tea. The tiled floor shimmered beneath the bare bulbs reflected in the polished surfaces.

Georges carried Verini to the sofa, help him sit down, then, weapon in hand, he checked out the room.

"Nothing. I can't hear anything."

Verini was shaking like a leaf.

All the things from his worst nightmares.

Everything he had spent years struggling to forget Rubio had collected here in his empty house.

Georges padded over to him. In the harsh light from the low-voltage bulbs, the bruises from his bout against Esperanza looked cadaverous.

"There's no-one here. What do we do?"

"Look upstairs."

"We got here too late. Bendjema's long gone."

"Go and look."

Two minutes later, Georges reappeared: he had found no-one. He slid open one of the French doors and checked the garden around the disused swimming pool.

258

"They're not here. There's no-one fucking here!"

Verini struggled to his feet, using the shotgun as a cane.

"They have to be here."

He checked out the other rooms, careful not to linger over the photographs that lined the walls. Rubio standing with one foot on the running board of the Citroën Traction. Postcards from Orléansville dating from the 1950s. The bridge over the river Chélif near the Farm. The church square. Rubio in a vineyard surrounded by Arabs wearing *djellabas*. An older Rubio, wearing a suit, shaking hands with beaming Jean-Marie Le Pen.

And the knick-knacks.

An army-issue dagger on a shelf.

Next to it, the black beret he never had the right to wear.

A decorative goat-leather wineskin.

Everywhere, nostalgia.

He wanted to torch the house.

On the ground floor, an empty bedroom with a filthy carpet and traces where a bed had once been. The kitchen, and behind that a laundry room. Next to the washing machine, a door he assumed led back to the living room and the rest of the house. Georges pushed it gently. Concrete steps led down to a brightly lit cellar. He took the first step.

"There's a cellar. We . . . What the fuck are you doing? They're down in the cellar, there's nowhere else they can be."

Pascal had taken a step back, he was clutching Crozat's sleeve. "You O.K.?"

Verini shook his head.

"Don't let go of me. My legs have packed up."

Hands behind his back, Rachid was sitting in a chair next to a pile of crates. The windowless, low-ceilinged basement was hot. Various boxes and old furniture had been pushed back against the bare walls to make room for the bed, an oxygen cylinder, an I.V. drip, and a trolley on which sat an open pot of yoghurt and some orange peelings. The mingled smells of bleach, piss and acrid sweat, of sour wine and dust.

An oxygen cannula inserted into his nose, Rubio opened his eyes when he heard them. His eyes, as dark as ever, glittered in a wrinkled face almost as white as his hair. Rachid's M.A.S.-50 was lying on the bed at Rubio's feet. The Kabyle looked up at Verini, his chin trembling, his eyes red from crying. Pascal looked at what remained of Rubio who stared back at him. Unable to stand, Verini slumped onto a pile of crates and turned to look at Rachid.

"Has he talked?"

"He says he doesn't remember me. I told him what happened, but he just pretends not to hear. He's been hiding out in the cellar because he thinks people are trying to kill him. He doesn't recognise me."

Georges walked over to the bed, flinched and stepped away in disgust.

"Jesus, he's fucking shit himself!"

Rubio's voice, hoarser but still shrill, hissed between chapped lips.

"That you, Verini?"

Verini leaned on the shotgun as he got to his feet, he stepped closer but said nothing.

"It is you, I recognise you."

Rubio raised a bony hand lined with swollen black veins.

"The *bougnoule* wants to hurt me. Help me, Verini."

*Don't turn back, Verini.*

"The filthy Arab came here to hurt me. Verini?"

*Don't turn back, Verini.*

Rubio's eyelids were drooping with exhaustion.

260

Don't remember, Verini.

Forget what you've seen, Verini.

Go home, Verini.

*Don't turn back, Verini.*

Verini stared into Rubio's eyes and the man flinched. He placed the twin barrels of the shotgun between the old man's legs, resting on his balls.

"I haven't forgotten, you vicious old bastard. I'm going to burn your fucking house down. You won't be here to stop us spitting on your grave. I'm going to do what I should have done back in Algeria if I hadn't been scared shitless. If I'd known you were going to ruin the rest of my life. I'm going to finish you off the way you used to finish them off, I'll drag your body out onto the street in front of your house so all your neighbours know what you were."

There was no change in Rubio's expression, he turned his head to one side to dismiss Verini from his field of vision.

The Wall crept up behind Verini and begged him:

"That's not why we came here. The guy's not dead, so let's leave and take Bendjema with us. We'll go to the docks. Leave him here to rot. Are you listening to me?"

Verini raised the shotgun and leaned it against the bedframe, took his Opinel from his pocket, unsheathed the blade and activated the twistlock. The knife-edge fluttered against Rubio's wizened throat and still the old man looked away. Georges made to stop Verini but Rachid laid a hand on his shoulder.

"Let him do it. Please, Georges, let him do it."

The scrawny neck of a plucked turkey, scabs of necrotic skin in the creases, the irregular pulse of the veins. The blade sank into the soft folds. He pressed harder. The old man swallowed, his Adam's apple rubbed against the sharp edge, scraping away skin but drawing no blood.

The knife withdrew, the hand quivered.

Verini spat in Rubio's face.

Rachid picked up his pistol and slipped it back into his pocket. Verini took the shotgun. Georges pushed them towards the basement steps, then turned back towards the old man and walked back.

He bent down, making an effort not to breathe through his nose.

"Where's Roman? Is Roman working for you? Has all this shit been down to you, you old bastard?"

He grabbed the old man's flannel pyjamas and shook him.

Spittle trickled from his lips and still the old man stared at the concrete walls. Georges let him fall back, went up the stairs and stopped on the top step. He flicked the light switch plunging the cellar and the stairwell into darkness. For several seconds, he listened to Rubio's frightened whimpers, then closed the door.

He stepped into the living room and felt the blood pulsing at his temples chill. Hands on their heads, the two old men were kneeling on the bare tiles.

"Drop your gun, Crozat."

Roman's driver had a Mini-Uzi trained on Verini and Rachid.

Georges felt the barrel of a gun press against his aching neck. He let the Taurus drop to the floor and the huge bulk of Roman, spinning round to face him, made him shudder. The senior officer from Organised Crime was wearing latex gloves and aiming a S.I.G. Sauer directly at Georges' forehead. Seeing Crozat's bruised and battered face, he smiled.

"Should have stayed in hospital. Clever move, getting yourself fucked up in the ring. I had a good laugh. But you should have stayed in hospital like the Paki. You didn't pull your punches with him."

Georges was pouring with sweat.

"You feeling O.K., Crozat? You don't look too good."

"I don't know what you're talking about. I don't remember anything."

Roman burst out laughing. Rachid looked up.

"It's true, he took a blow to the head, he's suffering from amnesia. He doesn't remember you, doesn't remember what he did. Leave him be."

Roman glanced from the elderly Arab back to Crozat, a half-smile playing on his lips.

"That true?"

Georges gritted his teeth.

"I don't know you, I've got nothing to do with your dodgy dealings. Rubio's still alive, they didn't touch him, and you can't touch me or you'll go down too. I might not remember, but I know what happened. You can do nothing to me. Now let us go."

The driver suppressed a snigger. Roman pulled a pair of handcuffs from his pocket.

"Yeah, I don't think it's going to be quite that simple. O.K., fat man, hands behind your back."

Georges joined the two old men kneeling on the floor. Roman whispered orders to the driver who left the room and they heard him go down the cellar steps.

"It's not as though we didn't give you enough time. We've been watching you ever since you showed up on the hill. We've been waiting for an hour for you to come out of the cellar. And not one of you had the balls to waste Rubio? Shit, after all the trouble the *bougnoule* took to get you here!"

He crouched down within head-butting distance of the boxer.

"What got into you, Crozat? You weren't happy with our little deal? The cash, the whore? I'm guessing he was the one who put ideas into your head? The Arab?"

263

"I don't know why I worked for you, fuckwit, I must have been soft in the head."

Roman patted Georges' cheek gently as he might an old horse.

"Careful what you say. I might decide to have a little fun before I waste you."

With a jerk of his head, Georges pushed Roman's hand away and snapped his teeth; the vertebrae in his neck cracked, but he no longer felt anything. The driver re-emerged from the cellar; he too was now wearing latex gloves.

"It's done."

Rachid and Verini exchanged a curious, surprised look. Roman roared with laughter.

"What? We do your job for you and you're not even grateful? Rubio had friends who thought he might be useful, even at his age and in his state. Matters became a little complicated because of you and your *bougnoule* friend, Crozat. So these same gentlemen decided to do a little spring cleaning."

Roman turned towards the two old men, and lit a Marlboro.

"You don't think it's funny?"

Verini spat at Roman who slapped him so hard he went sprawling across the floor. Rachid hurled himself at Roman's legs only to be kicked towards the sofa.

"Jesus, they're bloody-minded old fuckers. O.K., we're not going to stand around all night. Let's make this a little score-settling between old men. No survivors."

He took Rachid's M.A.S.-50 from his pocket, aimed at Georges' stomach and pulled the trigger. Kneeling on the floor, The Wall was thrown back and managed to right himself before falling face forward, his head rebounding against the gleaming tiles.

The driver set his Mini-Uzi on the table and released the safety catch on Georges' Taurus.

Roman turned to Verini who was still crawling on the ground.

"You get to sleep with the fishes. You weren't supposed to be here, so we'll have to toss you out at sea."

Rachid managed to leap to his feet and scuttle to safety behind the sofa. A bullet from the Taurus embedded itself in the upholstery. Verini kicked at the polished bronze tray, sending the teapot and the glasses flying towards the driver's face. Roman bent down to stun him only to find himself lifted bodily off the ground as Georges buried his face in Roman's back and sent him crashing through the picture window before slumping back on the ground. The driver did not have time to finish him off. Rachid managed to pull the trigger of the shotgun, the buckshot ripped off the henchman's ear and sent him reeling through the window Roman had shattered. The driver got to his feet, one hand clamped over the mutilated ear now pissing blood, the other gripping the Taurus.

Roman was lying on his back next to the swimming pool, both hands clutching his throat. Blood spurted between his fingers as it drained from his face. The driver hesitated. Verini, his hands trembling, was pointing the M.A.S. directly at him; Rachid, having fired the shotgun, had not set it down. The driver slowly bent down, laid the Taurus on the ground and took a step back, and then another. The old men watched incredulously as he ran through the grounds of the house and vaulted the wall.

Verini helped Georges to sit up. Blood was pouring from the nylon tracksuit.

"You O.K.?"

"I can't feel a thing. Roman?"

Verini turned back towards the terrace. The heavy-set body of Roman lay splayed on the grass.

"Shit. He's dead!"

"The cuffs. Get the handcuffs off me."

Verini took off his jacket.

"Rachid, put pressure on the bullet wound."

Shaking himself from a nightmarish daze, the Kabyle suddenly dropped the shotgun as though he had been holding a snake. He wadded up Verini's jacket and pressed it against the wound.

Verini bent over Roman's body. Glass from the window had cut a six-inch slash across his throat, severing the jugular. For several seconds he stood, staring at the gash, at Roman's head which lolled at an unnatural angle, then, holding his breath, he crouched down and rummaged in his pocket for the keys. The corpse shuddered, and Verini abruptly recoiled, sprawled onto his back clutching the keys to the handcuffs.

Rachid gathered up the weapons and, with some difficulty, the two old men helped Crozat as he staggered out of the house, through the garden and along the road to where the van was parked. They slid open the side door and groaned as they heaved the heavyweight inside. Verini climbed behind the wheel and drove towards Cassis at top speed. It took forty minutes for them to reach the nearest hospital just outside Marseille.

Rachid got out of the van before it pulled up outside the casualty department. Verini ran into the hospital shouting that he had picked up an injured man by the side of the road. As soon as Crozat had been carried inside, he drove off without leaving a name, picked up Rachid and together they melted into the darkness.

# 5

The old men crawled into the bunk in the camper van where they slept for a few hours and woke at dawn. The white sun rose into a cloudless Mediterranean sky. Verini took a few steps, coughed and spat towards the sea. He remembered sailing these very waters before bringing the *Flomela* all the way to the Atlantic along the Canal du Midi. In his head, he could hear Nina Simone crooning "Flo Me La", the song after which he had named the boat. He thought back to when he had sailed her back to La Rochelle with his wife and kids, the moment when things began to go sour. This was the end of his dreams of sailing around the world, his dreams of never again setting foot in France. Money troubles, his wife's terror that one of the kids would fall overboard and her fear that they would become like him, savages incapable of living on dry land. Two years sailing from port to port, then the Balearics and the decision to head home.

He had tried.

The Mediterranean is deceptive. The beauty of its coastline belies the fierce storms offshore.

He remembered one storm in particular.

There had been others since.

The face of Provost and the technical department at the Aluvac factory which he thought he had forgotten. He remembered Gerbault and the factory library. And the question that had long since haunted him returned to trouble his thoughts. Were it not for the war, would he ever have had the courage to leave Nanterre, to take to the sea, to become the man he was?

He was a free man; what exactly did he owe to the war?

His anger?

And his freedom?

He splashed water from a bottle on his face and sat down on a rock. He was happy that the *Flomela* was still afloat. The boat he had built with his own hands was somewhere out at sea, tacking into the wind.

Rachid came and sat next to him, his joints stiff and crippled with rheumatism.

Far below, fishing boats plied the creeks and inlets. The whine of diesel engines floated up.

"Where are we?"

"I took the motorway towards Toulon. We're somewhere between Seyne-sur-Mer and Bandol. I turned off and took a road down to the sea."

"So, what happens now?"

Verini lit a Gauloise and offered the pack to Rachid. The Kabyle took one and coughed as he inhaled.

"You'll take the ferry. That's what you planned, wasn't it?"

Rachid studied the cigarette burning between his bony fingers.

"What about you?"

Verini spat out a wisp of tobacco.

"What do you think? I'll go to ground and see what happens."

Rachid went back to the van and returned with the guns. He waited until a fishing boat was out of sight and tossed them into the sea at the foot of the cliff.

"That guy, the one we let go, he could be a cop. What's he going to do?"

"I have no idea."

The Kabyle sat down again.

"He killed Rubio and we know it. He can't touch us. It's not as if I killed anyone."

"Someone did it for you. It's what you wanted, wasn't it?"

"Not like that."

"What difference does it make? Rubio's still dead."

Rachid folded his arms in his lap. Verini shook his head.

"What? You think it doesn't count because you didn't personally do it? You're warped, Rachid. You couldn't bring yourself to do it. You should be happy."

"You think? What about you, why didn't you do it?"

"Verini got to his feet and strolled along the jagged rocks. He stared out at the horizon, then walked back and stood behind Rachid.

"I didn't kill him back in Algeria. I didn't find him in '68 when I went looking for him. That's all that matters in this story. Killing him now wouldn't have changed anything. It would just have been one more murder. And even at seventy-two, I'm still looking for a way out. Just as I did fifty years ago. A way to save my own skin."

The Kabyle bowed his head.

"I don't know why I didn't shoot."

"Because he didn't remember you."

"He was lying. He knew who I was."

"Maybe. But that's not the real reason. You wanted him to be afraid of you, but he was just afraid of dying. He tortured you, other men tortured you at the Villa Sésini. How does killing one of them change anything?"

"Scores have to be settled. Otherwise we don't win."

"Win? You'd do better to think about your own death if you're worried about winning. Because it's coming and you're not ready. You'd have gained nothing by putting a bullet in Rubio's brain.

You're dying. You need to get to work, Rachid. You survived, not everyone did. Have you thought about Crozat? You could have killed us all with your bullshit revenge."

"You came along. You nearly killed him yourself."

"Stop trying to pretend that we're alike. That's something else you have to give up on before you kick the bucket."

"I'm going home to die. I've been planning this for a long time. I had only two things to do, two people I needed to see."

Verini laughed.

"What? Me and Rubio?"

"I was more scared of seeing you. Because I believe we were friends. In spite of the circumstances. It's the only thing I want to remember about the war."

"What about your plot to kill us all?"

"It was a war."

"Fuck the war. Colona said the same thing when they carted you off to Algiers. 'It's not about men, Verini, this is war.' Fuck's sake, who fights the wars? Huh? Scores are never settled. That's why you sat in that chair and couldn't bring yourself to kill Rubio. I've always thought that if I ended up in that state, I'd want a friend to come and finish me off. The only thing I could do was to let him live a little longer. We're not friends, Rachid, I won't be the one holding your hand when you pass away. And nor will Rubio. What did you think, that he'd cry and beg for forgiveness?"

Rachid picked up a handful of pebbles and threw them into the void.

"But there are men like you who fight wars."

"Don't give me that shit. The anonymous hero, the human face of horror! If you think like that everyone can cite heroes on their side and war becomes a spectacle of courage and humanity when actually it is a ragbag of the worst, the most despicable things a man can do. I don't want people to remember me."

Rachid was staring at the sea, Verini at the old Kabyle's back, the narrow shoulders, the grey hair.

"Forget the war, Rachid, before you die too. Get all that shit out of your mind. You've no idea who you are without it."

"Neither do you. It's not possible and you know it."

*

The white ferry was docked at the quay, its engines throbbing. Ticket and passport in hand, Brahim Bendjema joined Verini in the departures lounge. A crowd of families and Algerian tourists were streaming through the ticket barriers, dragging overstuffed suitcases up the gangway.

"They changed my ticket, so I've got a cabin."

Verini could not bring himself to look Rachid in the face.

"I don't know which of us is right, Rachid. You with your ailing memory or me with my attempts to forget everything. Our lives were never going to be similar. We tried, that's all that matters . . . As for the rest, I don't know."

He looked up at the Kabyle.

"What are you planning to do when you get there?'

"I want to go back and visit the Farm. After that, I'll see."

Rachid thought for a moment, a smile flickered across his ghostly face.

"The D.O.P. moved a few months after you left. When the Farm was evacuated, the A.L.N. launched a raid on the empty buildings. They razed it to the ground and torched the orange groves. It used to be a beautiful place. That will be my first port of call. How about you?"

"I'll wait for news about Crozat and about the villa, then I'll go home, or to my hide-out on the coast."

Verini smiled, he was about to add something, but changed his mind. Rachid looked at him intently.

"What were you about to say?"

"You know, the book I was trying to write was a sort of adventure story set during the war. But I could never quite structure it the way I wanted to. I couldn't bear to turn it into fiction, and on the other hand I'm no historian. Most of all, I didn't want to be a witness. A witness is helpless and people usually mistrust him. When I tried to write, I realised that that's how I felt over there."

Verini took a deep breath and tried to contain his emotions. He looked at the ferry, at the passengers on the gangway.

"I wanted to stay behind after the war, to live with the girl I met in the brothel in Orléansville. I wanted to stay to be a part of that country, that town, that farm. Because I already knew that I would never really leave."

"You were right to come back here. You've done good things here."

"I ran away."

"You never ran away from yourself. That's more than most."

Verini shook his head, dismissing this nonsense with a smile.

"Fine words. I don't even remember the girl's name."

"Adila."

"Adila . . . Shit, how come you remember?"

"You talked a lot about her. You wanted to be a taxi driver."

"Right. Can you imagine? I thought I could live there with her after you lot won the war, when peace came. I believed in your revolution."

Verini laughed, an embarrassed laugh that made him close his eyes.

"On the road up to the farm, just past the narrow gorge on the steep hill leading down into the valley, there's a large, round rock. If it hasn't been swept away by the river, there should be an army-issue trunk buried underneath that rock. I was supposed to collect it after I was demobbed. I often think about that trunk.

But after Algiers I never went back to Orléansville. I'm glad we left it there."

Rachid held out his hand.

Verini grasped it in his own.

"Don't you have a last word, Rachid?"

"I'm waiting for the last moment."

"Not long now."

Rachid handed his ticket to an attendant and went through the barrier. Just before he was out of range, he turned back.

"I was on the quays the day you sailed. I watched you smoke a cigarette standing in the stern of the *Kairouan*."

Pascal raised a hand in salute. Rachid disappeared into the crowd.

Verini watched as the ferry pulled away, scanning the decks.

Rachid appeared in the stern and Verini lit a cigarette. They could not see each other's faces, yet still they did not turn away. Then Rachid bowed his head and walked off down the deck with no farewell wave. Verini left the harbour before the ferry had rounded the jetty.

*

A few kilometres south-east of Cassis, set on the edge of a rocky inlet, the Camping des Oliviers was peaceful despite the children and the teenagers. Verini walked back up the beach and across the patches of yellowed grass to the camper van. He allowed himself to dry in the sun, only towelling his chest where the salt water tugged at his scar. He bit into a tomato and spread a sheaf of papers on the small table in the shadow of the van and of a maritime pine. He reread the pages, and began working on the next section, trying to remember precisely what the buildings had looked like. Had the prisoners' cells been to the left or the right of the farmyard? He was fairly sure they had been on the right as you entered; on the left was the barn with the farm machinery where the Citroën Traction had been parked out of the snow. He remembered it being a bitterly cold day.

Casta was drinking more and more, Philippe and I did our best to make sure he didn't get into trouble. The closer his demob came, the closer Sylvain came to breaking point. We huddled together because we were terrified at the idea of being separated. When Perret delegated me and the Corsican to take the money to Orléansville, Philippe volunteered to be part of the detail.

The others squaddies were taking the piss, suggesting we take a long holiday. We were excited, but we were scared shitless there would be an attack.

There were patches of black ice on the road, I drove as fast as I could. We started joking among ourselves. Dreaming about what we could do with all that money. Chapel or Casta – I don't remember which – shouted as we came to the narrow gorge. I think we'd hit a sharp stone. One of the front tyres burst and I lost control of the Citroën and piled into the rock face.

After the shock, once we were sure we were all alive and well, the silence and the fear took hold. This was the worst place we could be. Halfway between the Farm and the town, on the most dangerous stretch of road with no radio contact. I'm not sure know how we decided what happened next, but I don't think we said very much. After we got out of the car, we lugged the steel box out of the boot. We looked at each other and almost immediately we came up with a plan.

Once we'd made the decision, everything happened quickly. With the machine guns, we fired at the car, then we fired into the air, I tossed a grenade up the side of the rock face and we lobbed two others after we'd crawled down into the ravine and then we waited, with Casta acting as lookout on the road. That's when he dreamed up the next bit.

"They'll never fall for it. We have to make them believe."

That was when he said that one of us had to be injured.

"I don't give a shit. I can't carry on anyway, I'll never hold out until I'm demobbed."

Chapel came back breathless and Sylvain explained his plan. We tried to dissuade him, but he wouldn't listen. He wanted to do it, as much for the money as to get the fuck away from the Farm. Hurriedly we went over the version of events we would give. We were completely keyed up, but we were terrified too, and there was an intense thrill at the idea of fighting against our own army.

While Philippe kept watch, Casta took out his M.A.S. I was on my knees beside him, still trying to talk him out of it. He shot himself in the arm, dropped the gun and passed out for a few minutes. By the time he came round, the convoy had already shown up.

I was the last to leave the D.O.P. Before being demobbed, I was supposed to pick up the money and bring it back to France where the three of us would have divided it up.

We didn't really do it for the money, we did it for revenge. And once we'd pulled it off, the trunk didn't really matter. When I left, I was still planning to come back to Orléansville to find Adila and collect the treasure. Once I got to Algiers, I realised I would never go back.

All we wanted was for the three of us to leave the D.O.P. alive. Once we were safe and our military service was over, nothing else mattered.

I met up with Casta and Chapel when I got back to Paris. We had dinner in Philippe's father's restaurant. We didn't talk much about the million francs. Though it represented adventure, the money also represented Algeria. And that day, at that meal, Algeria had already become something we couldn't talk about.

The one person I did mention was Colona. The old *caporal-chef* might have been a raging alcoholic, but he had already guessed. I was convinced of that. We laughed, thinking about him. It was the only genuine laugh of that meal.

We never saw each other again.

If it wasn't swept away by the river or found by some goatherd, the steel box is probably still there buried under the rock.

Verini wrote on until mid-afternoon, then, exhausted by the heat and by his work, he climbed into the van and hoisted himself into the bunk.

He woke up at about 6.00 a.m. Slinging a towel over his shoulder and grabbing his sponge bag, he headed for the showers. After he washed, he stood in front of the mirror and dabbed his cheeks, his chin, his throat with shaving foam. On the first days, he had cut himself, but he had become accustomed to shaving again. He had kept his moustache and cut his hair short. The transformation took years off him. Every day, he was surprised to find himself greeted by this new, tanned face, by the down-turned wrinkles at the corners of his mouth which he straightened out, smiling at himself when he knew no-one was watching.

He dressed, taking the shirt that had been drying on a low branch of the pine tree, then he drove out of the camp ground, leaving the table and chair behind him.

A nurse greeted him at the reception desk. Monsieur Crozat was out of intensive care, she gave him the room number and the floor to which he had been moved.

Georges was watching a football match. He turned as Verini came in.

"Hi."

"So? You're finished with your lost causes?"

"Looks like it."

276

Verini set a box of cakes on the bedside table. He smiled at the boxer.

"How's the memory?"

Georges glanced over his shoulder to make sure the door was closed.

"Still nothing. I don't remember how I got here."

Both men smiled.

"What do the doctors say?"

"A couple more weeks. They had my medical records send from Fontenay hospital. I don't even need to pretend anymore, they know I took a knock to the head."

"What about the rest, before our little trip, the bout?"

"Nothing, and this time I'm not bullshitting."

Georges' voice dropped to a whisper.

"Anything new?"

Verini pulled up a chair and whispered.

"Nothing since the local paper published an obituary of Rubio saying he died peacefully in his sleep. I don't know who went to his funeral, no-one, hopefully. There's been no mention of Roman's name. No-one is looking for us, or if they are it's all under the radar."

Georges relaxed and took off his neck brace.

"I went and twisted my fucking neck again. The doc here says I've got the hardest skull he's ever seen. I don't know what they're dosing me up with, but I haven't had any more headaches. And they say the bullet wound is healing well."

Georges propped himself up on the pillows.

"The local police came by. I brazened it out with the amnesia. They haven't put two and two together, but then again people get shot all the time in these parts. I told them I remember going on holiday to convalesce after the bout in Paris. Said I had a rental car and a couple of suitcases but there's no sign of them now.

They suspect a carjacking. Your buddy, are you sure he got rid of the car?"

"He did. It's at the bottom of the Loire."

"O.K. Well, so far, so good. Nobody has mentioned you or Bendjema. My version suits everyone. You still writing your book?"

"I'm trying to finish it this time."

Georges pulled back the sheet and got out of bed. He took a few steps towards the window.

"You think we'll get away with it?"

Verini opened the box of cakes and bit into a sponge.

"Maybe."

"There's no way of knowing what's happening with our friend?"

"I'm not sure I want to know. But even if I did, I've no way of finding out."

Silence settled over the hospital room. Eventually, Verini got to his feet.

"I'll come and visit tomorrow or the next day."

"Don't put yourself out."

"I need to see you back on your feet. I'll drive you back to Lyons. The camping ground is pleasant enough and I'm in no hurry."

Verini laid a hand on the door. Georges cleared his throat and the words tumbled from his lips.

"I'm glad we met."

Verini turned and smiled. Crozat blushed. Verini stepped out into the corridor and his smile promptly faded.

*

The bus pulled up at the side of the newly paved road five kilometres outside Chlef*. They had been travelling barely ten minutes and already the bus had stopped twice. Bendjema had been chatting to another old man on the bus who did not seem

278

to notice that his Arabic was rusty. The old man remembered when the road had been a dirt track running up to the narrow gorge which had since been widened with the aid of dynamite. But he talked only about the road, not about the time when French army trucks came and went. He simply said that landmines had been found when the route was being resurfaced and that the valley was still full of them. He talked about the vestiges of war, not the war itself. The bus driver stopped when Rachid signalled to him.

The old Kabyle pushed his canvas hat down on his head and walked along the road, chewing dates he took from his pocket. Hearing a car approach behind him, he stopped, stood on the hard shoulder and watched it pass, then set off again. It was 5.00 p.m. and the sun was blazing, but already the jagged landscape was beginning to shear away its rays. Rachid shaded his eyes with his hand and looked out over the valley. The river Chélif was a pale golden brown, the tilled fields along its banks were a lush deep green. He spotted the huge round rock framed against the sunlight, halfway down the slope between road and river and perhaps a kilometre ahead. He left the road and took a goat track running parallel between the rocks about twenty metres downhill. This dusty track led directly to the rock.

He paused before he reached it, sat on a pile of stones, took a small bottle of mineral water from his pocket. He swallowed a painkiller, the strongest he had been able to get without prescription in Algiers. He massaged his scar as though the weal was connected to the tumour beneath and rubbing it might ease the pain. More than once he lost his footing. There were moments during the day, whole minutes here and there, that were swallowed up as though he had been asleep. He doubted that he would be able to spot someone following him. He doubted anyone was looking for him. Who would bother to waste a bullet on an old man in his condition? Under the name Bendjema, he was a historian neither sanctioned nor repudiated by the Algerian authorities. They would probably let him die in peace.

He walked on again. The path veered away from the rock and he had to scrabble on all fours over loose stones for a good five minutes. He arrived at the foot of the boulder which was three or four metres high and round only when seen in profile. Walking around it, he decided it looked like a sliver cut from a football the size of a house. He stopped to catch his breath and wait for his dizziness to subside.

He circled the boulder, hands pressed against the sun-warmed stone, checking for clefts and fissures. He crawled through the dust, a fine dry silt deposited there when the river Chélif flooded. He wriggled into holes and tunnels, burying his whole body beneath several tons of rock.

Behind a pile of branches left smooth and twisted by the waters, in the faint glow of a fissure where only a boy or a scrawny old man would fit, he spotted a metal object. A rusted handle. The corners of a corroded steel box. He cleared away the branches until he could reach the trunk, then extricated himself from the straitjacket of clay and stone. He dragged the box out of the hole, scanned the area to make sure no goatherds or children were on the path. A car passed on the road above.

He crouched down and studied the trunk closed by a padlock so badly rusted that he could easily prise it open.

Inside was a fine layer of dried mud which he brushed away with great care like an archaeologist. Beneath it, his fingers encountered something lightweight and yielding. He blew away the dust to discover what at first he thought was the spine of a book, its pages stuck together. He plunged his hand in and the sheets of paper promptly disintegrated. He removed several layers until he came to paper that did not crumble when touched.

He peeled away a sheet that was illegible and beneath it was another, half faded, bearing the portrait of a bearded man and next to this, three numbers.

A 500-franc note bearing the portrait of Victor Hugo, one of the huge banknotes in circulation back then.

He continued his painstaking work, peeling away the strata, and recognised 1,000-franc notes bearing the portrait of Richelieu with his moustache and his goatee.

He smiled and sat down next to the open trunk. The sun was sinking over the valley. He thought about the book Verini had wanted to write.

Worried that the night might overtake him, he got to his feet and shook out the contents of the trunk, which were whipped away by the wind. A cloud of silt and banknotes billowed out like ashes from a funeral urn, the scraps of paper fluttering and disintegrating in the air.

Rachid pushed the trunk back under the boulder and continued along the path. He followed it for an hour until he saw, on the far side of the paved road, the track that led up to the Farm. He clambered out of the ravine, crossed the tarmac and began to climb the hill, stopping regularly. The grounds had been replanted. There were new orange groves. But there were no buildings where the Farm had once stood.

In a patch of dry rocky ground with little vegetation, he could easily make out the foundations of the Farm. Rows of stones emerging from the soil tracing the line of the walls. The house itself was a vast pile of rubble. Opposite, small piles of stones marked out where the barns had stood. The rest had probably been carted away to build new houses.

He crossed the courtyard. There was no trace of the cells.

Within the foundations of the farmhouse, he stood on the lip of a area that had collapsed, a rounded crater that looked as though it had been made by a bomb blast. At the bottom of this hollow, between tufts of dry grass and goat droppings, were jumbled piles of cut stone.

Rachid climbed down into the hollow, crouched beneath the vaulted ceiling. The ceiling of the old cellar.

When the sun set, he lay down in the ruined basement, sheltered from the wind by stones still warm from the heat of the day.

He wished he had a gun so that it might all be over sooner. Then he decided he would probably see a sunrise or two, a sunset or two before he died. He could try and make the most of it, be attentive to the workings of his mind, this brain that skipped like a scratched record. Because he did not want to miss his final thought, the only one that mattered. The thought that opens or closes a door. The thought he had been saving for so long, the one on which he wanted to go out.

His mouth felt terribly dry.

It was dark now and though he could not remember them appearing, the stars were there.

The sound of stones made him sit up.

A shadowy figure dashed across the old farmyard.

He made no attempt to make sense of things and lay down again.

Wait for the last thought. Be present when it came. That was all that was left to do.

# 6

Georges pressed the numbers in the public telephone box and waited, counting the number of rings.

The call was answered on the fourth ring.

"It's me."

"You O.K.?"

"Yeah, a bit nervous."

"You still phoning from a callbox? It's been long enough, I think you can stop taking precautions."

"I prefer it this way."

"Are you ready?"

"Yeah . . ."

With a fingernail, Georges scratched at the glass wall of the cabin.

"I would have liked you to be here."

"The children are home with me at the moment. My wife's here too."

"Yeah."

"Good luck."

Georges spoke quickly, before Verini had time to hang up.

"What about your book?"

"I'm nearly finished. I've been wondering whether I should keep the names."

Georges gave a short, nervous laugh.

"O.K. I'll let you know what happens. After."

"O.K."

Verini hesitated.

"Take care of yourself."

"Tell your family I said 'Hi.'"

Crozat hung up, cradling the receiver for a moment after he did so.

He crossed the street, walking at first, then breaking into a jog.

Paolo was pacing up and down outside the door.

"You done? Can we go in now?"

The hall was half empty and smelled of the mussels and French fries that hadn't been cleared away from the night before.

A couple of light heavyweights were coming to the end of their bout and it was difficult to tell which of them would crumple from exhaustion first.

Georges and Paolo went into the dressing room, little more than a box room with two chairs and a table. Marco was waiting for them and had everything ready. Shorts, pumps, protective cup, robe, vaseline, mouth-guard and tapes.

They kitted out The Wall, who began his warm-up exercises. Someone from the local club appointed by the Boxing Commission came to check the tapes – not really knowing what to do or say – and left again.

Marco whispered in Georges' ear as he shadow-boxed. He was already pouring with sweat. Paolo jabbed at his shoulders, his belly, slapped his face to warm him up.

"Shit, I can't even bring myself to land a serious punch. You sure about this, Georges? We're all scared shitless here."

The Wall was no longer listening.

The sparse crowd whistled and cheered as they came in. Half the men there had witnessed the first Crozat–Esperanza bout the previous year. And every one of them knew that The Wall had almost died during the fight. That he might very well die during this one.

Six months it had taken to find a doctor prepared to give him a dodgy medical certificate.

Six months training, learning to protect his belly and his head. Protecting both at the same time was impossible. But he was fit, he'd learned to be defensive. To parry the blows between his fucked-up brain and his perforated stomach.

He climbed into the ring and the whole room fell silent. Fear and excitement. Everyone in Toni's corner stared anxiously at The Wall. It had taken long negotiations to persuade them.

The referee made a short speech since he clearly did not know the regulations by heart. Georges and Toni stepped forward and touched gloves. Georges leaned forward and whispered in his opponent's ear.

"Sorry about the Fontenay bout. This time, no bullshit tricks. A fair fight."

Esperanza nodded that he had heard, but he still looked unconvinced.

Georges jogged back to his corner, shadow-boxing. It felt strange to be apologising for something he could not remember.

When he spotted the man with the missing ear in the front row, the blood froze in his veins.

Every time he saw the guy, it had the same effect. At Ring 14, and the *commissariat* on the avenue de Maine where he had gone supposedly to consult a case file. The guy's name was Guyot, a young sergeant in the Organised Crime unit. Every time they ran into each other, Guyot gave him the same look that said he was just checking. That neither of them had shifted their position. That their secret was still buried. Guyot raised a hand by way of greeting and Georges jerked his chin in response.

Paolo and Marco were tense and nervous, babbling and bombarding him with vague strategies.

"This is your swansong, Georges, your last bout. Don't fuck about, you're here to box. And protect your head for Christ's sake."

"Marco, if Paolo here tries to throw in the towel, smack him in the mouth for me."

"Stupid bastard."

Georges looked across the ring to his opponent, refusing to even think about the girl he was planning to buy himself tonight.

"You gonna be alright, Georges? Hey, big man, you listening?"

"Don't sweat it."

The bell echoed faintly. The cop with the missing ear applauded with the rest of the crowd. Georges stepped into the ring, put up a low guard and charged headlong at Toni Esperanza.

# Acknowledgements

For Pascal Varenne, my father who shared his experiences and his secrets shortly before his death.

This book is for him, the meagre plunder of his ravaged memory, his steel box of old banknotes.

He was happy when I began this project and delighted to read the first chapter, which reminded him of London, of the adventurers and the boxers he loved so much.

In the hope of making him turn in his grave, I have not respected his wishes. My father had forgotten most of the names, with the exception of Rachid and Colona. There was another name too, one he could only utter between gritted teeth, one he would not have wanted to appear.

To this day, whether alive or dead, Rubio never knew that Mohamed and Pascal were looking for him with a gun in their pocket.

My thanks to Laurence Biberfield and Renaud de Rochebrune, to Viviane and her team.

# Glossary

## Arabic

*bled*: a village; (figuratively) a godforsaken place

*chèche*: traditional Berber turban which extends to cover the neck, worn in the desert

*djebel*: a mountain or a range of hills

*fellagas*: Algerian partisans of independence

*katibas*: literally meaning "battalions", this was the term used by the French for the enemy troops in North Africa

*méchoui*: barbecue of a whole roast sheep

*mechtas*: a hamlet or a group of shacks

*muezzin*: the call to prayer in Islam

*salat al-isha*: the night-time daily prayer recited by practising Muslims

*wilayah*: the name given to an administrative division, or province, of Algeria

## French

*adjudant*: warrant officer

*bamboula*: a once common racist term for North Africans

*brigadier*: bombardier (artillery) or corporal (infantry)

289

*capitaine*: captain

*caporal-chef*: corporal

*cocos*: Commies, Communists

*commissaire*: superintendent

*commissariat*: police station

*Francs-tireurs et partisans (F.T.P.)*: the Second World War resistance movement founded in 1941 by the French Communist Party

*frichti*: grub, food (from German *Frühstück*, breakfast, via Alsacien)

*grigri*: an amulet or talisman in animist religions (from West-African French)

*harki*: Algerian soldier who served with the French during the Algerian War, considered a traitor by resistants

*maquis*: while this has become synonymous with the Second World War Resistance, it literally means "scrubland" and by extension a hideout

*la Milice*: the collaborationist militia in German-occupied France during the Second World War

*mistral*: the cold, dry wind that blows in the Rhône Valley and the South of France

*pied-noir*: French colonial born in Algeria

*police judiciaire*: the equivalent of the British C.I.D./Criminal Investigation Department

*préfecture de police*: the local police headquarters

*sergent-chef*: staff sergeant

*soldat (de deuxième classe)*: private (first class)

*sous-officier*: non-commissioned officer, NCO

*yéyé*: French pop music of the 1960s

# Notes

The **Palestro** Ambush took place near Djerrah, on 18 May 1956. Forty members of the *Armée de libération nationale* (A.L.N.) ambushed a group of twenty soldiers from the French 9th Infantry Regiment, killing all but one of the French soldiers.

**Messali Hadj** was an Algerian nationalist politician who co-founded the People's Party of Algeria, and later the Algerian National Movement, in direct opposition to the ongoing efforts of the F.L.N.

**Jacques Massu** was a French general who served in the Second World War, and later in the Algerian War and the Suez crisis. He was sent with the 10th Parachute Division in Algeria to combat a wave of terrorist bombings coordinated by the F.L.N.

The **C.C.I.** (*Centre de coordination interarmées*), or the Armed Forces Co-ordination Centre, received organisational, coordinated intelligence from the police, military intelligence sources and from the torture centres ("interrogation centres"). A quasi-secret organisation, it helped mount the *putsch* of 1961.

The **D.O.P.** (*Dispositifs opérationnels de protection*) were counter-insurgency "protection" units created in 1957 by the C.C.I. in order to "gather information" – which became a euphemism for torture.

The ***commando de chasse***, or Harka Commandos, acted as shock troops. Working outside the law, they hunted down and killed members of the A.L.N.s.

The **A.L.N.**, or *Armée de libération nationale*, was the armed wing of the *Front de Libération National* (F.L.N.) during the Algerian War. After independence it became the basis for the regular armed forces of the republic.

**Jean-Jacques Susini** is the Algerian-born co-founder of the *Organisation de l'armée secrète*. In 1972 Susini was arrested and charged with masterminding the abduction and/or murder of Raymond Gorel in 1968 and was held on remand for two years before being acquitted in 1974. Controversially, he was granted an amnesty by President Mitterrand upon his election.

**Pierre Lagaillarde** (born 1931) was a French politician, and a co-founder of the O.A.S.

**Raoul Albin Louis Salan** was a veteran general of the First Indochina War who later co-founded the O.A.S.

The **O.A.S.**, or *Organisation de l'armée secrète* (Secret Armed Organisation), was a French paramilitary organisation during the Algerian War. The O.A.S. described themselves as "counter-terrorists" and used targeted assassinations and bombings in an attempt to prevent the secession of Algeria. The motto of the organisation was "*L'Algérie est française et le restera*" ("Algeria is French and will remain so").

**Guy Mollet** was a socialist politician who was Prime Minister of France from 1956 until June 1957 when his government collapsed over a policy of raising taxation in order to pay for the Algerian War.

**The Algiers Putsch**, also known as the Generals' Putsch, refers to the attempted coup in May 1958 by (among others) Generals Raoul Salan and Jacques Massu. An army junta commanded by Massu seized power in Algiers while Salan assumed leadership of a Committee of Public Safety. They demanded that General de Gaulle be named Prime Minister and that a government of national unity be established with extraordinary powers to prevent the "abandonment of Algeria". On May 29, the French President, René Coty, appealed to de Gaulle to become the last Prime Minister of the Fourth Republic. De Gaulle accepted with the precondition that a new constitution be introduced and that he be granted extraordinary powers for an initial period of six months.

**Maurice Thorez** was general secretary of the French Communist Party.

The **Villa des Roses** and the **Villa Sésini** were notorious "detention centres" in Algiers where alleged members of the F.L.N. were tortured during the Algerian War.

**Paul Aussaresses**, a French Army general, was a veteran of the Second World War and of the First Indochina War. His actions during the Algerian War caused considerable controversy.

**Bernard Courcelle** is the former head of the D.P.S., the so-called "security branch" of the far-right *Front National*.

**Bruno Gollnisch** is a French revisionist historian, lawyer and M.E.P., and a senior figure in the right-wing *Front National*.

**Chlef** is the Algerian name of the town the French had called Orléansville.

ANTONIN VARENNE travelled a great deal and completed an M.A. in philosophy before embarking on a career as a writer. He was awarded the Prix Michel Lebrun and the Grand Prix du Jury Sang d'encre for *Bed of Nails*, his first novel to be translated into English.

FRANK WYNNE is a translator from French and Spanish. His translations include novels by Michel Houellebecq, Marcelo Figueras' *Independent* Foreign Fiction Prize-shortlisted *Kamchatka* and *Alex* by Pierre Lemaitre.